Passion

Heart-stoppingly beautiful in yellow attire, she stood in the doorway of his church sanctuary, surveying the crowd. Perhaps the slant of her eyes or the provocative way she stood—with a hand to a well-rounded hip—set off alarms in his head. One thing was certain. Never in his ten years of preaching had Jourdan Watters ever seen temptation wrapped in such a breathtaking package.

Passion

by T. T. Henderson

Genesis Press, Inc.
Columbus, Mississippi

INDIGO LOVE STORIES are published by
Genesis Press, Inc.
406A 3rd Avenue North
Columbus, MS 39701-0101

PASSION

This book may not be reproduced in whole or in part, by mimeograph or any other means, without permission. Published in the United States of America by Genesis Press, Inc. For information, write: Genesis Press, Inc., 406A 3rd Ave. North, Columbus, MS 39701-0101.

ISBN: 1-885478-21-6

Manufactured in the United States of America

First Edition

Thanks to Deb for discovering me
To Tari for forcing me to send *Passion* out one more time
To Deon for taking care of me
And to Martha for her greatly appreciated assistance

Visit our Web page for latest
releases and other information.

http://www.colom.com/genesis

Genesis Press, Inc.
406A 3rd Avenue North
Columbus, MS 39701-0101

Indigo Love Stories

Chapter I

She was sin waiting to happen. Heart-stoppingly beautiful in yellow attire, she stood in the doorway of his church sanctuary, surveying the crowd. Perhaps the slant of her eyes or the provocative way she stood—with a hand to a well-rounded hip—set off alarms in his head. One thing was certain. Never in his ten years of preaching had Jourdan Watters ever seen temptation wrapped in such a breathtaking package.

The choir singing behind him became a faint humming as the woman inclined her head toward the usher. She followed him down the aisle. Her beauty sliced through the sanctuary like a beam of sunlight through storm clouds. Male heads turned in indiscreet appreciation of the yellow-clad woman, followed by sharp looks and sharper elbows from their significant others.

Jourdan tried not to enjoy the smooth sway of her hips and the graceful stride of her long, shapely legs as she made her way toward the altar—toward him.

"Have mercy," he mumbled.

The usher's white-gloved hand shook slightly, a lovesick grin on his dark wrinkled face, when he motioned to a vacant seat in the fourth row.

Jourdan closed his own watering mouth, hoping no one noticed the effect she'd had on him. It had been a long time since he'd allowed himself even a passing glance at a woman. Not since he'd married his late wife, Cece.

He had a sermon to deliver; he had to concentrate. Closing his eyes, he extended his arms wide.

Oh, Lord. I glorify your name . . . The stirring began in his right hand. The one gripping his Bible. From there, a familiar heat went blazing into his chest, surging through his hands, his feet, his soul. He laid his head back and accepted the power that spilled over and through him. Every inch of his being sensitized, he sought to connect with a power beyond himself, until finally the channel of light opened, raining sheets of divinity.

It was time to cast out demons, heal the sick, turn sinners into saints—all in the name of the Lord.

Opening his eyes, he met sin's golden brown gaze.

Sweet Jesus.

She radiated both worldly pleasures and childlike innocence. Even as the Holy Ghost surged through him, her powerfully seductive stare shot an arrow of lust straight through Jourdan. *What manner of temptress are you?*

Drawing a deep breath, he forced his gaze away from her to the sea of expectant faces looking for spiritual guidance. They wanted a sermon to set their souls on fire—they wanted to jump and shout and scream in the name of the Father.

The blood in Jourdan Watters' veins pumped with new vigor. He would not disappoint the congregation.

* * * * * * * * * * * * *

Passion Adams exhaled slowly—he had looked straight into her soul. She'd heard volumes about Reverend Watters from his now deceased wife, Cece. Skeptical that any man could deserve a woman's total love and devotion, Passion's curiosity had guided her inside a church building for the first time in her adult life.

The rich bronze of his handsome face met her expectations. But she wasn't prepared for the way her body responded to his deep, dynamic voice, nor to the dark, almost black intensity of his eyes that sent excitement right through her. There was no doubt—this man answered prayers she had yet to make.

Passion wanted him. Unfortunately, she knew she wasn't alone. One look around the pews told her every eligible sister in Zion Baptist Church had all but scratched and clawed her way to the front to be closer to him. Well, Passion didn't have to play that game. He'd notice her—most men did. But what would she say when it happened?

"You know, Laticia, I would be *so* 'shamed if I *ever* came to church with a skirt so short you could see *my* drawers."

Passion glanced sideways at the woman next to her, then sighed heavily. *Not again.*

"Oooh, I know what you mean, Rochelle. And ain't it a sin to show off cleavage in the house of the Lord?" Both women looked Passion down then up, only to meet her steady gaze.

"Don't go too low, sisters," came Passion's low hiss. "You might get burned."

She smoothed the bright wool of her skirt. Just the very top of her breasts was visible from the square cut neckline and her skirt went all the way to mid-thigh. It was one of her most conservative outfits by far.

For the thousandth time, she wished her looks didn't cause such reaction from other women. It would have been nice to have a friend her own age to talk to. Shirleen was great, but she had enough years on her to be Passion's grandmother.

The women turned their noses to the air and their attention to the divine Reverend Watters.

"Now, some of y'all need to hear this," the reverend teased. "You remember the story of Samson?"

"Uh-huh."

3

"Go 'head," a woman shouted from the congregation.

"How many of y'all know Samson was a strong man with a woman weakness?" He paused for a barrage of "amens."

"He told his parents to go down to the Philistine Village and get the woman called Delilah. She pleased him well."

"Well," a man sang out in appreciation.

"You know one of those women, doncha?" The reverend flashed a knowing smile at the men, then glanced briefly in Passion's direction. "There are still a few Delilahs around today, aren't there?"

A twinge of guilt tugged at her insides.

"Ooooh, chile! He sure got that right!" one of the women to her side said loudly.

Self-conscious all of a sudden, Passion raised up her chin a fraction, trying to ignore the sting of accusation.

"We all know how that story ended." The reverend took a step forward. "This woman ended up betraying Samson, because her loyalties lay with the Philistines."

He strode to the opposite end of the stage. "When we don't do God's will in looking for our mates, we do Satan's work trying to get rid of them!"

He paced across the stage, his black robe floating behind him. "Tell me you know what I'm talkin' about."

"Hallelujah!"

"Preach!"

"Tell me you *don't* know someone who's wounded his spouse by copulating and fornicating with someone else."

Passion knew a few lowlifes in high places who fit the description.

"How many of them, men and women, feel they are justified because their spouses betrayed them first?" His pacing stopped and he stared out at the audience.

"I'm telling you that the way to understand each other is to first understand the Father and what His plan is for our marriages."

Passion took a deep breath as his eyes met hers once again.

4

His dark, piercing gaze held hers for what seemed a full half minute before moving on. She exhaled slowly, allowing her thundering heart to calm down and quell her doubts. In his eyes she saw acceptance, for certain.

There was something delightfully invigorating about the way the reverend made Passion feel.

The organist played and choir members sang the hymn "Just As I Am."

*   *   *   *   *   *   *   *   *   *   *   *   *

Jourdan Watters stretched out a hand to his congregation. The calm satisfaction of a sermon well delivered settled over him. "I need all heads bowed, all eyes closed. Please, come to the altar so that I can pray for your marriage or relationship."

Deacons and ushers joined the dozen or so weeping members who came forward.

"Now . . . there are some of you who can say you have not accepted Jesus Christ as your savior. Won't you please come?"

He saw tentative movement throughout the audience and he motioned them forward. One by one, they made their way down aisles to the altar. *Patience, Jourdan. There's always one more.*

"If the Lord has laid it on your heart to deepen your walk with Him today, please obey."

The woman in yellow swung her stunning legs from behind the pew and rose to her feet, taking a tentative tug at her fitted skirt.

Jourdan reached for the water glass on the podium and took a long swallow.

Her head bowing reverently, she swayed her hips like original sin down the aisle.

Jourdan wiped perspiration from his brow with a handkerchief, as though he could remove the lustful thoughts causing confusion. A new fire boiled in his veins. He stepped down to pray with those who'd come forward.

Placing his hands on the shoulders of the first weeping man, he prayed; and the Spirit moved between them. He went on to the next and repeated his ritual. One after the other, he prayed his way down the altar, aware that she stood last in line—waiting for him. The closer he got, the more her sweet smell teased his senses.

It was a struggle to remain focused on the plump woman before him. Jourdan finished with the kindly older woman, then steadied himself as if to do battle with Satan. He approached the beauty cautiously, almost stopping when she looked up at him. Her eyes sparkled brightly, her face smooth and rich like sienna silk.

"What is your name Blessed One?"

"Passion . . . Adams." Her smile revealed perfect white teeth framed in luscious, raspberry lips.

Jourdan forgot his name—and what he was supposed to do next. *Oh yes.* Remembering, he placed his palm on the cool skin of her forehead and looked deeply into those honey-flecked eyes. "Do you accept Jesus Christ as your savior?"

"I do. But . . . what I would like . . ." Her voice flowed softly, huskily as she met his gaze. "Is you."

Jourdan's muscles tensed.

It was not the Holy Ghost he felt, but an ancient desire born when Adam first met Eve in the paradise of Eden. In chaos, Jourdan clutched at what remained of his self-control, trying not to lose himself in temptation.

Passion. She housed an abundance of it, he felt certain. A slice of panic seized him. Was this beautiful woman yet another gift from Satan to set back his ministry? Jourdan brought his Bible to his chest like a shield. "What manner of temptress are you?"

A brief look of confusion wrinkled her brow before her extraordinary eyes squeezed shut.

Dear God. Why had he said that?

Her lips quivered as Jourdan searched to find words that would erase the embarrassment he'd caused. He sought to comfort her by placing a hand on her shoulder. Yet she backed away, pivoted around, and headed up the aisle.

He blinked a few times and lowered his Bible to his side.

"That was a great sermon, Jourdan," another woman said, her voice piercing his daze.

He blinked twice and turned to her. Struggling for control, he smiled. "Thanks, Mom."

Evelyn Johnson would always be "Mom" to him. Over the years, he'd grown closer to his in-laws than to his own parents.

Evelyn eyed the beams above his head. "I see you've added some lights. Are you going to be televised soon?"

"We're working on it." Thankful she could bend his attention, he swelled with pride. Jourdan couldn't wait to reach out to the entire world via satellite to do the work of the Lord.

Each night for the past year, he'd had a vision. A huge wall of television monitors spewed murder and profanity upon the populace of Kansas City. In these dreams, the monitors suddenly brightened with pictures of encouragement and love as Jourdan spoke from the pulpit, spreading the word of God. Worshiping converts would fall to their knees before Zion Baptist's altar. Overwhelming peace filled Jourdan's heart, both in his dreams and now.

Not since his call to the ministry had a message been this clearly spoken to him: his destiny lay in saving sinners.

"Don't tell Dad about your TV plans." Evelyn chuckled. "He's already jealous because your church is bigger than his."

Jourdan simply smiled.

The sanctuary slowly emptied. Cranberry upholstered pews fanned out in four sections from the altar, sitting atop lush mauve carpeting. Behind the podium was space for an even larger choir than the present one. And Zion had room for a small band.

Despite generous lighting, Jourdan thought it seemed dark and hollow all of a sudden. The brightness had followed the lovely woman who'd stood before him only moments before. Passion.

He scolded himself silently. How could he be thinking about another woman?

"Jourdan?"

He focused on the serious mien of his mother-in-law.

"Will you be over for dinner?" she asked. "The district attorney will be there."

"I'll be by at about four-thirty." He planted a big kiss on Evelyn's cheek in an effort to cheer them both.

The weight of guilt had settled even heavier in Jourdan's chest. Her mention of Kansas City's incompetent DA caused him to remember an unsolved murder. His wife's.

Had it been only two months since she'd been killed? And here he was lusting after another woman.

* * * * * * * * * * * * *

Passion threw her yellow purse across the room, then her yellow pumps went flying into the closet.

She regarded herself in the vanity mirror. "Stupid, that's what you are!"

"Who's stupid?"

Passion turned to answer the silver-haired woman in the doorway. "Not you, Shirleen. Me."

"You right about that, chile." She giggled more like a child than a sixtyish woman. "What was you stupid about now?"

Passion smiled sheepishly and watched her plump friend finish an ice-cream cone. "Well, I went to see the reverend," she said.

Shirleen rolled her eyes in amusement. "What happened?"

"I only wanted to get a look at him, you know, so I could see what makes him so special." Passion sighed. "Cece was so fireworks-in-the-sky in love with the man . . ."

"You're gettin' off the subject," Shirleen scolded.

"I went for the altar call, meaning to tell him—"

"You didn't!" Shirleen gasped.

Passion shook her head quickly. "No. I didn't say anything . . . I mean I couldn't." She shrugged, helplessly trying to find the right words to explain what had happened. "I don't know,

Shirleen, I got there and all of a sudden there was this feeling between us—like nothin' I've ever felt before."

"Don't say it." Shirleen wagged a pudgy finger.

"I think I'm in love with him," Passion confessed. She'd thought about it all the way home on the bus. There wasn't any other explanation.

A sigh preceded the older woman's slow steps toward the bed. She sat down heavily and gave Passion a look of pity. "Does you really believe dat?"

Passion folded her arms. "Why else would I tell the reverend I'd accept Jesus Christ as my savior and, while I was at it, take him on the side?"

Shirleen burst into laughter.

Passion began to chuckle as well.

Shirleen wiped tears from her eyes. "I'm sorry. I 'spose that was pretty embarrassin'. What did he say? What did he do?"

"Asked if I was a temptress, then just stared at me like he knew I was a whore and . . . that was that." She lay down on her bed, flat on her back with arms spread wide like the fallen angel she imagined herself to be.

"Now don't you worry, chile. You surprised him is all. Anyhow, you ain't a ho', so stop puttin' yo'self down like dat."

"Shirleen, what do I do now?" Passion rubbed her still-flat stomach. "What happens when this baby comes?"

"We'll get along some kinda way, so don't you fret about it. We'll be fine, just fine. I gets my social security every month, you still have some of that money Miz Watters give to ya."

"I thought about giving the baby to its father. He's much better off financially. And—"

"Now don't go talkin' crazy . . ."

"Yeah, but her partial payment won't go that far."

Shirleen took Passion into her stout arms and started to hum and rock her as if she was comforting an infant.

"Shirleen?" Passion pulled away from the older woman.

"What, honey?"

"Do you really think I deserve a good man after the things I've done?"

Shirleen looked Passion straight in the eyes. "Baby, nobody deserves one more."

But did she? Passion left the bed to stare through the security bars on the window. She looked in disgust at the graffiti-splattered buildings and overturned garbage cans, hearing teenage boys talking trash in the alley.

She wanted to be somewhere safe and clean. A place where children and drug addicts didn't end up shot or stabbed in the alley below her window. Somewhere nice to raise a child.

Passion Adams had never known peace. She was determined that this child would.

"I'm yo friend," said Shirleen. "And I'm tellin' you, ain't no man gonna respect you 'til you respect yo'self."

"One thing's for sure. Reverend Watters hasn't got an ounce of respect for me now. I mean, he acted just like I expected him to, I guess. But it hurt when he asked me what kind of temptress I was. Like I'd asked him to throw me down right there in the church or something. It's like he could see every sin I've committed."

"You only done what you had to do, remember dat." Shirleen gave Passion one of her serious business looks. "You mine now. I'll look after you, and we'll both look after that young'un in your belly." She stood beside Passion at the window and put an arm around her. "You don't need no man to take care of you."

Passion, a little startled, turned to face the short, plump woman. "Shirleen, I know I can take care of myself. No man has ever given me anything out of the kindness of his heart. But once, just once, I'd like a man to look at me with love instead of lust— like I had more to offer than tits and a . . ." She stopped at Shirleen's censorious look. "You know what I mean."

"I knows what you mean, sugah." The old woman's hand went to her breast and her eyes clouded in remembrance.

Passion had grown familiar with Shirleen's brief moments of reverie, knowing her thoughts were of William. Even after his death, she seemed spellbound by her husband's deep, lasting love.

Passion let her forehead rest on the cold glass of the window, feeling deep inside her that Jourdan Watters was the one man who could give her spellbinding love.

"I want a man to wake up on the pillow next to me every morning, instead of a quickie before midnight and a promise for next time. I want to have that man's children. I want a life like Cece Watters had." Passion stood straight and looked directly into her friend's eyes. "And, like you said, I deserve it."

Chapter II

Jourdan Watters nearly knocked over the chair in his in-law's dining room. "My wife is dead! I will *not* have you casting aspersions on her good name, Mr. Reed."

He resisted the urge to slug Kansas City's district attorney in his long, straight nose.

"If there is one thing I do know about this case, Reverend Watters, it's that Cece is no longer with us." Edmond Reed rose from the table and adjusted the cuffs of his shirt. His steely glare looked straight into Jourdan's. "However, my office has found evidence that links your wife to some very shady characters and I have every right to release those findings to the public."

"My daughter's shooting was an accident, Mr. Reed." Evelyn Johnson circled the table, collecting dirty dishes. "You said that yourself."

The district attorney slid into his suit jacket. "Granted, my initial investigation did indicate the bullet came from the same gun that someone fired into the restaurant. But, I'm not so sure the shooting was a random act. Only your daughter got hit. Usually, in these situations, there's more than one victim."

"Usually, Mr. Reed, good Christian women do not end up dead for no reason," Jourdan challenged.

Small, beady eyes made Reed look mean. But it was the callous way he discussed a heinous crime that made Jourdan dislike him. "Thou shalt not kill" was one of the Ten Commandments. "Admit it, there's no link between my wife and any *shady* characters. You're clutching at straws."

"We have solid leads—"

"It's been two months since the shooting and you don't have a single shred of evidence to convict anyone of her murder. This is just another one of the cases the state won't be able to solve, isn't it?"

"Now, wait a minute . . ."

Amos Johnson interrupted. "Gentlemen, we're getting nowhere. I would suggest, Mr. Reed, you continue to review your evidence. There's no possible way our Cece would do anything illegal or immoral. I'm certain you will come to the same conclusion, once you've given the situation more thought." The older man placed a hand on the district attorney's back. "We've been praying the Lord will bring the truth to light."

"No disrespect intended, Reverend Johnson." Reed frowned. "But I'm growing tired of all this Bible-thumping crap." He shrugged off the older man's hand. "If you people honestly think prayer works, then why is Cece laying six feet under right now?"

Evelyn covered her mouth with a trembling hand.

Jourdan assisted her into the nearest chair. "You have absolutely no respect for human life, do you, Reed? You don't care about people dying in the streets. They're just anonymous faces to you. No wonder you can't convict real criminals. You can't come up with enough compassion to care for their victims."

Reed's nostrils flared. "You don't know what you're talking about. There are so many loopholes—"

"Perhaps the next DA will find my wife's murderer."

Reed pointed a thick finger at Jourdan's face. "Do *not*

13

threaten me, Watters. Don't think I'm unaware of the things you say to reporters, damaging my reputation. I'll be reelected because I'm the best man for the job!"

Jourdan suppressed the urge to break Reed's offending finger. His blood boiled, his precious control fading fast. "Think what you will, Reed, but I know the truth." He headed for the front door, and flung it open. The cool September night breezed in. "You'd better leave. I'll be praying for a miracle to shatter the stone you have where your heart should be."

"If you want miracles and deliverance, then come to me." Reed's finger now jabbed at his own broad chest. "I offer peace of mind with each drug dealer I convict. I put rapists and murderers behind bars to bring harmony to your neighborhood. He snatched his overcoat from the rack by the door and shoved his arms into it. "The only miracles I've seen are those I've made happen!"

"Dangerous words from a mere mortal." Jourdan's eyes narrowed.

"What about you, Watters? You tell people their money will buy them salvation." He bent toward Jourdan, his eyes slits of anger. "People actually believe that crap and throw money at you by the truckload."

"It's not about money. It's about faith. In this world, people have to have something to believe in."

"Believe in me. I'm the one who's gonna find your wife's killer." With that, Reed stalked into the dark night.

Jourdan slammed the door behind the abominable man.

"Jourdan. Son. Calm down." Amos motioned for his son-in-law to join him on the sofa. "I know how you feel, but Cece's murderer will be found, despite Mr. Reed."

Jourdan, seated, breathed in deeply and rubbed his temples. He calmed himself and smiled at the white-haired man. "Of course, Dad. I know better."

Years ago, Amos Johnson impressed the seventeen-year-old Jourdan with his ability to use his voice and words to lead a group of people to the Lord. People looked at Amos with respect—despite his small stature—and were awed by his sermons.

Jourdan's own father had been a Missouri pig farmer with a work ethic as strong as his back. Alex Watters believed in settling disputes with his fists, not his head. Unfortunately, Jourdan had inherited his lightning temper. Not a good thing for a man of his size. At six-foot-three and a hundred-and-ninety pounds, a careless punch from Jourdan could easily knock a man unconscious.

Jourdan would rather emulate Amos. His calm wisdom was quietly dispensed and always correct. Only once had he seen the old man ruffled. The funeral of his only child had brought the dignified man slowly to his knees at the gravesite. His cries of, "I love you, Cece. Daddy loves you, baby girl," had ridden winds of grief, as his tears rained down the side of the casket, following his beloved daughter into the depths of the earth.

Jourdan's heart had nearly burst from grief that day, partially from the pain he saw on the old man's face, but mostly from his own. Cece, dear Cece—his wife and best friend—was gone. How easily she'd made the transition from a friend into a loving, devoted wife. He believed deep in his heart that he'd returned her devotion, had been a good husband.

The only thing he hadn't given his wife was a baby, although they'd tried everything, even in-vitro fertilization. Cece had blamed herself when it hadn't worked.

Guilt sent tight, gripping fingers to squeeze Jourdan's heart. He'd buried his disappointment at not being able to conceive a child with his wife in the details of building a television ministry.

Allowing the dream to consume him night and day made it easier to put aside his own pain, but left precious little time to comfort Cece. She'd needed him. He'd let her down.

His dream for a television ministry was on the brink of coming true, but he couldn't revel in it. The woman who'd meant everything to him the past five years wouldn't be around to share in his success.

He rubbed at the ache in his chest and vowed to honor her memory and ensure her killer was brought to justice. Respecting a long mourning period was all he could do for her now.

"You look tired, Jourdan," Evelyn observed. "Why don't you go upstairs and lie down?"

"No thanks, Mom. I need to get home." He gave her a big hug. "Dinner was great, as usual. Even Reed couldn't spoil the taste of your pot roast."

"He's only trying to do his job, Son. Remember that," Amos said. "Don't go getting upset if he doesn't do it as well as you'd like him to."

"I can't believe you think it's all right for him to drag Cece's name through the mud."

"I don't agree with the way he's going about the investigation, but he'll soon discover he's barking up the wrong tree."

"He's totally inept." Jourdan headed toward the door. "Luckily, the election isn't far off."

"Perhaps." Amos accompanied him out the front door. When they reached the relative privacy of the driveway, he spoke again. "Your mother-in-law is worried about you, Son."

"Why? I'm fine."

"Seems you were looking a little odd this morning after church. Anything you'd like to talk about?"

Jourdan tensed. Had Evelyn seen or heard what the woman in yellow had said to him? No, Dad. There's really nothing to tell."

"Fine, fine. Just had to be sure."

Jourdan got into his Lincoln Town Car, backed out of the driveway, and pointed the car toward home. He barely noticed the chilly interior, his head whirled with unbidden visions of the woman from church. Passion. The name suited her.

He wondered if she'd come again to Zion Baptist. Would he have a chance to apologize for hurting her feelings? He'd be

16

careful not to get too close, though. She was much too bright and beautiful for him to trust. And it wouldn't be right to show interest in any woman. Yet, he couldn't shake the feeling his past might be trying to repeat itself.

*   *   *   *   *   *   *   *   *   *   *   *   *

As if the sun laid a warming caress on Passion's face and shoulders, she still glowed with immense feelings of peace and contentment during the examination. Already, she'd made her decisions about the child.

Clarissa Hartman removed the ultrasound gadget from Passion's yet-flat belly. "The baby's heart sounds good and strong."

The doctor's reassuring words sent Passion's spirits soaring even higher. Her eyes watered with emotion. There was really a baby in there.

"Have you given any more thought to adoption?" The doctor set aside the instrument and took a seat in a rolling chair.

Passion sat up slowly. "I'm going to keep it. I don't see how I could do anything else."

Doctor Hartman smiled. "That's commendable, given the circumstances."

Commendable or stupid? The doctor thought she was a single woman who'd decided to raise a child on her own. She was partially right; Passion wasn't going to tell her any different.

How could she possibly explain that her pregnancy resulted from a good deed which had taken a strange turn? The circumstances were too unreal to believe—even for herself.

Adjusting her clothes, Passion welcomed the warmth of her red sweater after the chill of the examination room. "Thanks, Doctor."

Passion slid from the table and walked out to the lobby where her elderly friend sat flipping through a *Jet* magazine.

Shirleen looked up expectantly. "Well?"

"I heard the heartbeat." Passion grinned, still overtaken by the miracle.

"You keepin' it for shore, ain't you?" Shirleen pushed out of her chair to hug Passion.

"Yeah, but our worries are just beginning." Passion wouldn't abandon the child. This baby was hers now, but she hated the thought of raising it in such a bad neighborhood. This baby deserved better than that.

A little guiltily, she wondered if she owed Reverend Watters the truth. She should have told him when she'd had the chance. Then again, how would he have taken the news that she carried his child, when he considered her a *temptress*?

Just the thought of the way he'd spoken the word hurt her all over again. She'd done the right thing in not telling him.

"I seen the cutest baby clothes in Kmart the other day."

* * * * * * * * * * * * *

The two women walked toward the building's exit.

"Shirleen, we can't afford to . . ."

"I said, we goin' shoppin'. There ain't no use in you arguin'."

That was the truth. Passion had never met anyone more stubborn than Shirleen.

She remembered sneaking over to her older friend's apartment when she was twelve, asking to spend the night. When Shirleen had asked why, she'd told her about one of her mom's boyfriends coming into her room, feeling her up. Shirleen had insisted Passion go back and teach him a lesson—no arguments.

Later, Passion grew terrified when the hall light sliced the dark in her bedroom and the tall man loomed over her. She'd almost hated Shirleen for making her return. She took a deep breath, smelling cigarettes and stale alcohol, trying to remember what her friend had told her.

As soon as his rough hand began to slide down her tender breasts, Passion remembered, she slipped the weapon from under the sheets. A shard of light gleamed on the small, dark

18

dome peeking from his boxer shorts. She swung at it as hard as she could.

He screamed and held himself, crawling out of the room. Shirleen never did get her rolling pin back.

Passion now followed Shirleen outside, the cool crisp air bringing her out of her reverie. She looked down at the old woman as they walked. Shirleen was stubborn, for sure. Even a heart attack last year hadn't kept her from doing her volunteer work at the hospital.

She always said she owed a debt to doctors for making her husband's last days as painless as possible, so she'd do what she could for others. And did.

Furthermore, Shirleen had never judged Passion for the things she'd done in the name of survival. She was always around with a soft shoulder and a "Hush, now. It's gonna be all right," in the worst of times.

"Shirleen?"

"Yeah, sugah?" Her bright eyes sparkled and her plump, brown cheeks were flushed with the autumn air. Wisps of gray hair blew around her face.

Passion smiled at her friend, not knowing quite what to say.

"You welcome, honey. You welcome."

The bus ride home from the doctor's office was thirty minutes with twice that number of bus stops to endure. Passion decided the first thing she would buy, if she had money, would be a nice big car. She wasn't very patient about waiting on buses.

They entered their apartment building, once the bus reached the projects. It worried Passion, Shirleen getting winded walking up the stairs. She'd been having difficulties lately. Passion made a mental note to check on an apartment on the first floor or to get a lease in a building with a working elevator.

"Phew. Somebody been layin' the perfume on thick." Shirleen's nose crinkled as she paused to catch her breath.

Passion noted the unmistakable scent of Obsession for Men

drifting down the stairwell, blending with other, more unpleasant odors. "Yeah. Reminds me of a certain well-oiled snake I know."

Shirleen snorted in disgust. "You mean, pretty-boy Dre Woods?"

"One and the same." Passion unlocked their apartment door and tried to forget her unpleasant past with Dre. When she'd first left home and found herself on the streets, she'd considered him her savior. He'd fed her and given her a job.

At fifteen she'd danced half-naked in his club, too naive to know her feelings of discomfort were well-founded. Still, it had been at Midnight Dreams where she first met Bob Anderson. Convinced he was in love with her, and she with him, she foolishly believed he'd leave his wife and marry her.

It had taken two years for her to come to grips with reality. When she left him, tearful and disillusioned, Dre Woods comforted her and took her in again.

Looking back, she could see with extreme clarity how Dre had manipulated her into thinking he was a kind, caring man. In reality, all he really cared about was how he could use her and the rest of the women he brought in off the streets.

When Dre decided to expand his business to drug dealing and pimping, Passion knew the time to go had arrived. There was no way she'd let the likes of his drunken, ill-mannered clientele so much as touch her.

Instead, she dressed nicely and invited herself to business parties at high-profile hotels. Nice places to meet nice men. She'd met many, but they were all married.

At some desperate point, she'd decided it was better to share a man than not have one at all. After two long, loveless liaisons, though, she aspired to become more than a professional mistress.

The last time she'd run to Dre, she'd witnessed the true beast he'd become. Thank goodness for Shirleen's return from Colorado.

She could hear Shirleen breathing hard behind her as they walked inside the apartment. "You doin' all right, Shirleen?"

"Yeah, sugah." She sank onto the worn sofa. "Just has to catch my breath."

"You need to see your doctor." Passion stood with hands on her hips.

Shirleen waved her away—swatting—as if a fly buzzed around her ear. "I'm okay. It's you I worries 'bout."

Passion rolled her eyes. "Don't start." She should never have mentioned Dre's name. The first time Shirleen set eyes on him, she'd decided he wouldn't do anyone any good.

"Hear me out, now." The dear woman's eyes clouded with concern. "That Dre's been followin' you around for eight years like a dog chasin' a bone."

Dre did have an uncanny talent for finding Passion, no matter where. "I hate to admit it, but I think he's still got a thing for me."

"That may be, but he been actin' crazier and crazier every time he sees you."

"Only I could get a pimp to fall in love with me, when he's got a whole harem to choose from," Passion muttered.

"Well, he may be in love, but that don't mean he won't hurt you."

Her friend told the truth about his strange behavior, but Passion still felt some debt to the man for saving her when she'd been down and out. "I don't think he'd hurt me."

The old woman shook her head. "That's prob'ly what that young girl thought too, 'fore he beat her to a pulp."

Passion cringed. The memory of the young dancer's bleeding, battered face being pounded under Dre's fist still made her nauseous. And he'd done it for what? Twenty bucks the girl had tucked inside her bra to keep for herself.

"Dre said it was business. He had to keep the girl's respect," Passion said hollowly.

"You kin believe that if you wants," Shirleen grumbled. "But one thing's for shore."

21

"What's that?"

"He gonna have to come through my wide behind to get to you. And that's a fact."

Passion reached out to hug her dearest friend. She silently thanked God for Shirleen, the one person in the world who loved her unconditionally.

Chapter III

"What in the world is you up to, chile?"

"Oh, hi, Shirleen." Passion looked up from the book and noticed her scattered notes. She'd been thinking nonstop for the past four days trying to figure out how to re-introduce herself to Jourdan Watters. "Sorry for the mess, I'll pick it up."

"Okay." Shirleen puffed her way past Passion. "But, you still . . . ain't answered . . . my question."

"I got to thinking about what Reverend Watters said in his sermon. About how we need to know God's plan for our marriages and all that." Passion followed Shirleen into the kitchen and began to help put away the food. "I went about this thing all wrong last time."

"I see you had my Bible out on the floor," Shirleen chided. "What did ya find out?"

"Near as I can tell, a woman's got to do whatever her husband says, believe what he believes, and not screw around on him."

Shirleen chuckled.

"I figure that doing what a man says shouldn't be too hard,

as long as I want to do it. And I have no desire to do any screwing around. I've had enough of that to last a lifetime. I want respectability."

No man had more respectability than Jourdan Watters. A powerful speaker—a man of God, not driven by the needs of the flesh. A faithful husband. She needed and craved his decency.

The thought of his powerful bronze arms around her and his dark, piercing eyes staring into her own made her more excited than she'd imagined possible. No wonder his wife had said she'd do anything for him.

The tough part would be winning his heart. Passion feared she'd already lost hers to him.

"I figure I'll join the church, maybe even the choir," she said to Shirleen. "That way he'll notice me and see me as a respectable, marrying kind of woman. What do you think?"

"I think you nuts." Shirleen giggled. "If the man's gonna fall in love with you, then he just will. Ain't nothin' all your planning gonna do 'cept get you near him, which I suspect is the first step. After that, it's up to him what he's gonna do."

"I guess you have a point, Shirleen. But when I was up at that altar and he touched my face . . ." She closed her eyes and said breathlessly, "It was awesome how much electricity sparked between us."

"Yeah, well. Don't go mistakin' paradise for a preacher. It ain't the first time you got a man all hot and bothered, you know."

"It's the first time a man did that to *me*." Passion smiled.

"Oh, and by the way." Shirleen closed the cabinet, then sank into a chair to fan her overheated face. "What you s'pose he'd think about that child you carryin'?"

"He'll be thrilled." Passion put away the plastic grocery bags, hoping her words were the truth. She didn't have much time.

October had brought winter weather and an extra five pounds to Passion's waist. It wouldn't be long before her stretch pants became uncomfortable. She could barely zip up her favorite pair of jeans.

Unless she missed her guess, her pregnancy would become obvious soon. Not much time to win a husband.

"Don't be too sure 'bout that," Shirleen cautioned. "Where you goin'?"

"To church. The choir practices on Wednesday nights." Passion left the kitchen, tossing the words casually over her shoulder. She sensed Shirleen's pursed lips and wagging head.

"I sure hopes you know what you're doin', chile."

Passion knew exactly what she was doing. Making a future for herself and this baby. By rights, Jourdan Watters should be part of it.

She knew the feelings that stirred within her had been mirrored in his eyes. Despite her need to have him as her husband, she'd have to wait for the right opportunity and not give in to her impulsive nature.

* * * * * * * * * * * * *

Thirty minutes later, Passion entered Zion Baptist Church and found comfort in the high beams and solid walls of the old building. Even with contemporary accents, the old, dark wood and impressive surroundings were a testament to the dedication and support from the church's members to their charismatic minister.

A smiling man approached her, ceiling lights reflecting on his shiny brown head. "May I help you?" he asked.

"I'm Passion Adams. I've come to join the choir."

A wider grin spread on his face. "Always delighted to have a new singer. Bless you for doing the Lord's work, Passion. I'm John Singletary, the choir director." He extended his hand. "Do you sing alto or soprano?"

"I'm really not sure," she answered honestly. The only singing she'd done was to accompany Mariah Carey or Whitney Houston on the radio.

25

"Not to worry. We'll figure it out." The kindly man ushered her into the sanctuary where the other choir members were chatting.

Her presence attracted odd glances and a flurry of whispers among a clutch of women. Two women looked familiar. Weren't they the ones who'd attacked her attire?

Anger heated Passion's face.

Not now.

Getting defensive wouldn't help in reaching her long-term goal. Still, she couldn't help but send the women a frosty glare before taking the empty seat two rows down from them. She concentrated on carrying a tune.

The music powerful, the song lyrics uplifting, she clapped and swayed with the choir. For a moment—a brief moment—she actually felt part of the group. This was the most fun she'd had in a long time. It would be like starring in "Sister Act" when they all had their robes on.

"Great job, Passion," said a beautiful woman in braids and a pound of mascara after practice ended and the choir had filed into the hallway.

No daggers shot from this female's eyes and her friendly tone was laced with warmth.

"Thanks." Passion couldn't remember the woman's name, but smiled in response to the honest compliment.

"Oh, Reverend Watters," the woman called to the preacher as he exited Bible study across the hall.

Passion's heart skipped a beat. Braids was after *her* man. She watched as the young woman tossed a braid over one shoulder and shimmied her partially exposed breasts in the reverend's face.

Tacky. Passion checked her watch. Only ten minutes before her bus was due. *Come on, Princess Jiggles, out of the way.* The reverend dismissed the woman with a polite smile a moment later.

Perfect.

Passion stepped up beside him. "Reverend?"

He turned to her. A hint of black stubble accented his bronze skin. His wonderful eyes attracted her like magnets.

Frantic feelings welled up inside her again.

"Passion Adams, isn't it?" He smiled. A more than "just-polite" smile, Passion noted. Her stomach did a flip-flop of joy. "I'm surprised you remembered."

John Singletary rushed by, buttoning his coat as he ordered, "Hey folks, better get on home. It's starting to snow."

"We'll be leaving in a bit, John. Drive carefully," the reverend said to the retreating man.

"Oh, and Passion . . ." The choir director stopped. "We'll see you Sunday morning. It's not often that I get a new recruit who can actually sing." He grinned and left.

The reverend shot an eyebrow upward. "You joined the choir?"

"Yes." Her mood brightened with his reaction. She could tell he was impressed. "I figure it's the least I can do for the church."

"I appreciate your willingness to get involved," he said, obviously reassessing her.

Passion looked at the floor, nervously. "I, uh, also noticed in the bulletin . . . you need a secretary for the church office."

"As a matter of fact, we do." With a wary look on his wonderful face, Jourdan asked, "Are you interested?"

She noted a frown of suspicion drawing his eyebrows inward.

"I don't have much experience, but I learn fast." She dropped her voice. She was sounding too perky. "I'd be happy to interview for the position." She inched closer to him.

Jourdan cleared his throat and shifted from one foot to the other. "That won't be necessary, Miss Adams. The job doesn't pay much above minimum wage. I'm afraid we'll take anyone who wants it."

"Since you've made it sound so attractive . . ." Eyes on his delicious five-o'clock shadow, she extended her hand and gave him her best smile. "I accept."

Passion resisted the urge to feel the roughness of his face beneath her hand. She did allow her eyes to wander down his strong physique. The outlines of his muscled arms beneath his black sweater flexed easily as he moved his Bible from one hand to the other to take the fingers she offered.

Passion exhaled slowly to ease the pressure in her lungs and the dizziness in her head caused by his firm, warm handshake.

"You're certainly full of surprises." His full lips turned up at the corner, his dark eyes twinkling. "Will you accept my apology, as well?" he asked, releasing his grip.

"For what?"

"It appeared I hurt your feelings when we first met." His forehead creased with concern. "That was certainly not my intention."

He was apologizing? To her? She waved a hand dismissively. "Don't give it another thought. I'll be looking forward to seeing you next Sunday."

"Next Sunday?"

"Yeah, you know. When you preach and I sing?" she teased.

"Of course." He laughed the nicest laugh Passion had ever heard.

"Well, I've got a bus to catch." She backed up slowly.

"Good night, Miss Adams."

"Passion," she corrected and turned toward the doors.

It was going to be a great bus ride home. She bundled her jacket and pulled its hood over her head to avoid the big snowflakes plummeting to earth in a whirling white frenzy. Beneath the street lamp, she looked at her watch. The bus should arrive any time now.

* * * * * * * * * * * *

Jourdan stood rooted to the spot, after having watched Passion Adams walk out the door and into the snowy night. Their conversation had convinced him that he'd misjudged the woman. Passion had a kind, generous spirit. She'd joined the choir and volunteered to be the church secretary. If he'd been thinking, he would have asked her assistance for the upcoming holiday feast for the poor. These days there were too few volunteers for all that had to be done.

He realized now why he'd reacted so strongly at their first meeting. No use blaming it on her extraordinary beauty. He couldn't trust his own reaction, not in her presence. Even now, his physical attraction to the woman pressed uncomfortably against his slacks.

His lustful needs were his own problem. He should be thanking the Lord for Passion's generosity, not damning her as a spawn of Satan. He willed the tightness in his BVDs to subside.

"Down, boy," he instructed.

"What's that, Reverend?"

Startled, Jourdan wheeled around to meet the curious gaze of Sister Martha Biddle. "I, uh . . . I was just saying 'oh boy,'" he stammered awkwardly. "Miss Adams volunteered to fill our secretarial position."

"Oh?" The narrow-faced woman smoothed her flowered print dress and raised a precisely drawn eyebrow. "How interesting. She doesn't seem the type."

Her catty voice made Jourdan instantly angry. "What do you mean? What *type* makes a good church secretary?"

"Oh, don't mind me." Mrs. Biddle recovered sweetly, waving a white-gloved hand. "Just an old woman talking too much."

Jourdan eyed her skeptically.

"Have you seen my nieces?" Sister Biddle inquired.

"Your nieces?"

"Rochelle and Laticia."

As if on cue, they both rounded the corner and stood smiling beside their aunt.

Jourdan glanced at his watch. "It's getting late, ladies, and the roads are slick. We'd best be on our way." The last thing he wanted was to be snowed in with Sister Biddle and her rampantly wagging tongue.

29

"How sweet of you, Reverend," Martha Biddle crooned. "Isn't it sweet of him, his concern for our safety, girls?"

Both of them voiced their agreement with overzealous exclamations and exaggerated smiles.

Jourdan smiled wearily. "Shall we go?" he asked, forcing pleasantness.

Stopping by his office, he grabbed his coat, then herded the twittering ladies from the church and into the parking lot. Cold wind stung his cheeks and penetrated his coat. He cleared the snow from Mrs. Biddle's windshield and noticed the lone figure with hunched shoulders standing beneath the street lamp. Passion.

Mrs. Biddle thanked Jourdan profusely—making too big a fuss for such a small courtesy—before driving away.

Jourdan started his Town Car, turned the heat on full blast, then scraped the car's windshield. Finishing quickly, he tossed the scraper onto the back seat with frozen fingers and drove across the street to the bus stop.

Passion stamped her feet and blew on her mittened fingertips to stay warm. She looked around for a less frigid place to wait for the bus without much luck.

"Miss Adams."

She whirled toward the familiar voice. "Yes, Reverend?"

"Would you like a ride?"

Gratefully, she entered the car and sank into the leather seats, welcoming the lukewarm air that blew from the vents. The car smelled faintly of aftershave. She inhaled discreetly, enjoying the fresh, manly scent.

"Thanks." She smiled. "Looks like the bus got stalled somewhere."

"It's pretty slick out here. Which way is home?"

"Tenth and Washington." And to think, she hadn't even planned this. She hoped it would take a very long time to get home.

"I wish I'd known you were still out here. I would've finished up earlier."

"How could you have known?" Passion excused him graciously, touched by his concern.

They sat in silence for a while. Passion stared out the window, yearning to stare at his handsome silhouette.

"Where are you from?" Reverend Watters broke the silence.

"Never lived anywhere but Kansas City." In fact, she'd only been out of the state once, but now wasn't the time to mention it.

"You have family here?"

"Just my mother." At least she thought Sherrie Adams was still in town. It had been years since she'd last seen her. From time to time she thought about dropping in for a visit. Inevitably, she found a reason not to. No way would Passion discuss her family with the reverend. "I really enjoyed your preaching." Flattery, yes, but true.

She caught his smile as the car passed beneath a street lamp.

"I was wondering, though," she said. "A few weeks ago, you spoke about God's plan for marriages. What did you mean by that?"

"Just that God planned for men to be the head of the household. Of course, some men think that means ordering their wives around and making them beg for spending money."

"You don't?"

"I don't." He warmed to the subject. "I think it means a man must take responsibility for leading his family down the right path, setting the example for his children."

Passion shivered at his mention of children. She wondered again if she should tell him about the baby. The child was much more his than hers.

Passion lay a protective hand over her stomach, unwilling to give it up. Hoping the three of them would become a family.

"Do you ever wish for children, Reverend?" She held her breath.

"All the time." His reply had been softly spoken, with undertones of sadness. "My wife and I . . ."

The dark car and his deep voice wrapped Passion in a blanket of sorrow. He grieved for Cece—his loss.

Shaking her head, Passion wished he already knew. Cece had intended to tell him about their deal before she was killed. Now that task fell to her. Passion took a deep breath.

"Jourdan—"

Fierce lights of an eighteen-wheeler pierced the windshield, the driver blaring his horn.

Passion jolted.

Jourdan applied the brakes; a car at the intersection ran a red light. The Town Car fishtailed, barely missing the sliding vehicle in front of them. Passion braced her hand on the dash, trying not to scream.

Horns honked. Lights flashed. Snow whirled. Cars came at them. Metal crunched metal. And they stopped.

Miraculously, they'd missed all the other cars, instead sliding into the curb.

"You okay?" Jourdan asked not two seconds after their abrupt halt.

She nodded, her fingers pressed protectively against her stomach.

The sound of the driver side door opening and the cold rush of snowy air made Passion open her eyes. Twisting around, she saw two cars in the intersection, their bumpers and lights entangled in unwilling introduction. The reverend was running, sliding, running toward a third car that rested on its side.

A small arm appear from the window. *Oh my God. A baby!*

The reverend freed the child from its car seat the same moment Passion slid up beside him. "Give it to me." She panted warm clouds in the cold air. "Are there other children?"

"I don't see any," he replied, handing her the screaming child. "The woman is out cold."

Passion sniffed the air. "Is that gasoline?"

"Yeah." He ducked into the car's interior and braced himself against the door panel. "I need to get her out of here before it explodes or catches fire." He looked at Passion. "See if you can find some help."

She clung to the blue snow-suited bundle, carefully placing one foot before the other. Halfway across the street, she slipped on an invisible patch of ice. Gripping the baby tighter, she struggled to keep her balance, but lost her footing. She landed heavily on her butt. Panic ripped through her gut. *My baby!*

The child in her arms stopped crying. His little eyes were wide as he stared at her.

"Scared you too, huh?" Passion smiled weakly at the little brown face trimmed in white fringe.

The baby rewarded her with a beaming toothless grin.

Carefully, Passion held the baby in one arm and lifted herself with the other. Thankfully, she seemed to be okay.

She approached two male drivers of other crashed cars. They argued over the damage to their vehicles. "Are you guys all right?"

"Yeah, but my car—" The one in the expensive cashmere overcoat spun around.

A twinge of discomfort twisted her gut at the sight of her former employer. "Oh . . . Dre . . . Nice to see you again." She smiled but didn't mean it.

A slow grin spread across his thin features. Weaving unsteadily, he narrowed his eyes in appraisal up and down Passion's body. "Mm, mm, mm! You're sure lookin' good, sunshine."

His voice had a liquored lilt.

Passion bristled at his endearment. Many years ago, on the night he tried to steal her virginity, he'd called her that. Shirleen's rolling pin had rid her of his disgusting advances.

"What can we do for you, lady?" the other man asked impatiently.

"There's a blue car over there." She pointed. "A woman is unconscious. We smell gas. Can you help get her out?"

The stranger immediately moved in that direction, his own troubles forgotten.

Dre remained. His slit eyes looked over at the reverend. "Who is *we*?"

"No one," Passion said quickly. "Just someone giving me a ride home."

"You don't have to lie to me, girl. That's your new sugar daddy, isn't it?" His hand wavered unsteadily in the snow-flurried air.

Frowning in irritation, Passion tried to dismiss him. "No. I've decided I don't need anyone to take care of me anymore." True. She didn't want Jourdan for his money. Her desire for him ran much deeper than his pockets.

"You could always come back to me." Dre staggered in her direction.

Passion assessed his high yellow coloring, his beauty salon waves, and his gold hoop earring. There was nothing about this lowlife that appealed to her. "I wouldn't feel right about that, Dre. You've done enough already."

"So when you gonna show a little gratitude?" The way he said that made the hair on the back of her neck rise. He'd clearly gone way past drunk tonight. He shouldn't be out in the snow, driving his own car. "Where's Tracks?"

"Around." Dre tugged at the waistband of his slacks. "Told him I had to see my lady tonight. Told him to stay nearby in case I needed a relief driver."

Damn his possessive soul. He'd been following her.

He took a step toward her and slipped.

Thank goodness for booze and slick Italian leather shoes. Passion backed away slowly from the cursing man as he struggled to his feet. She watched in amusement as he dusted the snow off his suit and straightened his collar. Even drunk, he had to look good.

The baby wriggled restlessly when screaming sirens and flashing lights filled the night. "Go home, Dre. It's cold."

Dre held onto the car handle and gestured helplessly. "I just wanna talk to you, sunshine. Can't we talk?" He glared at the bundled baby, as if noticing the child's presence for the first time.

"What you doing with that brat?" he yelled.

Terrified screams rose from the baby's small lungs.

"Shush, shush, little bit. He's not going to hurt anyone. It's okay." Passion continued to back away. It was too cold for the child to stay out much longer. She needed to get to the warm car.

"I've gotta go." As she turned, the reverend walked up to her.

Jourdan sent a quizzical look in Dre's direction. "Who're you?"

Dre released his grip on the door handle and offered his hand to the reverend. "Dre. Doctor Dre."

Passion rolled her eyes at his street moniker.

Jourdan hesitated visibly before shaking his hand.

"Passion's a real good friend of mine." Dre's eyes were dark and haunted in the sparse light of the street lamp. "We go way back."

"That's nice," Jourdan said failing to offer anything about himself.

When her eyes met Dre's, Passion sent him a poisonous look. "We'll talk later. Much later."

She quickly changed the subject. "The baby's not hurt, Reverend, but he's hungry. Do you suppose there's a bottle in the car?" Passion noted firemen hosing it down with some foaming substance.

Jourdan held out his arms. "The baby's father is here."

She looked past him to the somber man following beside the stretcher. "Is his wife going to be all right?"

The reverend frowned. "If it's God's will."

Tugging the snowsuit's hood, Jourdan tried to protect the baby's face. Black curls defied his efforts to cover them. He looked at Passion with sad eyes. "She's carrying another child."

Shielding the small face from snow with his shoulders, he headed toward the ambulance. leaving Passion empty-handed. And alone with Dre.

Crunching metal made her turn around. Dre's Beemer was being elevated for towing.

"Damn," Dre groused, clearly unhappy about his prized possession being totaled. The front end looked like a squashed soda can.

"Where's Tracks and our ride?" He searched the street for a moment, before staring at her. "How 'bout it, sunshine? You and your boyfriend got room?"

He hunched his shoulders when two policemen walked past. "I'm in kind of a hurry," he added.

"You know you can't leave the scene of an accident, Dre." She folded her arms against another gust of chill wind.

A second invasion of blue uniforms increased Dre's anxiety. He pulled his collar up past his ears and made like a turtle.

Passion had half a mind to point him out, just to avoid answering his question. The last thing she wanted was to have him and the reverend in the same car.

Thankfully, Tracks appeared. Ignoring Passion, he spoke quietly to Dre. "Let's go, man. I got a car waiting."

Dre stalled.

"Cops are crawling around here waiting to slap cuffs on somebody. *Let's go.*"

Passion breathed a sigh of relief when Dre finally complied.

Within minutes of Dre's flight, Passion and Jourdan were back in his undamaged car, driving away.

"I've had enough excitement for one evening. How about you, Passion?" He removed his gloves and rubbed his palms together vigorously.

"Absolutely," Passion agreed. "Oh, and by the way, thanks."

His forehead creased in confusion. "For what?"

"You finally called me by my first name." She gave him a big smile.

"Oh, did I?" He also smiled, then shifted the car into drive.

Large snowflakes splattered the windshield. The warmth of the car cocooned them in a world all their own. It wouldn't be long before they reached her apartment building. Not much time to tell her tale. How in the world was she going to do this?

"Would it disturb you too much if I called you Jourdan?" Passion held her breath waiting for his answer.

"No."

"Good." Yet, she was disappointed his answer had been directed toward the window, not to her.

"So, Jourdan." She tried to keep her voice cheerful. "Do you accept confessions?"

"I'm not a Catholic priest," he answered with a chuckle.

"I know. But would you listen if I gave one?" Passion's heart beat like rumbling thunder, partially from Jourdan's nearness, partially for what she was about to reveal.

He gave her a quick, curious glance. "I'll listen," he said, his voice low and deep. "What do you want to confess?"

"A lot of things." She stared straight ahead, not daring to look at him. "I hate my mother. She stayed drunk or high and prostituted herself to make money."

"That must've been awful," Jourdan sympathized.

She shrugged. "Most of the time, I took care of myself, so it wasn't a big deal to do it when I left home at sixteen." Passion reflected for a moment. "I guess it's true what they say."

"What's that?"

"The fruit doesn't fall far from the tree." She hung her head and squeezed her eyes against the sting of tears. "I was a mistress to several married men I didn't love. I used them to stay alive." She paused. "I guess that's the same thing."

Jourdan didn't reply.

Why had she admitted her dark past? Maybe he needed to know what kind of woman was carrying his child. And maybe, if she laid all her cards on the table now, she could discover if her hopes of a lifetime with him were realistic.

"You know, the first time I ever stepped inside a church was the Sunday I met you?" she asked.

He remained silent. Probably wondering how long it would be before he could get her out of his car, Passion feared.

Just when she thought she'd drown in silence, he spoke quietly. "Did you mean it when you accepted Jesus Christ as your savior?"

His sermon had moved her and she had meant it at the time. "Yes."

"Then, your slate is wiped clean. The Lord is gracious and forgiving." The sincerity in Jourdan's words was unmistakable.

"Do *you* think badly of me?" His acceptance meant everything to her at the moment.

"No, Passion. I don't." He directed his immediate response to her. "I think it's remarkable you survived."

She released a long sigh. "It's comforting to hear you say that." So much for the small stuff. Passion wondered how he'd react to the big things she'd yet to confess. "My apartment building is just in the next block."

As he and Passion neared her apartment, Jourdan reminded himself of his vow to respect a long mourning period. Passion's confession had all but undone him. He'd longed to stop the car, take her in his arms, and comfort her with kisses.

She'd cried no tears, but the scars of her life were laid bare with her words. He wanted desperately to ease her pain, but like with Cece, he held back. Passion was still more stranger than friend—more fire than ice. He knew to touch her would increase his need to possess her.

Jourdan parked the car and studied the apartment building. Despite the coat of new snow at its base, the old stone dwelling appeared ready to crumble from its foundation upward.

"I'll walk you in," he offered.

"Wait." Passion grabbed his arm.

Mesmerized by the probing beauty of her eyes in the dim light, he met her gaze and sensed another confession in the offing. "Yes?"

She opened her mouth, then swallowed and let her hand slide from his arm. "You're a perfect man, aren't you?"

"No." He laughed nervously. "Hopefully, just forgiven."

Seriousness mixed with yearning scored her comment: "That's what I want. Forgiveness."

"The Almighty forgives our sins." Could He forgive a preacher's forbidden desires?

Passion smiled. "It's not necessary for you to walk me inside." Looking away, she opened the car door. "I've done it a thousand times."

"I insist." It wasn't chivalry. Greedy for her presence, weak of will, Jourdan wanted a few more moments with her.

"All right. I give." she said in a playful swoon.

It came too easy for her, Jourdan decided. The voice toned for seduction. The body suited for sin. Her simplest gesture took his breath away—and she knew it.

Not since he'd lifted Bobbi Mae's dress, in the back of the barn, had he been so tempted by desire. His father's stern lessons about fornication had been whipped indelibly into his hide that night. Nothing short of a glacier would cool the heat in his veins tonight.

They went inside and climbed the stairs. Rustling paper and hollow footsteps echoed as they made their way to the third floor.

Jourdan crinkled his nose at the strong smells of the first two floors. Nearing the third, the mouthwatering smell of fried chicken met his nostrils. Passion stopped. The wonderful aroma drifted from her apartment.

"This is it." She pointed at number three-twenty-three. "Thanks again for walking me up. You didn't have to." Her voice was as inviting as a warm fire.

"My pleasure." *Careful, Jourdan. Remember Cece.* He retreated a step.

"I appreciate the ride home, too. It certainly wasn't dull." She took a step forward.

"Right. It wasn't." He smiled easily, trying to memorize the way her dark, shoulder-length hair went this way and that. He wanted to dive into those exquisite eyes and not surface for a week.

"It smells like Shirleen's been cooking. Would you like to come in for supper?"

Despite the protest of his stomach, he declined, her company far too intoxicating as it was. "No thanks. I'd better be going. It's snowing harder out there."

"You're right. Be careful driving home, Jourdan." She stood on tiptoes and kissed him gently on the cheek.

Her cool hand slid down the side of his face like hot ice. The gentle pressure of her body ignited flares of desire. Jourdan, yet determined, took another step back. "I'll be going."

Resolve formed swiftly in her extraordinary eyes. "Before you do, I really have something important to tell you." She flattened her palms on his chest.

"No more confessions." He placed a finger on her soft lips and instantly regretted the action. His control shattered and gave free reign to his need. Instinct drove him. Jourdan swiftly, urgently kissed her tempting lips.

His tongue dove hungrily into the sweet, dangerous honey of her mouth. Her arms circled his neck and her hips pressed against his. He encouraged her closer—his hands beneath her open coat sliding on the tight fabric covering her hips.

Passion's moans vibrated against his lips. Blood rushed to his head. He plundered the brown velvet of her neck with kisses, reaching up beneath her sweater until he felt the soft, warm weight of her breasts in his hands. His manhood throbbed like a sinner knocking at the gates of heaven.

Dear God, what was he doing? Cece was barely cold in the ground.

He released Passion quickly. His breath came in ragged gusts as he studied her confused face. "Passion, my wife . . . I can't—this isn't right."

He raced down the stairs before he could read her reaction.

Bursting out of the building, Jourdan threw himself backward onto the thick pile of snow in the small yard. He swore the stuff sizzled beneath him. He lay there, letting the big snowflakes cool his face. Only when the cold began to creep into his back and legs did he stand.

Never in his life had he felt this out of control of his emotions. From the moment she'd walked through his church doors, he'd been fighting the feeling of wanting. Wanting what he could not have.

It was time to focus on practical matters. Not only did he have to tend to his ministry, he also had to make sure Cece's murderer was caught and brought to justice.

Yet Passion had joined the choir and had become the church secretary. There would be no avoiding her. He only hoped she would forgive him for tonight.

Chapter IV

"Here you go, Eddie."

District Attorney Reed heard the popping gum before he deigned a glance at his secretary.

"How many times have I told you to call me Mr. Reed when we're in the office?" he asked irritably.

"I don't know." Vanessa's hands flew up in futility. "A thousand?"

Reed looked at the papers she thrust beneath his nose. "What's this?"

"Gawd." She rolled her eyes. Layers of mascara gave them a dramatic slant. "You forgot you asked me for these telephone records?"

"I didn't forget." Not in the mood for her flippancy, Reed snatched the papers from her curved red fingernails. "You might want to remember who signs your paycheck."

"My check has a signature *stamped* on it, thank you very much." Vanessa bobbed her head, sending long braids into motion. "Don't get testy with me just 'cause you're getting all that heat from the newspapers."

Surprised she read the newspaper at all, Reed asked, "What do you know about it?"

"I know Reverend Watters hates your behind—that's what I know." Vanessa eased herself into a chair opposite Reed and crossed one dark chocolate thigh over the other.

Reed took an appreciative look at the slender leg. It was a good thing she typed well, was efficient as a machine, and didn't mind a little slap-and-tickle after hours, otherwise he wouldn't put up with her insubordination.

Shifting his attention back to his desk, he shuffled through the records she'd given him and spoke without looking at her. "Watters has reason to hate me. I'm about to expose him for the forked-tongue liar he is."

Vanessa stilled her incessant chewing. "What're you talking about?"

He puffed his chest in satisfaction and tapped a finger on the papers. "These records show that Cece Watters, the reverend's wife, was making regular calls to a penthouse leased by Dre Woods."

"Who?"

"Dre Woods. Pimp and drug pusher."

"Oh." Vanessa's crossed legs exposed a fair amount of thigh as her short skirt rode up. "So, how do you know it was Cece making the calls?"

Reed let a wide grin spill across his face. He hadn't been this happy since his wife lost the house in the divorce settlement. "Because they all happened between seven and eight o'clock on Wednesday evenings."

He watched in enjoyment as Vanessa held up her palms in a "so-what?" gesture.

Leaning across his desk for emphasis, he delivered his point. "Watters has Bible studies at Zion from six-thirty until eight-thirty every Wednesday, so it couldn't have been him."

"Okay." Vanessa mimicked his position, exposing her cleavage. "If Cece Watters made the calls and is now dead, why would the reverend be afraid of anything you find out about it?"

Reed stared down the neck of Vanessa's blouse, growing aroused. "Watters would do anything to protect his precious image. He's got plans, big plans to expand into television ministry. Why, he even drives ten miles below the speed limit to avoid traffic tickets. The last thing he wants is to have his wife's name associated with a scandal."

Lust abundant, Reed took one velvety breast in his pale hand and felt her shudder beneath his touch.

"He's a good preacher. I go to his church. Ow!"

Releasing the tight squeeze he'd given her for that comment, Reed rose from his chair.

Vanessa rubbed her bruised flesh. "What was that for?"

"For not knowing what you're talking about." He crossed the room to the coatrack.

"So why do you think the preacher's wife called on a pimp? You don't think she was hookin' for him, do you?"

Reed slid into his suit jacket and overcoat. "I'm not ruling it out. We all know it's those quiet ones you've got to watch." He winked one hazel eye.

Vanessa rose and smoothed the tight material of her skirt. "I sure hope you figure it out. Because it looks like your job is on the line if you don't solve at least one murder this year. And who knows?" She sent a red-lipped smack in his direction. "The next DA might not be as talented as you."

The phone rang in time to keep him from throttling her on the spot. "Hello," Reed barked into the receiver.

"This is Sergeant Casey."

"Yeah, Sergeant."

"I'm calling to let you know the FBI just apprehended the suspect in the Watters case in Miami."

It was about damn time. "Did he have anything to say?"

"Yes, sir."

Reed could imagine the man puffing his chest in pride.

"We got a full confession. He says he was hired anonymously for $200,000."

"Yes!" Reed dropped the receiver gingerly and smiled smugly at his secretary. "We got us a conspiracy, darling."

"That's great, Eddie."

Reed followed her sashaying backside out of his office. "I gotta go. I don't know how long I'll be gone, so take messages."

"Okay. Oh, by the way, I'm leaving early today. I get my nails rebased every other Friday."

Reed suspected she'd be rich if she didn't spend half her paychecks trying to look good. Still, he'd bet ten to one she'd have all of his correspondence completed in half an hour, so she could leave. "Fine, but be at my house at eight tomorrow night."

"Is that an order or a request?" She put her hands on her hips.

Reed stabbed a finger toward Vanessa. "Don't start that crap." Next time he'd have to get a secretary with a lot less sass.

Heading for Dre Woods' ill-gotten, grand estate, Reed steered his Mercedes out of the parking garage and popped in his Wynton Marsalis tape. Excited, he whistled along with the trumpeter.

Jim and Tammy Faye Bakker would be nothing compared to the scandal he was going to expose on Reverend Watters.

The press would love him again, making him a shoo-in for the next election.

Time flew, his destination just a turn away. Reed suppressed a laugh as he pulled into the long driveway. He took the stairs two at a time to reach the big double doors of the huge home, then went solemn.

Damn Dre Woods. Reed would have to work another lifetime to afford a home this lavish now that his wife and her trust were gone.

His insistent knocking went unanswered. Fridays were

45

probably big business in Woods' line of work; it could be hours before he returned.

Reed slapped the steps irritably with his size eleven shoes as he went back to his car. Fine. He'd be here every day until he caught the little slimeball at home.

* * * * * * * * * * * * *

At home, Shirleen sat frowning on the worn sofa, her arms crossed beneath her ample breasts. "I knows you ain't goin' back to dat church."

"I have to. I'm doing a solo." Passion swallowed back a lump in her throat and glanced away.

Shirleen would scold her if tears welled again. Her dear friend had seen the cardiologist today. He'd told her she needed a triple bypass operation—soon.

Passion picked up her purse and coat from the sofa. "Plus, I have work to do."

"After what that man did to you?" Shirleen had tired, sleepless circles beneath her eyes. Passion felt guilty for keeping her up nights. But as quiet as she tried to be, Shirleen was up at the slightest sound, insisting on making tea and talking with her.

It hurt so bad that Jourdan had run away after he kissed her. It affected Passion's ability to sleep. Now, she had Shirleen to worry about as well.

"It wasn't Jourdan's fault." A pang of guilt and sadness shot through Passion's bruised heart. "He's right. Only a Jezebel would go after a man whose wife is barely dead. Worst of all, Cece was my friend. I should have more respect."

Shirleen reached up to take Passion's hands "Now, I wants you to listen to me good. You didn't do nothin' wrong. It was just bad timin', is all. If you go in that church, hold your head up high, hear?" She raised double chins.

Passion hugged Shirleen, trying to hide all the emotions building up inside. "All right, Shirleen. But you've got to prom—"

"Don't you worry none about me, now." Shirleen struggled to her feet to retrieve her needlework. "I just gets a little tired now and again."

"Just the same, get some rest. And take it easy on the stairs. It'll be a while before another low income apartment comes open."

Passion had tried repeatedly to bribe the gap-toothed super into giving them an apartment on the first floor, to no avail. He'd scratched his hairy white belly, said a quick "no-can-do," and slammed the door in her face. It was a small setback, but nothing would keep her from helping her friend.

"In the meantime, I found a real nice apartment to rent with a six-month lease for when you get out of the hospital."

Shirleen spoke softly, not turning around. "I knows I needs this operation. But I feels bad takin' your money, Passion honey. You sure you wants to do this?"

Passion crossed the room in two steps to hug the woman. All the money she had was the $5000 Cece had paid her for carrying her baby. She'd intended to use it to take computer classes, but that seemed trivial now.

"It's the very least I can do." She readjusted her purse on her shoulder and walked away quickly, before the two of them started crying all over again.

Passion left the apartment and trudged through the hard, dirty snow to the bus stop, irritated that the lazy super had neglected to clear the sidewalk. She hoped he fell on his wide, fat behind the next time he stepped outside his door.

The small, nervous knot in Passion's stomach grew larger as she climbed the bus steps and found a seat. Even after the painful past three days, she had some sadistic desire to see Jourdan again. She couldn't help remembering his deep, soft kiss melting every bone in her body, despite efforts to the contrary. The solid strength of his arms alone had kept her standing. She'd never known such intense feelings and, quite frankly, wasn't willing to give up on his company so quickly.

47

He'd felt it too. She needed to let him know that she could wait a while. After he'd mourned his wife properly, they could be together.

Passion knew that nothing short of all of him would ever be enough for her. He was everything she'd ever dreamed of. Solid. Respectable. Desirable. Unfortunately, he wanted nothing more to do with her.

It would be hard to face him today.

She should get off the bus, cross the street, and get on the next one going home to avoid the inevitable discomfort of their meeting. Except it was too late.

The bus pulled to a stop in front of Zion; she stepped down onto the pavement. Nauseous with tension, she steeled herself to see him again.

"You going to stand there looking sick, or are you coming in?"

Passion looked at the smiling face. "Oh, hi, Vanessa. I'm coming in." She was still Princess Jiggles in her tight knit dress.

"Good. I know you ain't worried about singing today." Vanessa guessed incorrectly about the source of Passion's tension. "'Cause you can bring down the house with that voice you got."

"Thanks." Her first assessment of the woman was blessedly correct. Vanessa was kind.

Passion walked inside with her. She liked her, despite her earlier play to be Jourdan's girlfriend. Passion figured Vanessa jiggled for attention, not because she was serious about any one man.

"Check it out, Passion." Vanessa wore a devilish grin as she pushed the stretchy fabric of her skirt down her thighs. "Watch these old dogs start salivatin' when you and me walk past."

Passion couldn't help but smile as Vanessa switched her bottom in an exaggerated swing while passing the group of men chatting in the hallway, her head held high and aloof. They suspended conversation for several seconds until they could no longer watch without turning their heads in obvious enjoyment.

48

Passion couldn't hold her laughter in. By the time they reached the robe room, she held her sides to keep them from splitting. "Vanessa, you ought to be ashamed."

"Sorry, girl." Her hand slapped the air while she laughed as well. "I couldn't help it. Did you see Deacon Jones? His eyes nearly bugged out of his head."

A fresh wave of laughter doubled Passion over. She knew the other choir members in the room were wondering about their sanity. It felt good to laugh. She wasn't about to let them spoil their fun.

Passion had had enough of Laticia, Rochelle, and the rest. Instead of getting angry, she'd adopted Vanessa's don't-give-a-care attitude. If they couldn't accept them as they were, that was their problem.

"What are you ladies finding so amusing?" Sister Martha Biddle approached them with a pinched expression.

"Not a thang, Mrs. B. Not a thang." Vanessa chewed noisily on her gum.

Sister Biddle's precise eyebrows shot up; she didn't approve. "You'd best get your robes on. We'll be going out in a moment." Her words were crisp and to the point. Turning on a heel, she strode to the opposite side of the room and began whispering with her nieces.

"Why she gotta be in people's business all the time?" Vanessa threw a robe over her head in a huff.

"Maybe she hasn't got anything better to do," Passion replied.

"Yeah, well, just because her dead husband was a deacon, don't mean she owns the church." Vanessa raised her voice just loud enough for the group of ladies to hear. Martha Biddle pursed her thin lips and led the group out the door to the choir pit where John Singletary awaited.

Moments later, Passion and Vanessa stood with the rest of the choir, singing as the last of the congregation filtered through the double doors of the sanctuary.

Passion centered on Jourdan. His eyes were closed, his face upturned in reverence as he prayed. "Say just one prayer for me," she pleaded silently.

"That is one *fine* man." Vanessa whispered between songs.

Passion smiled obligingly, nodding in agreement.

Jourdan finally opened his eyes and approached the podium. "Hallelujah, hallelujah." His deep voice vibrated throughout the sanctuary. "How many of y'all know that God is good today?"

"Amen," came the resounding reply.

"Praise, God." He looked down at notes placed next to his Bible. "It looks like we have a special treat this morning. One of our newest choir members will be singing for us. Passion Adams. Why don't you come on down, Passion, and minister to us in song?"

Jourdan extended his hand in invitation. A small smile reached the corners of his mouth and his dark eyes softened as they looked in her direction.

Passion relaxed a little. He didn't seem upset with her. She stepped within a foot of him and took a microphone from the stand. In a brief meeting of their eyes, Passion felt the power of his undisguised lust reaching to devour her. Head swimming, knees shaking, she wanted nothing more than to act on his invitation. He turned away quickly and took a seat in the pew at the edge of the stage.

Somehow, Passion found her mind and the strength to remain standing. She wondered if the sea of gawking faces had noticed her reaction.

The music started. She tried to remember the words.

* * * * * * * * * * * * *

Elbows on his knees, fingers folded in front of his face, Jourdan hugged the edge of his seat, breathing heavily. He listened to Passion sing to his flock, to their Lord. Awed by her delicate, golden-brown features and the faint, airy fingers of her perfume that drifted to him, he was wrapped in memories of their desperate encounter in the apartment hallway.

Her fingers held the microphone in a death grip, he noticed. Taut knuckles were her only indication of nervousness. Passion's lips parted in song.

Jourdan wet his lips, as if the action itself could bring back the sweet nectar of her kiss.

Her rich, powerful alto filled the sanctuary and the empty places in his heart.

Individuals in the crowd rose to their feet, releasing their mounting joy. Several threw their hands upward, others streamed tears.

Jourdan closed his eyes, trying to concentrate on his sermon, but again found himself weaving visions of himself and Passion within the words of Bible verses. In his thoughts she sang only to him, her voice sending tender notes to touch him like whisper-soft kisses.

He grabbed his chest a second time. *Lord, I'm in trouble.*

He forced her from his thoughts. He spread his arms, pleading for the light. Within moments, torrents of bright waves washed over him, offering temporary deliverance from her spellbinding temptation.

Her song ended and he opened his eyes, trembling with renewed conviction. If nothing else, he owed it to Passion to preserve her dignity. She hadn't deserved being groped in the hallway of her apartment building.

Guilt rolled his gut for Cece. More so when he remembered Passion's plea for forgiveness for past fornications. How could he have allowed himself, afterward, to take such shameless pleasure in her? From now on, she could trust him not to take advantage of her. Even if it meant steering a wide berth around her to keep his fleshly desires in check.

* * * * * * * * * * * *

After church Passion entered the crowded hallway, feeling ambivalent about her successful debut. The thunderous applause

51

of the audience had sent her soaring on heavenly clouds of joy only to come crashing to earth when Jourdan dismissed her quickly to get to his sermon.

Passion looked from left to right, making her way toward the big double doors. She nodded and said "thanks" for the hundredth time as yet another male church member patted her on the back.

"You tore that song up, sunshine."

Passion pulled her jacket closer to fight the sudden chill the voice provoked. The smile dropped from her face at the sight of her praiser who wore an Armani suit, sunglasses, and an entire bottle of Obsession. "Since when do you go to church, Dre?"

"Since I found out you were trying to make time with the preacher man here."

"Don't be silly." Twitching her nose, Passion pushed her way out of the heavy doors, welcoming the fresh, cold air of October. Unfortunately, Dre followed.

"I'm being silly?" The gold on his fingers sparkled in the bright sun as he pressed them to his chest. "You're the one trying to fit in where you don't belong."

Passion crossed her arms and took a long look at him. "And just where is it that I belong? With you?"

A smile slid across his face and he pulled a thin cigarette from its gold case. "I can think of a lot worse places."

"Well, I can't." Passion turned her attention to the street she had to cross to reach the bus stop. An unending stream of cars seemed to crawl down the street. Passion exhaled impatiently and tapped her foot on the pavement.

"How can you say that when I took you in, when you were sixteen, and cold and starving?" His use of guilt blatant, Dre lit his cigarette and blew the first puff of smoke in her face.

She'd been driven into the harsh, Kansas City streets in the middle of January, in fear of her red-eyed, knife-wielding mother. Shirleen had moved to Colorado—too far for her to travel at the time. Hunger and desperation sent Passion into the underworld of Dre Woods.

"I don't mean to sound ungrateful, Dre. But I did work while I was with you."

"You were a moneymaker all right. Tips thrown at your feet every night." Dre's smile brightened. "Don't make it sound like a prison sentence. Come on, sunshine, I'll give you a ride home and we can talk about the good old days." Dre pointed to a shiny black Lexus sitting in the church parking lot.

"Got a new car?" Passion asked, not really caring.

"Best one on the lot. Had it customized by an associate. You don't really wanna ride the bus, do you?"

"Not really." It was out of her mouth before she considered the implications.

"Good." Dre took her arm firmly and guided her over to the gilded car.

Tracks emerged from the car to open the rear door for Dre and Passion. A knit cap covered the big man's otherwise bald head. His eyes, as always, were wrapped from temple to temple in sinister-looking sunglasses.

Passion noted the parallel lines of scars on the man's cheeks. She'd heard that a gang had whipped him for stepping into their turf when he was eighteen. When he'd left the hospital, twelve of the gang members turned up murdered. No evidence was found, but everyone believed Tracks was guilty. Passion knew Dre paid well for the big man's reputation and protection.

"Hop in," Dre ordered. "I won't bite . . . unless you say where." His million-dollar smile gleamed in the sunlight.

Passion kept both feet planted on the concrete and pulled her head out of the car. "It's a little too flashy for me. I mean, gold door handles and locks? Besides, here comes my ride." Passion saw the bus in the distance. If she hurried, she could still catch it.

"I can't let you walk away from me again." Lips in a thin line of determination, Dre's bony fingers caught Passion's arm in a viselike grip.

Passion, irritated, grew wary of the icy glare he'd turned on her. "Why, Dre? Since when do you care so much about me?"

The ice behind his eyes melted.

"Truth is . . ." Dre's Adam's apple bobbed as he swallowed. Taking two ringed fingers, he ran them gently down the side of her face. "I've always cared about you."

Passion didn't like the desire that rang in his voice, nor the searing heat of his traveling fingers. "You mean to tell me, that of all the women you have working for you, I'm the only one you want?"

"Yes." He didn't even blink.

She feared as much. Chills ran up the back of her neck and arms. Her senses were on red alert. For the first time, she was afraid of what Dre might do.

"Surprised you, didn't I?" His fingers finally relaxed their grip on her arm.

"I'll say." Passion, forcing nonchalance, adjusted her coat and purse. She looked longingly at the bus as it closed its doors with a loud *tk-shhh* and roared down the street. "Look, Dre, I'm really flattered and all but—"

"I know what you're going to say, so stop right there." Dre held up a palm.

Passion looked at him curiously.

"You think you're too good for me, sunshine, don't you?"

"I didn't—"

"I know you do. You got some kind of high-and-mighty idea that if you go legit, people will look at you different—that you might get a preacher man for a husband."

His words made her uncomfortable. "Dre, I don't think—"

"Well, I got news for you." His gaze was black and cold as onyx. "You can't hide your fine face in a crowd of ordinary people and you can't disguise the curves of your body beneath choir robes." His stony glare heated as he scanned the material of her clingy jersey dress. His breath came in fast bursts. "And you can't bury the fire of your soul in a church of ice-cold Christians."

"Don't talk about what you don't know, Dre." She tugged her arm loose and backed away.

Dre reeled, his lip curling. "And you think you know somethin' about these people?"

"I'm one of them now. I don't believe in your world, Dre. I never did."

A slow smile brought up the corners of those thin lips. "You mean to tell me, you didn't like your weekly trips to the beauty shop? Or that plush penthouse all to yourself?"

Passion didn't answer. In truth, she'd enjoyed every luxurious moment of his lavish accommodations, except for Dre's persistent advances.

"What do you suppose the good folks in there would say if they knew you used to be an exotic dancer?"

Her heart panged with old embarrassment. "I was young and naive back then. You forced me into it."

"Did I?"

"As I recall, you kindly offered me the choice of dancing for you in exchange for food and shelter, or a box under a bridge." Passion fought to keep her anger at bay. He was sewer slime—preying on the young and unfortunate.

"I saw how you smiled at those men. You wanted them to want you."

"I've got to go." She backed away.

This time he didn't try to stop her. He simply leaned toward her, dropping the butt of his cigarette from his fingers. "Would these people pray for you, Passion? Do they really care about you?"

Passion watched streets and buildings blur through her tears. "I don't want to hear this."

Dre leaned closer, not touching. "How about that preacher man? What do you think he'd say if he knew?"

Passion swallowed the lump in her throat. She wanted to believe Jourdan would accept her, although she hadn't included this part of her life in her confession.

"He'd let you warm his bed every night, then curse you for tempting him when he got caught."

"Stop it, Dre." He'd landed too close to the truth. Jourdan had held her, until there had been no world outside his arms, then pushed her away like some demon that needed to be purged from his soul.

"Be my lady, Passion," Dre whispered, his breath hot and insistent against her face. "I'll give you the world."

Passion didn't pull back when he took her in his arms this time. Suddenly, it was tolerable, almost pleasant to have someone want her just the way she was—someone who couldn't be scandalized by her past. Someone who would love her.

Sense pushed its way through her foggy thoughts. He was manipulating her again.

She shoved him away. "No."

Monitoring his expression, Passion was surprised to see him smile. "It doesn't matter if these people ever accept me. I'll deal with it. But, Dre, I'm not going with you."

"Suit yourself, sunshine." He crossed his hands in front of his crotch. "But when the preacher man don't deliver, you know where I'll be."

"Yeah, burning in hell," she wanted to say, then thought better of it and headed back to the church.

* * * * * * * * * * * * *

Vanessa, just outside the double doors, waited for Passion to reach the top of the steps.

"I'd say you got yourself an admirer, girlfriend." She shoved a piece of gum between her moist plum lips then offered a stick to Passion.

"Not one I want to keep." Passion refused the gum and continued to watch Dre warily. It wasn't until he climbed into his car and Tracks drove out of the parking lot that she relaxed a little.

"Nice ride, though," Vanessa said appreciatively, watching the Lexus glide down the street.

"Yeah."

"So what's he do? Deal a little white powder?" There was no accusation in her inquiry. Just genuine curiosity.

"Runs a topless bar. Calls it Midnight Dreams," Passion answered evenly. It was a relief to be able to talk so comfortably. "Sells crack on the side, I think."

"I ain't asking unless you're tellin', but I sense you have stories to tell." Vanessa winked her dramatic brown eyes. "You wanna have lunch? There's a buffet just up the street."

It would be another twenty minutes before the next bus. With her church work finished for the day, Passion wasn't anxious to freeze her butt off in the cold. She smiled at her new friend. "Let's go."

Passion found it very easy, too easy to tell her abbreviated life story to Vanessa. Nothing surprised the woman. She just clucked understandingly about how a woman has to do whatever's necessary to survive these days.

"There's one thing I don't understand, Passion." She pointed a long, red fingernail.

"What's that?" Passion finished the last of her lemon meringue pie.

"Why did you leave your last man? You said he had enough money to put you up for a long time."

"That's right."

"What made you leave all that to live with your friend in the projects?" She tossed a wayward braid from her face as she worked on a piece of fried chicken.

"A nice lady made me an offer I couldn't refuse." Passion smiled at the wide-eyed look Vanessa gave her.

"Come on, girl. Don't leave me hangin' like that. What lady?"

"Cece Watters."

The chicken bone slid from Vanessa's fingertips and her mouth fell open. "Reverend Watters' Cece Watters?"

"Yep." Passion took a long sip of her water. She knew stalling would drive Vanessa crazy.

"Stop all that drinkin' and tell me what in the world you're talkin' about." Vanessa slapped at her hand playfully.

Passion put her glass down slowly and smiled at the Kodak moment of Vanessa hanging on the edge of her chair. "What would you say if I told you I was carrying Reverend Watters' baby, but I've never slept with him?"

"I'd say you were having delusions of being the Virgin Mary, that's what I'd say."

"Not the Virgin Mary, but perhaps the Surrogate Passion."

That did it. Vanessa tipped her chair too far and fell under the table with a clatter.

"Oh no. Are you all right?" Passion couldn't help laughing as Vanessa struggled to her feet on three-inch heels.

"Oh yeah. I'm all right. But . . ." Vanessa planted her butt firmly onto the chair once she'd set it upright and downed a healthy swallow of her iced tea. "I coulda swore you just told me you're carryin' the reverend's child."

"Not so loud," Passion cautioned. "He doesn't know yet."

"For real?" She wagged her head in disbelief when Passion nodded, then stopped suddenly.

Passion shook her head slowly, watching in amusement while Vanessa threw back her head in a hoot of laughter.

"I don't believe it. This is too fresh." Her continued laughter drew the attention of other customers once again. Finally bringing herself under control, Vanessa leaned toward Passion conspiratorially. "You mean to tell me Cece Watters hired you to carry her baby, didn't tell her husband, and neither have you?"

Passion leaned in as well. "Yes."

Vanessa went pensive. "I'm curious. What happened to make Cece do this surrogate thing?"

Passion studied her emptied plate. "She and Jourdan tried in-vitro fertilization twice. It failed both times."

"Those procedures are real expensive, aren't they?"

"Very." Passion didn't want to go into how much her procedure had cost Cece. "Apparently, the reverend didn't think his wife could handle another failure, emotionally or financially. So, she turned to me."

"Where'd she get the money?"

Passion shrugged. "I think she had a small trust from her grandparents, or something."

"Are you gonna tell him?"

"When I get a chance."

"How much were you gonna get paid?"

Passion sighed, knowing she'd never see a dime past the $5,000 downpayment, now earmarked for Shirleen's operation. "Enough for me to get a degree and a nice apartment for my friend Shirleen."

Vanessa shot straight up in her chair. "Shirleen Jackson?"

"Yeah. Do you know her?" Passion knew Shirleen had a lot of friends, but she'd never mentioned Vanessa.

"She plays cards with my mom every Wednesday."

"Miss Nellie is your mom?" Passion couldn't believe what a small world it was.

"She sure is."

"So you're the one who . . ." She covered her mouth to keep from blurting out what Shirleen had told her.

"I'm the one who what?" Vanessa smiled.

"Is it true you bet your stepfather fifty bucks you could stop traffic, and went into the middle of the street in your underwear to prove it?"

Unintimidated, Vanessa lifted her head. "First of all, I wasn't wearing underwear. It was a thong bikini. I bet the old goat that my butt could stop traffic because he said it was too big to be attractive." She paused and a suggestive smile curved her lips. "Not only did I cause skid marks to cover the road, but I had a date every Friday and Saturday night for two months."

"Heyyyy." Vanessa snapped her fingers and rose from her chair. "Come on, girlfriend. I'll give you a ride home."

They swapped stories and laughed all the way back to Passion's apartment building. As Vanessa pulled the Ford Escort to the curb, Passion found herself already regretting the loss of her company. "You want to come up and have some coffee, girlfriend?"

"No thanks. I've got a date."

"On a Sunday night?" *The woman is always going out.*

"Yeah, well. I ain't gettin' any younger and I still haven't found Mister Right."

"Sounds like you're having a good time looking," Passion teased.

"And what about you? You find your Mister Right?"

Passion answered her steady gaze with her own. She remembered Jourdan's cold response; it stabbed an ice dagger to her heart. "Yeah. Problem is, he thinks I'm Miss Wrong."

Vanessa covered her hand and squeezed. "Maybe, the problem is he's too busy being Mister Perfect to remember he's just a man."

No doubt Vanessa had caught her looking at Jourdan for a little too long. Her new friend had a way of paying quiet attention to everything around her.

"Thanks for everything, Vanessa." Passion climbed out of the small car. "See you next week."

She watched her friend disappear down the street.

Chapter V

Jourdan threw his keys onto the small table in the foyer then slammed the door behind him. He took two steps into the darkness of his house and tripped, barely keeping his balance. "Doggone it!"

He reached for the wall beside him and flipped the light switch. He stood staring at the offending object on the floor. "Stupid rug." Cece had filled the house with them. She'd said it accented the wood floors. Jourdan had been tripping or slipping on them for the past two years. He should just throw them out or give them to Goodwill or something. Better yet, give them to Cece's mother.

It was time to start putting away old reminders of Cece. He had to relegate her to memory, a cherished memory, and to think of his future. *What about Passion?*

He slid out of his coat and hung it in the coat closet beside the stairs. Turning to his right, he headed for the kitchen. It was the first Sunday this month he'd had to fix his own dinner. He'd spent two nights with his in-laws and one with Sister Nellie, who tried to fix him up with her daughter—Vanessa.

Jourdan loosened his tie and undid the top button of his shirt while he circled the island in his kitchen. Soon the glaring light of the refrigerator matched his own unblinking stare as his mind wandered.

He'd watched Passion this afternoon, in her pink dress and purple coat, collapsing into the arms of that no-good drug dealer. Jourdan slammed the refrigerator door and paced the tiled floor of the kitchen.

Had to be a drug dealer. No one else went around town in a black Lexus with gold wheel covers and a window design that said DOCTOR DRE. "Doctor, hah." Jourdan spat into the air. "Since when is it medicinal for a drug to fry your brain and turn you into a walking zombie?"

He rubbed his fingers through his thick hair, hating how disgust and jealousy slowly burned in his chest—as if personal feelings had the right to be there.

An urgently growling stomach reminded Jourdan of his reason for being in this particular room. He went back to the refrigerator and pulled out some leftover rice, a fresh stalk of broccoli, and a steak. If he broiled it, the latter wouldn't take long to cook.

He shoved his steak in the oven, the rice on to warm, and his broccoli in a steamer, then went to the living room to turn on some music. Rarely was his mood ever dark enough that the Wynan's couldn't shatter it.

Music followed him upstairs. Singing along, he changed into casual slacks and a comfortable shirt, pushing Passion from his mind. It was only as he looked around his bedroom, about to turn off the light, that he thought of her again.

They were Passion's dark locks he wanted to spray across the cool tan linen on his pillow, the warm softness of her skin to fill the aching emptiness of his arm—and her sweet voice, the last thing he wanted to hear at night.

The buzzing oven timer brought Jourdan out of his reverie. He stood straight and sighed heavily. He'd made a promise to

God to do his best to protect her, especially from himself. If only Passion didn't spell temptation.

Just as he reached the landing, the doorbell rang, grabbing his attention. He walked the few steps to open the door.

In the shortest black spandex dress ever made, with enough makeup to launch a new line of cosmetics, stood Vanessa.

"My God," Jourdan said, his mouth hanging open in shock.

"Hi, Reverend." She giggled coquettishly. "I just came over to see how you're doing tonight."

Jourdan didn't know what to say.

"I couldn't stand the thought of you eating alone." She looked past his shoulder and shrugged a little. "Can I come in?"

"Of course." Jourdan stepped back and gestured her in graciously. No need to be rude.

"I, uh, think something's done."

Jourdan creased his brow. What was she talking about?

Vanessa pointed a curved red fingernail toward the kitchen. "Your oven's buzzing."

"Oh, yeah."

Jourdan tapped a finger to his forehead and headed toward the kitchen. He turned off the stove, slipped on an oven mitt, and rescued his well-done steak.

Vanessa moved toward him like a cat stalking a mouse. Her breasts bubbled over the tight material of her dress as she walked. "I won't be in your way, will I?" She slipped out of her short coat, revealing bare shoulders that were the hue of dark chocolate. She placed her coat on a chair, bending over a bit more dramatically than necessary.

Jourdan attended to his food, pretending not to notice the curves she tried hard to reveal. What was going on? First, Passion, and now . . . but this was different. Vanessa might be attractive, but she didn't make his blood boil. It wouldn't bother him at all if Dr. Dre held her in his arms and kissed her, except as a shepherd he'd fret over a threatened lamb in his flock.

He looked at the woman and smiled his most reverent smile.

"Would you care to join me for dinner?" Jourdan asked cordially, predicting her answer.

Her eyes popped wide open. "Why, I'd love to, Reverend." She took a seat at the small kitchen table and crossed her legs, revealing a long length of thigh.

Jourdan placed his own dinner on the counter, then put another steak in to broil before joining his guest. "How's your mother? Her knees doing better?"

"She's much better. In fact . . ." She presented her spandex-bound breasts over the table. "She's been telling folks you healed them."

"Jesus heals. I'm just a vessel." Jourdan focused on her face to keep from staring rudely at the bounty she'd laid before him. "You're still working for the DA, Vanessa?" Perhaps she could tell him if any progress had been made on Cece's murder case. After she replied in the affirmative, Jourdan asked the question uppermost in his mind. "Has Reed given up on his theory about Cece having anything to do with unsavory characters?"

"I don't think so. He was looking at some telephone records. They showed she made calls to a penthouse owned by a pimp named Dre Woods." She batted her dark eyes sweetly. "But I'm afraid Ed—er, Mr. Reed doesn't know what to make of them."

Dre Woods? Doctor Dre? They had to be the same man. But what did he have to do with his wife? And what business did he now have with Passion? Was her life in danger as well? "Is that all Reed has to go on?"

"At the moment." She settled back in her chair. "Would you have a soda or something, Reverend?"

"Oh, sure." He sifted through his refrigerator until he came across two colas. Filling glasses with ice, he returned to the table.

"Thanks." Vanessa lifted an ice cube from her glass and slid it from her throat to her cleavage in one long, languid motion. "It's kinda hot in here, doncha think?" She looked at him through heavy lids.

Jourdan cleared his throat and checked on the steak.

"Probably the oven," he said, not certain of how she expected him to react. But Lord, he knew he wasn't about to pounce on another woman. He figured the best way to handle Vanessa was to be blunt. He pulled the steak from the oven.

"What brings you here tonight?" He eyed her warily. "I get the feeling it's not because you're afraid I'll die of loneliness."

She dropped what was left of the ice cube into her glass. "You got me there."

"Well?" He served her a perfect steak with rice and broccoli, then turned back to retrieve his own.

"Let's just say I'm testin' out a theory." She unfolded her legs and turned her attention to the food before her.

Jourdan took his seat, asked the blessing over their meal, and proceeded to quiet the roar in his stomach. "A theory?"

"About you. You see, I figure you're still upset about Cece's death. That's why you don't pay attention when women flirt with you."

"What kind of man would I be to chase after women so soon after my wife's death?" A remnant of guilt washed over him as he thought of Cece, of Passion, and of his vow.

"Okay. Gotcha." Vanessa nodded her head, sending her braids bobbing up and down. "Just had to check. To make sure there's no *particular* woman you don't want."

Jourdan swallowed a piece of steak and spoke cautiously. "Particular woman?"

"Yeah. Passion."

He took a deep breath. "Passion?"

"Sure. She's in love with you, you know?" She shot him a look that said it should have been obvious.

His heart beat with intense rhythm. "In love with me?"

"Don't worry. I'm sure she'll wait until you're ready for a relationship." Vanessa waved her nails over her plate. "But it'd mean a lot if you were at least nice to her in the meantime."

Exasperated and unsettled, Jourdan stared at her. "And you know all this because . . ."

65

"Because I'm her friend."

"This love thing. Why didn't she tell me herself? She's not the type to send someone out to do her talking."

Vanessa plucked a napkin from the holder in the middle of the table and wiped what was left of the lipstick from her mouth. "Her pride would get in the way of telling you." She shot him a meaningful glance. "And no one should go without the things they want. Not for something as silly as that, wouldn't you agree?"

"No, indeed."

Did Vanessa know about his embarrassing display in the hallway? How could Passion be in love with him after that?

How could he remain in control of his life, his ministry, his soul, when she consumed every part of him just by being in the same room?

No more playful seductress about her, Vanessa rose to leave. He found her unadorned smile very becoming. It was all Jourdan could do to keep pace as she whipped her coat from the chair and headed for the door.

"Thanks for dinner, Reverend. Give some thought to what I said."

Would he be able to think of anything else?

Vanessa stopped. "Is there any reason you can think of for Cece to call a pimp's penthouse?"

"Not one," he admitted, truly baffled by the information.

She shrugged and walked briskly out the door he held open. "See you in church, Reverend."

Jourdan acknowledged her absently, wondering how his life had become so complicated. It was all too much—love and murder intertwined, twisting about him all at once. He needed to stay away from Passion, but she seemed to be a link to Cece's murder. He had no choice but to question her about this Dre Woods character.

* * * * * * * * * * * * *

The early morning sun sliced through the wrought iron of Passion's bedroom window casting prison-like bars onto her wall. She stared at the water-stained ceiling and ran her fingers through her hair. The thick, spongy feel of new growth near her scalp told her it was almost time for a perm.

Passion threw the quilt to the side and crawled out of bed. Shoot. The last thing she needed to worry about was her hair, although she noted as she passed her dresser mirror that it looked as if Don King had styled it.

Quickly, she searched her closet for the perfect outfit. Nothing too dressy. The brief note left in the church office was written by Jourdan. He wanted to see her on an urgent matter, but failed to name a time or place. She'd check his office when she got to Zion, since she hadn't been able to reach him by phone.

The enticing aroma of bacon reached her just as Passion pulled out a pair of black jeans, a casual T-shirt, and a beaded black and white vest. Her stomach growled in protest at the necessity of a shower delaying breakfast.

She showered and dressed quickly, then made her bed, anxious to dig into the big breakfast Shirleen had waiting for her.

The first bite of the soft, tasty biscuit nearly melted in Passion's mouth. "Mmm. Shirleen, how do you make these so perfect every morning?" she asked, dabbing at the margarine that dripped from the corner of her mouth.

One plump fist went immediately to an ample hip, the other pointed a cooking fork in Passion's direction. "You'd know if you stayed in dis here kitchen long enuf for me to teach ya somethin'."

Passion took a bite of the perfectly seasoned scrambled eggs. "I told you, Shirleen, cooking's not my thing."

In truth, she'd never had much chance to explore the many things that most women took for granted, like cooking or sewing or simply taking pleasure in a quiet evening with family and friends.

Life as a mistress had been a lonely affair, lived on the fringes of respectability. Perched in plush apartments like gilded birdcages, awaiting a man's brief attentions and inconsistent affections—she wouldn't recommend that sort of life to anyone. Thank goodness, things were changing.

"Maybe not," Shirleen commented, giggling. "But you sure got the hang of eatin' all right." The older woman assessed Passion for a minute longer than necessary, grabbing her attention.

"What?" Passion felt uncomfortable under her stare.

"Oh, nothin'." She turned back to the stove. "Don't forget. I got my pinochle game dis evenin'. I'll be home late."

Passion resumed chewing. "I remember. I'll probably be late . . . hanging out with Vanessa for a while."

"Mmm hmm."

Her tone made Passion nervous. *Get a grip, girl.* Meeting Jourdan wasn't like committing a crime . . . not that she could convince Shirleen of that. Her friend balked every time Passion mentioned telling Jourdan about the baby, since he'd left her distraught in the hallway. It seemed she wanted to keep the child even more than Passion did. Perhaps it was because she and William never had children.

Picking up the last biscuit and taking a hasty swallow of orange juice, Passion rose from the table. "Gotta go."

"There's some leftover beans and rice in the refrigerator for your lunch. Make sure you keep that baby fed," Shirleen said, wiping down already immaculate counters.

"Thanks. Maybe for dinner." Passion hugged the woman briefly, wishing she'd stop working herself to death.

"Mmm hmm."

There she went again. Passion grabbed her coat and purse and wasted no time dashing out of the apartment. Shirleen couldn't possibly know. She would've said something. It wasn't like her to hold her tongue when she disapproved of something.

Passion wondered for the hundredth time what Jourdan wanted. Surely, he'd be at church today. She boarded the bus and squeezed into the only seat available in the rear and immediately wished she hadn't. The smell of stale smoke clung, like stink on a skunk, to the unkempt woman in the next seat. Passion's heavy breakfast became instantly disagreeable. Although she didn't get sick at regular intervals with this pregnancy, certain odors made her stomach do flip-flops.

Rising as delicately as she could, Passion made her way to the front of the bus, making a quick comment to the woman about standing being more comfortable, so as not to hurt her feelings. The woman gave her a blank stare and turned to the window.

Thirty minutes later the bus deposited Passion in front of Zion. She pushed her way in through the double doors. Associate pastors and other workers were sprinkled here and there in the hallways and sanctuary, but Passion searched futilely for Jourdan.

She entered the glass enclosed office, greeted immediately by Sister Martha and her love for lavender water. The scent permeated the room.

"Come on in, Miss Adams." Her words dripped with saccarine. "Take a seat right here at the desk."

Passion did as instructed and hoped the software on the computer was the same as Vanessa's. Every night for the past week, she'd been getting lessons from her friend on how to move through Windows.

"I don't know too much about this machine," Sister Biddle disclosed. "Sister Harris used to take care of it before she went traveling with her husband."

"That's okay. I've been taking classes," Passion said. It was stretching the truth a bit, but hoped it made her sound halfway competent.

"You're in college, then?" Martha's eyes widened in surprise.

"Technically." Passion smiled nervously. Why was it every time she told a little white lie, she always had to back it up with another?

Enthusiasm fell from Mrs. Biddle's face, like Satan from

heaven. "I see," she said. "My nieces are both at the university." Looking down her nose, she gave Passion the distinct impression nothing but a four-year degree would meet with her approval.

"That's nice." Passion tried to sound interested. "Shall we get started?"

"Certainly, if you think you can figure it out."

It was a dig. A sugar-coated one, but a dig nonetheless.

Play nice, Sister Biddle, you old . . .

Passion placed her hand on the mouse and moved the cursor around the screen. The darned thing flew off into oblivion with only the slightest wrist movement.

"Looks like you might need a few more classes."

Passion could feel Sister Biddle's pinched mouth turn up into a smile behind her.

"Just have to get a feel for this mouse," Passion explained, trying to sound knowledgeable. "It seems extra sensitive."

"You're probably right." Sister Biddle circled the desk to stand behind the monitor. "My nieces thought about taking this job, but they teach Sunday school, and that's enough with their studies. Do you know Laticia and Rochelle?"

Did she ever! The thought of Ditzy and Doodle teaching small children was enough to send shivers up her spine. Zion was desperate for volunteers, but what were Jourdan and the rest of them thinking? "I believe I've made their acquaintance."

The linen-suited sister preened like a bird arranging its feathers, before taking a seat across from Passion. "Chances are you'll see them often. The reverend really can't do without their assistance."

"Is that so?" Passion chuckled to herself. Hard to imagine the two of them being any help. They weren't particularly smart and they were jealous of anyone they perceived as more attractive—which really didn't take much.

It was an uncharitable thought and, for a moment, she considered praying for forgiveness. Naw. Better not push her luck. She and God hadn't been that tight over the years. Passion played around with the columns and graphics. She was pretty sure she could handle this.

"So tell me, Miss Adams—"

"Passion."

"Such an interesting name." Sister Biddle looked as if she'd just eaten something distasteful.

Passion peered over the monitor at the woman. "My mother was an interesting woman."

"Was?" She sat forward in her chair. "Is she deceased then?"

"No. I just haven't seen her in a while," Passion stated precisely.

"Pity."

"Yeah," Passion agreed unemotionally. Why she picked now to mention her mother was a mystery. She couldn't help but feel Martha Biddle was trying to catch her off-guard, uncover some critical piece of information to spread all over the church. The less said about the scandalous Sherrie Adams, the better.

The click of computer keys filled the silence in the room for long seconds.

"So—Passion?"

She ceased typing. "Yes?"

"What do you usually do for a living?"

"I'm between jobs. That's why I took this one."

"It doesn't pay much." The mock concern in the thin woman's voice was sickening. "How do you make ends meet?"

"I have a roommate. We do okay."

"Ah. I see. And your roommate, what does he—"

"She," Passion corrected quickly. *The woman's workin' my last nerve.* She tried to focus on the computer, certain if she didn't, Martha Biddle would fall victim to her rising temper.

Undaunted, Sister Biddle pushed forward. "What does *she* do?"

"She's retired. Mostly volunteers at the hospital at her church, when she's not visiting friends."

"Her church?" Sister Biddle perched her birdlike butt on

the edge of her seat, once again. "You're not of the same denomination?"

"We're both Baptist." At least Passion considered herself one now. "I just prefer this church."

"Any particular reason?" she asked.

Passion actually felt her control snap. She sat back and crossed her arms. "Is there any particular reason why it's any of your business?"

"Excuse me?" the old bird asked, with obvious offense.

"You just grilled me like I was O.J. Simpson on trial."

I probably shouldn't have said that.

"What's the verdict, Sister Biddle? Am I worthy enough to serve God in the same sanctuary as you?"

And I definitely shouldn't have said that.

Martha Biddle stood up in a huff. "It's too bad your mother isn't around to teach you some manners, young lady!" She grabbed her purse and smoothed her salt-and-pepper French roll.

"Unfortunately," Passion said sarcastically, "that's the last thing she would've taught me."

Eyes wide and cheeks puffing with indignation, Sister Biddle searched for a reply. "Take care, Miss Adams," she finally managed to squawk. "I'll be watching you."

"Like a vulture, I'm sure," Passion said tongue-in-cheek.

The woman stalked out of the office.

Ruffling the feathers of Sister Biddle wasn't the smartest thing to do if she was going to be accepted here, but it had been an absolute delight to put the old busybody in her place.

She made a mental note to stay out of her way. All-out war with her and her nieces wouldn't accomplish anything. The only thing she wanted from this place was Jourdan Watters.

Which reminded her—she had to find him.

Passion turned off the computer and walked down the hallway to Jourdan's office. Her light knock went unanswered. Disappointed, she turned to leave.

"Passion?"

Jourdan was rushing down the hallway to meet her. "Please, I need to speak to you."

She got all warm and tingly, just looking at him. "I got your note."

"Good. Good." He held open the door to his office and gestured for her to enter. While not huge, the room was warm and comfortable, from his big, cherry wood desk to the African-American art on the walls, to the leather wing chair he offered.

"Sorry I wasn't here earlier. I've been running around like crazy trying to organize the holiday feast and the television deal."

"It's quite all right." Passion tried to contain the frenzied emotions dashing around her insides. "I thought . . . if you'd like . . . we could talk over lunch."

Jourdan glanced at his watch and sent her an apologetic frown. "I'm afraid I don't have time. I've got a meeting with the general manager at channel seven in forty-five minutes."

His deep chestnut eyes warmed with sincerity. For a moment, Passion lost herself in their depths. "If I can help with the feast, Jourdan, I'd be happy to."

"Really?"

He looked so delighted, Passion nearly laughed. "Yes. What can I do?"

"I just need someone to supervise the volunteers."

Passion leaned in closer to enjoy his pleasant male scent, warmed by his smile. "Consider it done."

"Thank you again for your generosity, Passion." Jourdan looked away suddenly and cleared his voice. "I suppose I should get to the topic I wanted to speak to you about—Dre Woods."

Her warmth evaporated. Passion sat in chilled astonishment at the mention of Dre's name. "Dre? What about him?"

"He was the friend who went way back, right?"

Did she detect a bite of accusation in Jourdan's tone? "Yes. The one you met after the accident."

73

"Would you know if he ever owned or rented a penthouse in Crown Center?"

Panic hit her. How did he know? "I . . . yes, he did." Suddenly, the room felt less cozy than closed in. "Why do you ask?"

Jourdan's demeanor darkened. "The DA says there were calls made from my house to that location. Do you have any idea why Cece would call Dre Woods?"

Passion took a deep breath and sank back in her chair. *So that's what this is about.* He was trying to solve Cece's murder and thought she could help. Disappointment swallowed her whole. "Cece wasn't calling *him*."

"Who then?"

"She called me."

It was Jourdan's turn to be shocked. "You?"

"I was staying at the penthouse, waiting for Shirleen to move here from Colorado. Why's the DA so interested in those phone calls?"

Jourdan's bronze features hardened. "I think I should be asking that question."

Bristling, Passion hopped to her feet. "You can't possibly think I had anything to do with Cece's death."

Pushing his chair back, Jourdan rounded his desk to face her. "I don't know what to think, Passion. You were living with a drug pusher—"

"I was *not* living with Dre. He has his own house."

"You want me to believe he put you up in a penthouse for nothing?" Jourdan fumed. "I may be a man of God, but I am not naive to the ways of the world, Passion."

His allegation stabbed like a piercing hot needle. After all his talk about forgiveness and having a clean slate, in the end, he was as judgmental as Mrs. Biddle and her nieces.

Passion threw the one thing at him she hoped would hurt most. "You don't know anything about me. And, Lord knows, your head was so deep into your ministry three months ago, you didn't know what was going on with your own wife."

Passion took vengeful pleasure in watching his face turn from stone to stunned in the split second before she walked out of his office.

* * * * * * * * * * * * *

"Sweet Jesus." Jourdan pushed the few papers on his desk to the floor. If he were a cursing man, he would string a few together right about now.

Why was he never able to say or do the right thing around Passion? The mere thought of her living in or around Dre Woods sent jealousy and anger pounding through his chest with equal intensity. He'd wanted to take her in his arms and kiss her to prove she wanted him and not some thug from the street.

He couldn't blame her for being angry; he'd all but called her a prostitute. And her jab about paying more attention to his pulpit than Cece. Regret whirled through him like a Kansas twister, although he knew she'd only tried to meet him hurt for hurt.

And for all his fury, he hadn't gotten any answers. He knew for certain now that she and Cece had some kind of history, and the mystery deepened as to the past Passion and Dre Woods shared. But how much of this tied in to his wife's murder was anyone's guess.

Jourdan checked his watch. He had half an hour to travel across town to the television station. Desperately, he hoped the drive would help soothe the tangled emotions only Passion could cause.

* * * * * * * * * * * * *

Passion thought she'd left her naivete on the doorstep of her seventeenth birthday. But . . . again she'd hoped for something impossible, only to have it shattered against the hard core of reality. Jourdan would never love her. That much was obvious. He'd practically accused her of murdering Cece. Just because she hung around with Dre, when necessary, didn't make her a killer.

Tears burst as she retrieved Vanessa's computer reference books and left Zion. If only her desire for Jourdan could be purged with the simple act of crying.

When she reached the bottom step, a black Lexus stood ready to take her in. Tracks held open the rear door. Dre's ringed fingers patted the leather seat beside him. "Need a friend, sunshine?"

Impeccable timing. As usual, he lurked at the bottom of her pit of despair, making escape too easy.

Too weak to fight, she slid into the car and pushed at the tears on her cheeks. "When you pick me up again, would you at least drive your own car?" she admonished, eyeing Tracks.

Dre leered. "You mean, you want to be alone with me? How delightful."

"No." Passion placed her books on the seat between them and gave him a pleading look.

"Yo, Tracks," Dre spoke loudly to his bodyguard. "Next time you're gonna have to get lost."

The driver remained silent, but smiled, revealing a gold tooth.

Passion tried to explain, "I just meant that it's embarrassing to be picked up and chauffeured around like I'm some kind of princess."

Dre looked intently into her eyes. "You'll get used to it again."

Passion threw her hands out in exasperation and turned her attention to the city as it unraveled beyond the church. She wiped the tears from her cheeks, but could do nothing about the gripping hurt that encased her heart.

Dre sat with one of her books in hand, slowly turning the pages.

"Where are we going?" she sniffed.

"Wherever you like," he answered simply.

Passion could hear the paper rub between his fingers as he turned a new page. His fingers slid slowly and deliberately down one page, then up again to take hold of the next. The pages turned at frequent intervals, too quickly for him to read the book, she decided.

"Take me home."

His stilled fingers drew her attention. He sat staring at the piece of paper she'd used to mark her place in the text. She knew what the note said by heart.

Call me. I need to talk to you. Jourdan.

He'd printed his telephone number in a neat, meticulous hand. She'd been so excited.

Dre's shoulders stiffened. "Jourdan?" The word barely escaped his compressed lips.

"My pastor." Passion tried to make it sound as if it were the most normal thing in the world, Jourdan's asking her to call.

"Is he the one who's got you so upset?"

Her heart tapped vigorously. "No," she lied, not wanting him to know she'd failed at love again.

Dre's eyes threw daggers of disbelief into the air. "Told you he wasn't about nothin'. You're coming home with me. You know I'll treat you right."

Passion pulled her wits about her, struggling to appear upbeat. "It's okay, Dre. Just got a little shook up about some scripture he quoted."

The lines around his mouth softened a little. "Don't throw yourself at another no-good man." Inching closer to her on the leather seat he said, "Remember who takes care of you in your time of need."

Jesus carries in times of need—or so Jourdan had preached in his sermons. Passion sent a tentative prayer up to her new-found Savior, even as she accepted her old one's kiss to her cheek. Dre's possessiveness hadn't waned a bit, but at least his anger was abating. "Dre, I'm not throwing myself at anyone. Not even you."

"That's all right." He nodded, his earring bobbing. "You'll come around."

She couldn't help but smile at his persistence, wishing she

could feel more for him than mere gratitude. Despite all his manipulating, his love for her was real. She knew it.

Passion placed a palm over his knuckles. "I appreciate everything you've done for me, Dre. I hope you know that."

He lifted her hand to his mouth and slowly licked a trail from wrist to fingertip.

God, she hated when he did that. Yet, it forced her to get a grip on her emotions. Somehow, she managed to keep a smile plastered on her face and endure his disgusting affection.

"I can give you so much more." His thin, pink lips were still wet.

Passion wanted nothing, only to put this day behind her. "I'll keep that in mind," she said wearily. "I really need to check on Shirleen."

"She's grown. She can look after herself," Dre said, instantly irritated.

"The doctor says she needs a heart operation—triple bypass —next week." Passion knew the surgery wouldn't come a day too soon to ease her worrying.

"My heart bleeds. No pun intended," he added unsympathetically.

"She's going to need a comfortable place to stay when she gets out. Someplace without stairs."

"So?"

Passion studied him objectively. He'd do anything for her. He'd said so. "So ... I only have enough money to keep her in a nice apartment for a few months. I'll need a good job to keep us out of the projects after that."

"What do I look like? Job service?"

"No, but if you could give me a small loan—just enough for me to take computer classes at the community college—I promise to pay you back."

"Loan sharkin' ain't one of my specialties." He moved closer to her. "But I might make an exception in your case."

Relief flooded her heart. The school's financial aid office had frowned on her lack of credit history. What they had offered her wouldn't cover the cost of books. That was why Cece's money had been so important.

"Thanks, Dre."

"Wait just a minute, now. Hold on." His smile glittered brightly. "We haven't talked about a payback schedule."

Uneasiness gripped her. "I told you, when I get a job, you'll get your money."

"I'm no sucker. I need a guaranteed payback." He crowded her, giving her a smoldering look that said, "Show me the money."

"What did you have in mind?" Passion knew she wouldn't like whatever he said.

"You've got to be my lady. I'll give you the cash for that lame degree you want, and the old biddy can use one of my nicest condos. She can stay as long as it takes to recover. If you move in with me."

Passion closed her eyes in resignation, cursing herself for not seeing this coming.

"For how long?" she needed to know.

"What do you mean, for how long? For as long as I say."

Passion was running out of options. Lacking hope for a relationship with Jourdan, she couldn't get on her feet without financial assistance. And Shirleen needed a nice place to rest during her recovery. Was selling her body and soul to Dre Woods any different from what she'd done in the past? Was it really such a high price to pay? At least this time, she'd actually benefit from the deal in the end.

Cold comfort.

She regarded him soberly. "There's something you've got to know."

"What's that?"

"I'm pregnant."

The smile slid from his face like an avalanche.

"Don't worry." She wriggled uncomfortably in her seat and

sealed her fate. Hating the words as she spoke them, she said, "I'm not going to keep it."

"That's a relief." Dre's pinched expression relaxed. "What do you need? A couple hundred to get rid of it?"

Passion gritted her teeth. "I'm going to give it away after it's born."

Disgust marked Dre's features. "But you'll get all fat and swollen."

"Live with it." Passion nearly choked on the words.

Her heart wrenched at giving the baby away, even to its father. Still, she refused to bring a child into Dre's dark world.

The babe in her womb chose that moment to offer a flutter of activity, as if it knew her dilemma. Gently, she placed a hand on her stomach. It was the first movement she'd felt and she wanted to remember it forever.

Even if it kills me, you'll have a better life than me, little one.

She'd meet with Jourdan. It was past time he knew about his baby.

Chapter VI

Jourdan, in awe, studied the plans laid out on the oval conference table. His heart full, he wanted to fall to his knees right there and thank the Lord. He prayed Cece somehow witnessed the moment. It was a victory he wanted desperately to share.

At least Sherman Townsend, his good friend and attorney, stood by him. "You're going to donate your old television cameras to Zion and send someone in to run them every Sunday?" he queried channel seven's general manager.

"That's right, Reverend." Win Cummings placed a tanned hand on Jourdan's shoulder and smiled broadly. His silver hair gave his square features dignity. "You'll have everything you need. By the way, I understand the lighting in your place can be rigged for broadcasting."

Jourdan stood proud. "They can. One of Zion's own members designed and installed it."

Sherman stepped forward and took the general manager's hand. "The contract looks fine, Mr. Cummings. We'll be expecting your people in the next week."

"Absolutely, Mr. Townsend." Cummings turned to Jourdan. "Reverend," he said, extending his hand, "I look forward to a long partnership with you and Zion Baptist."

Jourdan reciprocated the gentleman's firm handshake. "I can't tell you what this means to me."

Outside the television station, Jourdan looked at his attorney and gave a hoot of laughter. "Can you believe it, Sherman? I'm going to deliver The Word to all of Kansas City."

Sherman's thick, salt-and-pepper eyebrows rose in amusement. "First, they gotta turn the TV to the right station."

"They will." Jourdan could see his breath reach out into the cold, crisp day. "I know they will."

At least this one thing went right. If he could find Cece's killer and come to grips with his feelings for Passion, his life would be just about perfect.

* * * * * * * * * * * *

Life wasn't near enough perfect, Shirleen decided. From the couch she watched Passion fumble with her bag. *Dat chile ain't happy.* "You gonna be workin' late agin tonight?"

"Uh, yeah." Passion flung the bag over her shoulder; her eyes darting here and there around their sparsely furnished apartment. "I'm making flyers for the holiday program."

One more lie to pile up on t' others. Shirleen shook her head sadly. *The chile must really be in trouble to carry on so. She been actin' funny about a week now.* It was high time her conscience kicked in, and she spilled the beans. "Well, I gots pinochle myself."

"I know."

Her reply came a bit too fast and eager for Shirleen's liking, but she knew she wouldn't get anywhere today. Patience and a nice long rope. That's all it took for folks to hang themselves.

"I vacuumed, put up the laundry, and dusted. You need to rest. I'll see you later." Passion about tripped on her way out the door.

"Mmm hmm," Shirleen hummed softly. Shaking her head once again, she began to vacuum the missed places. Lord, Lord. *What kinda trouble could that chile be into now?*

Shirleen quickly turned off the rattling motor. Had the phone rang? Another long ring sent her in motion. She grabbed the princess phone from the wobbly end table just as it rang for the third time.

"Hello?"

"Well, well, well. If it ain't the wicked witch of the Midwest."

Shirleen shuddered, recognizing the voice. "Dre. How you gets my phone number?"

"Whoa. Slow down. Don't get your tent in a twist, old lady," Dre chided. "Your lovely roommate gave it to me."

"Passion?" Shirleen began to get a sick feeling.

"Yeah, who else?" Dre sounded impatient. "Let me speak to her."

"She ain't here."

"Don't mess with me, old lady!" His impatience grew to irritation. "I'm not in the mood for your games."

Shirleen parked a plump fist on her hip. "I said she ain't here. And iffen she was, you couldn't talk to her."

Dre replied in the foulest, heathenest language Shirleen had ever heard. She held the phone at arm's length until he finished.

"Now, you gonna listen to me," she began. "You stay away from Passion. She don't want nothin' to do with you. And I sure don't wanna see yo ugly face up in my home no more."

Silence hung on the other end of the phone for a moment, followed by Dre's haunting laughter. "You don't know, do you?"

"Know what?" Shirleen could barely breathe, her chest tightened painfully.

"Passion's moving in with me," he said, smug satisfaction filling his voice. "I was just calling to see when to pick up her stuff."

"Like hell!"

83

Shirleen slammed the phone onto its hook and trundled to Passion's bedroom. Two suitcases sat neatly inside the vacant closet, obviously packed. A hand to her bosom, she tried to calm herself. It wouldn't do if her heart pounded its way out of her chest right now. She had to think things through.

"No wonder the chile didn't tell me nothin'. I woulda wrung her neck! She must be plannin' to sneak out dis evenin'," Shirleen said to herself. Uh, uh. No way. She wasn't about to let the only family she had leave her. "There ain't no need in Passion wantin' a man so bad, she hasta takes da lowest one on earth."

What to do? What to do? Shirleen paced the worn carpet, pushing gray hair away from her face, puffing to catch her breath. She stopped suddenly with an inspired thought. Grabbing her coat from the rack and her purse from the table, she said a small prayer. She knew exactly who could help.

* * * * * * * * * * * *

Reed squinted against the bright day as the black car approached. Yeah, it was Woods all right.

He crumpled the french-fry packet and tossed it inside the car beside the empty hamburger bag. He preferred restaurants that served rich, foreign dishes to fast food, but time was of the essence today. Too much rode on a conviction in Cece Watters' murder. Now that the police had bagged the trigger man, Dre must confess to ordering the hit.

Reed had been here every day for the last five, trying to catch the scumbag at home. Still, he leaned casually against his five-year-old Mercedes, trying to appear in control as the gleaming Lexus finished its long crawl up the driveway to the Woods residence.

The car stopped just a hair too close to Reed's back bumper. Tracks emerged from the driver's side, his dark face unsmiling.

To hide the sudden uneasiness he felt in the man's presence, Reed gave him what he hoped was a menacing smile.

Tracks ignored Reed and opened the rear car door closest

to the walk. Dre slid out slowly, clearly unhappy to see the district attorney invading his territory.

He extended a hand back inside the car to assist his companion. Blond, almost white, shoulder-length curls framed the barely brown face of the girl. It wasn't hard to tell, even with her fur on, that she was built like the proverbial "brick house." He had to give it to Woods, he sure knew how to pick his hookers—dancers—whatever she was.

"Why, Reed." Dre sneered. "You have the drool of a dog without a bone."

Reed wasn't amused. "Don't worry, Woods. I may be a dog, but I don't take my meals from the trash, no matter how attractive the packaging."

The woman looked seriously wounded by his words. Reed was surprised she understood what he'd meant. She looked dumb as a doorknob.

Dre took two angry steps to face him, although he had to look up to do so. Nothing pleased Reed more than intimidating little pip-squeaks like Woods.

"I want you to state your business and get the hell off my property," Dre spat venomously.

Reed opened his arms wide and hunched his shoulders. "Is that any way to talk? I'm kind enough to come and talk to you personally, instead of hauling your butt into the nearest police station."

Dre retreated and looked away in disgust.

"You could invite me inside your modest home and offer me a drink, at least." Reed smiled, enjoying the obvious displeasure he caused the man.

"Fine," Dre said through gritted teeth. "Just give me a minute."

"I've got all the time in the world," Reed said graciously. All of a sudden he didn't want this moment to end. He'd savor every second as Dre broke down and admitted being hired to kill Cece Watters—every pure-gold second.

85

"Come on, Chante," Dre ordered his companion.

Hostility was clear on the woman's face as Dre tried to kiss a golden cheek. "How come you let him talk about me like that?" Her pretty head jerked angrily.

Reed chuckled under his breath as the little weasel got a mouthful of hair for his effort.

"Take her for a drink and come back in about an hour," Dre instructed Tracks. He waited until the Lexus was well down the drive before giving his attention to Reed. "This better be worth my time," he growled, then climbed the stairs to the huge double doors.

Reed dismissed the petty threat, following the man into the house. The less time Woods spent at his criminal activities, the better for Kansas City.

They entered a room just off the foyer. It was full of the most exquisite artwork Reed had ever seen. His ex-wife would have been envious. He removed his overcoat and laid it neatly on one arm of the jade leather couch which sat in the middle of pure white carpet. "Nice. Very nice."

Dre busied himself at the bar in one corner of the room. "What'll you have?"

"Something expensive." Reed sank comfortably into the soft cushions of the couch and placed his large shoes on the glass cocktail table.

"Do you mind?" Dre approached with drinks in hand.

"If I scratch it, I'm sure one good sale of crack will get you a new one," he said dryly, taking a long swallow of the caramel-colored liquid in his glass. A low sigh escaped his lips as the Johnny Walker Black warmed him down to his belly.

Dre sat opposite him, taking huge gulps of his drink. A double, Reed noted.

"What's this about?" Dre demanded.

"Don't be impatient, Woods." He took another slow swallow of his drink and watched the man grow more fidgety by the second. Deciding the time was right, he removed his feet from the table, pulled a cassette tape from his breast pocket, and laid it where his heels had been. "I need some information."

A small twitch formed in the corner of Dre's left eye. His gaze never left the cassette. "What kind of information?"

Reed sat back to enjoy the show. "Seems there's a penthouse in Crown Center with your name on the lease."

"Nothing illegal about that." Dre looked him straight in the eye.

"No? Cece Watters made regular phone calls to that apartment for a couple of months before she died. It might be significant."

Dre choked out a laugh. "You think I had something to do with Cece Watters' death?"

"I know it for a fact. It wouldn't be the first time you've ordered a hit." Reed watched carefully for any reaction.

"I've never been convicted." Dre appeared confident.

"Why'd she call you?" This still remained a mystery to Reed, although it was a nice coincidence.

Elbows on his knees, Dre leveled beady eyes at him. "I never talked to the woman."

"Bull."

Their eyes locked in a determined stare-down.

"I'm telling you straight up. I never knew her."

"Don't mess with me, Dre." He picked up the cassette and waved it back and forth. "I'll use this if I have to."

Dre's answering smile hardened Reed's resolve. "I'm not leaving until you tell me what Cece Watters was to you and why you had her killed."

"Then you'll be here a lot longer than either of us wants you to be."

"Quit giving me that, Woods. I know you did it."

"Is that a fact?" The smile wouldn't leave his face.

Reed grew tense. All he needed was the weasel's confession to wrap up this murder investigation with a tidy little bow.

Intimidation time. "You remember Teardrop? Your trigger man?"

"Who?"

"Go ahead. Be cute. You know who I'm talking about." Reed warmed to the subject. "In case you've been wondering whatever happened to him, I've got him in custody."

He watched for any sign of nervousness. Dre didn't budge.

"And, on this tape . . ." He picked it up and rattled it. "He's told us a lot of things that can put you away for quite a while, Dr. Dre."

"Then why aren't I being hauled away in handcuffs right now?" Dre rose to refill his glass.

Reed grew weary of this game. He wasn't winning. He dropped the cassette to the table with a clatter and rose to his full six feet, four inches. "I think Cece Watters gave one of your working girls a hard time."

Dre's expression turned blank.

"Maybe the Reverend Watters had something going on with one, and his wife found out." A guess, but he had to be on the right track.

Dre chuckled. "Go on. This is very amusing."

"I think the reverend asked you to kill Cece so he could avoid a scandal."

It began as a gurgle in Dre's throat. Soon he laughed uncontrollably, trying to balance his drink before finally placing it on the bar.

Reed tugged at his collar. He went crimson hot all over. "What's so damn funny?"

"You. Ha, ha, ha. You really are stupid. Ha, ha. The preacher man would be the last one I'd ever help." He doubled over, holding his stomach while the waves of laughter overtook him.

Reed tightened his trembling fists. "Aren't your hits usually anonymous? Maybe you didn't know it was Jourdan Watters."

Dre went into coughing fits before he finally regained his

composure. "My clients may *think* they're anonymous, but I know every one of 'em by name."

The knowing glow in his eyes gave Reed pause. He knew, didn't he? No wonder he wouldn't buckle. Of its own free will, his right fist sent a smashing uppercut to the hard bone of Dre's jaw.

Dre doubled over in pain instead of elation. It was of small satisfaction to Reed.

Snatching his coat from the sofa, Reed took long, angry strides from the room, cursing the day that pimps and preachers began walking the earth. He couldn't nail the murder on Dre without implicating himself.

* * * * * * * * * * * * *

Dre heard the door slam in his foyer. Still clutching his throbbing jaw, he stormed to the window. Reed was tossing his coat inside the car. It took only milliseconds before the white Mercedes squealed down the driveway.

"No-good, pompous politician." He spat blood with the words. He made his way back to the bar to devise a makeshift ice compress with his monogrammed handkerchief.

Bracing himself for the shock of the cold, he placed the ice pack carefully on his jaw. He slowly began to shift his mouth from side to side. Nothing seemed broken, except a crown from one of his molars, which he deposited into his palm.

He sank into his wing chair and stared at the forgotten cassette lying on the table. He picked it up with his free hand and rattled it.

Reed was set on convicting him of Cece Watters' murder. True, he'd received an anonymous phone call requesting the hit and, unless he missed his guess, he'd just confirmed who'd made the call. Reed had had guilt written all over his face.

Dre walked over to his component system and pushed the tape inside the player. Hearing a faint voice, he increased the volume. Soon the deep, sultry voice of Toni Braxton filled the room. "The sorry son-of-a . . ." He nodded his head in triumph. Reed had been bluffing as well.

Dre poured from his liquor bottle and tried to make sense of last July's hit. Teardrop had executed it. Badly. He'd gotten Cece Watters instead of Reed's estranged wife.

Thanks to the incompetent hitman, Dre never received the money. Teardrop had left Kansas City after that, a smart move since Dre was still anxious to teach him a lesson.

Things soured further, when the cops took Teardrop into custody. As long as he didn't talk, Dre would walk.

Reed was primed for extortion now. Dre would get more than $200,000, the price of the hit.

There was still the nagging question of why Cece Watters had called the penthouse. If Reed hadn't lied about that, she'd have to have been talking to Passion.

Just before Cece's death, Passion had disappeared for days. She hadn't offered an explanation. Had she been meeting the reverend on the sly?

Instantly, the image of Jourdan Watters blurred Dre's vision. He flinched in pain and unclenched his jaw. It was all too obvious whose baby Passion carried. The preacher's wife must have been calling to confront her.

Dre downed his drink. The liquor stung his mouth like hell. He'd put up with Passion's past boyfriends, knowing the relationships would only last a while, at best. If she took up with a preacher and turned into one of those Christian hypocrites, she'd be out of his reach forever.

Dre noticed the salty metal taste of blood, so he headed for the bathroom to rinse out the nastiness.

In the mirror, he examined the tender spot beneath his cheek. Despite the ice, a slight swelling covered the bone. He replaced the ice pack and decided to lie down to see if it would help.

Reclining on the waterbed, Dre closed his eyes and imagined Passion next to him. He'd decided to take her in anyway—

pregnant or not. But there wasn't any way in hell he'd be taking care of a preacher's kid.

If she changed her mind about giving it up, he'd call a friend and see what could be done about staging a kidnapping.

He'd make a tidy profit selling the baby on the black market, and with Shirleen, the old witch, out of the way, he'd have Passion all to himself.

His plan was so pretty he allowed himself a cautious smile. Surprisingly, it barely hurt at all.

The front door downstairs opened and Dre heard the childlike giggling of his new conquest. The fifteen-year-old runaway from Philly would be ready for the streets in a couple of days. His dancers had to welcome the advances of the male customers, not shy away. All the big money came from lap dances and after-hours love sessions. This one had the long legs to do justice to both.

There was a sudden clatter, then more childish giggling floated up the stairs. Apparently she'd tripped on the stairs and Tracks was helping her up. Dre closed his eyes and sighed. *I'm getting too old for this crap.*

Unwilling or not, Passion wasn't prone to infantile chatter or giggling. She was one hundred percent mature woman. It had taken eight years to get her there, but her ex-suitors had sung her praises. Dre couldn't wait to take her to his bed. Nothing would stop him this time.

The commotion at his bedroom door forced him to open his eyes again. The blond hung drunkenly on the knob to peer inside. "Hi, Dre, honey." Her voice was annoyingly high-pitched. "Tracks said you'd want to see me." She stumbled a few steps into the room and threw her arms open. "Here I am!"

Dre laid his melted compress on the end table and wiggled into a sitting position on the king-size bed. Her small breasts were pushed up enticingly by a black lace bustier, and her leather skirt stopped just past her point of pleasure. She wasn't as fully developed as he liked, but she'd do for now.

Dre patted the satin comforter beside him. "Come here, Chante. Let Dr. Dre teach you all about supply and demand."

Chapter VII

"Damn." Reed slammed a large fist on his desk, then rubbed his sore eyes in exhaustion.

"I see you're in a good mood," Vanessa said between pops of gum.

Reed noted the color of the day was plum. Her eyelids, lips, and fingernails were drenched in it. "If you don't have something relevant to say, get the hell out."

"Hmmph." His secretary entered the room and flung herself into the chair opposite him. "For your information, I know who stayed at that penthouse in Crown Center before Cece Watters was killed."

Reed studied her with dawning interest. "If you're telling the truth, I'll kiss you."

Vanessa leaned an elbow on his desk, chewing gum noisily. "I'm telling the truth, but it's gonna cost you more than a kiss."

"Don't play games with me, Vanessa." His eyes narrowed dangerously. He'd spent a long sleepless night wondering when he'd hear from Dre Woods again and if he'd have to go back into private practice in a month after losing the election.

She shifted to a comfortable position to impart her news. "I really don't think Reverend Watters had anything to do with his wife's murder."

"Get to the point!" Reed pounded on the desk. He didn't need her and the pimp telling him what he already knew.

Vanessa held up a palm and cocked her head to the side. "Chill, okay?"

The district attorney held his tongue between his teeth. Experience had taught him not to rush. "Proceed," he said with practiced patience.

"So, anyway, I had a long talk with this new woman from church last Sunday. She told me how she used to be hooked up with this guy who had her livin' large in a penthouse in Crown Center."

Reed leapt up and yanked the secretary up by her shoulders. He could hardly breathe when he asked, "What was her name?"

"Whoa, big daddy," Vanessa teased. "I like it when you're physical."

"Please." He shook in anticipation. She held his entire career in the palms of her hands.

"Get this." Her voice filled with amusement. "Her name is Passion."

"Passion?" Reed frowned. "I don't have time for jokes, woman."

"I ain't jokin'." Her expression was as serious as a heart attack.

"Okay." Reed sat down slowly, trying not to get his hopes too high. "Did she happen to mention any conversations with Cece Watters?"

"Sure did." Vanessa examined her nails, as if they had had a chance to get damaged.

Reed's heart thundered like a racehorse on the home stretch. "And?"

"And—it seems when Cece couldn't get pregnant on her own, she hired Passion to be a surrogate mother. Except the reverend doesn't know a thing about it."

Reed jumped up and danced a jig around his office. "That's it, that's it!"

Vanessa smiled. "What now? You gonna just call the murder a freak accident, then leave it at that?"

"Hell no."

"Why not?"

Must he explain everything, as if she were a child? "Because, Vanessa my sweet, this is a perfect motive for Passion to kill Cece."

"What?" She gaped at him like he'd gone crazy.

"She's carrying Watters' baby. She decides she wants to keep the baby and become the new Mrs. Watters. She's connected with Dre Woods. She asks him to snuff Cece. It's all so simple."

Vanessa rose from the edge of the desk and shook her head. "You're gonna lose the election and be hauled off to the Larned State Hospital, all on the same day, if you keep this up."

Annoyed at the thought of being housed with his drooling cousin Elliott didn't sit well at all.

"Sometime, Vanessa, we're going to sit down and have a discussion about how you should keep your smart mouth closed."

"Hey. Far be it for me to tell you how to do your job, Eddie. But this time you need to think a little harder about how you're going to prove your case."

"What's to think about? We have a motive, we have a suspect, we have a conviction."

"It was much easier to believe when you said a crazy man got upset over the service at brunch and decided to take revenge on the buffet table."

"It's no coincidence Cece Watters was in the line of fire. It was planned."

"What makes you so sure?"

"Never mind." Why'd she have to ask so many damned questions? "Just get to the cleaners and pick up my navy blue suit, would you?"

"All right. But . . ." She headed out of the office. "It seems like you're ready to pin Cece's murder on anybody who's even halfway connected to Dre Woods."

Reed gave her a mean glare, sending Vanessa on her way. He sat down heavily. This was his last chance. It wouldn't work, but if the grand jury bought it, he'd have time to come up with something else.

* * * * * * * * * * * *

Shirleen Jackson worried with her coat buttons in the frosty air and stared at Reverend Watters' door. Plumb silly to fret over her appearance right now, but Passion's foolishness had her scared to death. She needed help and figured the best defense against Satan's own was a man of God.

She knocked and waited, trying to pull air into her lungs. Placing a hand to her chest, she tried to calm herself. It seemed like every little action gave her pains.

At last, he answered the door.

Shirleen looked up at the tall, handsome man. She couldn't fault Passion for taking a liking to such a fine gentleman. He was so good-looking, she barely managed to introduce herself.

"Please, come in, Miss Jackson." He stepped back and ushered her inside.

"Nice place you got here, Reverend." Shirleen allowed him to remove her coat before sitting down in the living room. The pillow-backed sofa felt good; the short walk from the bus stop had winded her something awful.

Jourdan hung up her coat and addressed her politely. "Can I offer you a warm drink, Miss Jackson?"

"Shirleen," she prompted. "Everybody calls me Shirleen."

He smiled graciously. "All right, Shirleen. I'm sure you're chilled. Can I get you a cup of tea?"

Shirleen waved away his kind intentions. "Naw, sir. I'm doin' just fine."

He sat in the opposite chair. "Tell me what brings you here. Are you a member of my congregation?" With the burgeoning memberships, it was getting harder and harder to know each person individually.

Shirleen wagged her gray head. "I goes to the First Baptist Church on t'other side of town. But my friend goes to Zion."

He nodded his head and listened intently.

"I believes you know Passion Adams?"

Jourdan straightened his spine. "Yes. Yes, I know her. Has something happened to her?"

If she wasn't mistaken, his eyes were looking real panicky and he was holding a bit too tight to his knees. He did care about the girl. "No. Least not yet."

"What do you mean, not yet?" He pushed forward in his chair.

"Well, Reverend, Passion is like a daughter to me and dat's why I'm here. I believes you're the only one who can help me now."

Shirleen told him about Dre Woods' attempt to win Passion's affections. "He gots it in his head, she gonna move in with him."

It seemed like a fire had ignited inside the reverend. He jumped to his feet and started pacing.

"I'm glad you came to me, Shirleen. I certainly don't want a member of my fold to fall into demonic hands. Unfortunately, it's up to Passion to make her own choices, whether we like it or not."

This wasn't the kind of talk for a smitten man.

"Just so." Shirleen nodded. "But I suspect she's movin' in against her will."

"What makes you say that?"

Shirleen wanted to smile at the look of hope that lit his face. "Passion don't like the man anymore'n I do. I'd just bet he gots somethin' over her and is forcin' her to do what he say."

Jourdan frowned. "Do you think he'd hurt her?"

She spread her hands and hunched her shoulders. "Anythin' possible with Dre. It wouldn't be so bad, Reverend, if Passion was da onliest one we had to worry about." She sighed. "But she gonna have a baby."

A sneeze would have blown Jourdan over.

"Passion is pregnant?"

"Yessir. 'Fraid she is." Shirleen pushed herself off the couch with some effort and walked over to the reverend. "I can't imagine what dat godforsaken Dre Woods would do to a innocent chile, can you?"

"No. I can't," Jourdan Watters said, a hard edge to his tone.

"Will you come by dis evenin' for supper and talk to her?"

"I'll be by around seven. How's that?"

"Fine. Dat'll be just fine."

Shirleen, her faith in the reverend intact, followed him to the coat closet and bundled up tightly against the afternoon wind. Her legs became wobbly, her head started to spin; she smiled. The reverend would use his influence to keep Dre Woods out of their lives and everything would be fine.

"On second thought," said Jourdan, taking his own coat from the closet, "I'll take you home. No need in you taking the bus when I've got a perfectly good car."

"Oh, dat's so kind of you, Reverend." She tried to steady herself. It wouldn't do to fall down at a time like this.

The ringing telephone stopped Jourdan the moment he touched the doorknob.

"I'd better get that," he apologized.

"Go 'head. I gots time." She leaned heavily against the wall after he left and closed her eyes just for a moment. Yessiree. It was time for these young people to be together—make a life together. She thought of William. He'd be proud of her.

* * * * * * * * * * * * *

Leaving Shirleen in the front hall, Jourdan went for the phone. His thoughts were troubled from the news of Passion's pregnancy. That, and her new involvement with Woods.

He picked up the receiver on the third ring. "Hello."

"Reverend Watters? District Attorney Edmond Reed here."

Jourdan's burden increased. "I don't suppose you have a lead on my wife's murderer?"

"As a matter of fact I do."

Elation went through Jourdan. Finally something was happening. Cece would be vindicated after all. The light of God removed another shadow from his life.

He grabbed a pencil and paper from his desk, poised to take down the details. "Tell me what you've got."

"No can do, Reverend." Reed laughed.

"I don't have time for practical jokes, Reed."

Mirth rang apparent in the DA's voice. "You can't fault a man who's solved the murder of the year for being happy now can you?"

Jourdan took a deep, temper-abating breath. "Tell me what you've found."

"I'd be happy to."

There was a long silence.

"Well?" Jourdan tapped his pencil impatiently.

"I can't tell you now. If you're watching channel seven at nine o'clock, you'll get your answers."

There was a click, then silence, and finally the inevitable tone of a cleared line.

Jourdan slammed down his receiver and held back the flooding temper that raged within him. Reed probably didn't have anything to disclose on the murder, he reasoned. The man probably would announce another harebrained theory that led nowhere. Could be he'd pieced together the connection between the pimp, Passion, and Cece. If so, then the man had more brains than Jourdan gave him credit for.

A sound from the front hall reminded him of his guest, Shirleen, and the reason for her visit. He wondered if Passion's baby belonged to Woods. If so, why had she propositioned Jourdan at his own pulpit? It churned his stomach to think her sole purpose in volunteering at the church had been use him to escape Dre Woods. But . . . what other explanation could there be?

His first impression had been correct—she was a temptress out to bag a preacher.

And what of Shirleen? Had she shown up to further Passion's cause?

Composing himself, he went back to his visitor. He noticed her labored breathing and pale face. Immediately, he regretted his suspicions of the woman. Clearly, it had sapped her strength to plead for her friend's safety.

"Are you feeling all right, Miss Jackson?" He guided the woman through the open door, wondering which doors would open and close, once he'd finished with Passion Adams.

* * * * * * * * * * * *

Edmond Reed walked up to his secretary, pressed a pack of gum into her palm, and kissed her cheek.

"What's this for?" Vanessa asked, thrilled with the small gift.

"For giving me a brilliant lead in the Cece Watters murder. And because I haven't heard you pop any gum today."

Vanessa followed her elated boss into his office. He hadn't been in this good a mood for a month of Sundays. Her suspicion of his involvement in Cece's murder warred with her desire to see him happy.

She closed the door carefully behind her and slid up to Eddie. "You tellin' me there's reason for celebration?"

He put one large hand on the small of her back and pulled her near. "Yes, there is." He planted a hungry kiss on her lips.

Vanessa purred her approval. "I'm all ears, Eddie." She sat on the edge of his desk as he took his place in his desk chair.

"Remember those phone calls from the Watters house to the penthouse?" he asked, arms folded behind his head.

She nodded.

"Cece was calling Passion Adams."

Vanessa rolled her eyes impatiently. "So tell me somethin' I don't know."

"I ran a check on the Adams chick and found her medical records from the free clinic—Dre's girls go there for regular check-ups."

"To make sure they don't have any diseases and stuff?"

"That's right." Reed grinned widely. "We couldn't find any records of her visiting an obstetrician or gynecologist there, but we found some at the downtown Medical Center. She's definitely pregnant."

Vanessa shifted impatiently. "So you found records of her donor-egg implant?"

"They only do that stuff at specialized fertility clinics. We've checked everywhere in town. She hasn't been to one. The story she told you doesn't hold water." Reed sat forward on his chair and ran a hand up and down her thigh. "You know what that means?"

"What."

"She and the good reverend were having an affair. Passion got pregnant and insisted Watters divorce his wife. The good reverend had Cece killed to get her out of the way."

"I still think that's stretching things a bit."

"No one asked you to think." He pulled his hand away abruptly. "Crimes of passion happen every day."

"How're you going to prove this? Did the hitman give you information?" Somehow, she doubted it.

He twisted his mouth into a wicked grin. "I've called a press conference for tonight to let the city know their DA is on top of this case. I'm telling them the trigger man is in custody, then I'll haul the reverend and his mistress in for interrogation. She'll confess to being pregnant with his child, he'll deny it, but the grand jury'll have enough motive to indict for conspiracy."

"I don't mean to be negative, Eddie, but isn't that hopin' for a lot?" She left the desk and shoved her way into his lap, encircling his neck with her arms.

Reed immediately removed her arms and glared at her. "I'm the one with a law degree here. I certainly don't need a lowly secretary telling me how to try a criminal case."

"You're trying somethin' all right." Vanessa released a loud breath as he stormed from the office. Lowly, her behind. He was taking himself straight into another pitfall. And damned if she knew why she cared.

Folding her arms, she walked slowly back to her desk. Maybe if she prayed hard enough, Eddie would see the light.

In the meantime she should warn Passion and Reverend Watters. It wouldn't be fair for them to be blindsided by her boss's groundless accusations. Vanessa laid a hand on the telephone and took a deep breath.

No answers. Not at the church, not at the reverend's house, not at Passion's apartment. Where could they be?

* * * * * * * * * * * * *

Passion pushed the shrimp around her plate, for once not able to enjoy the plush atmosphere of her favorite Kansas City steakhouse.

Dre, on the other hand, nearly made love to the remainder of his filet mignon.

"What's the matter, sunshine? Aren't you supposed to be eating for two?" His tone lacked concern.

"I'm not feeling well." Since she'd agreed to move in with him, it was all she could do to keep nausea at bay.

Tossing his napkin onto the empty plate, Dre motioned for the waiter. "Let's go then. I can't have you tossing your insides all over this nice restaurant."

"Thanks." She hoped he caught her sarcasm. Still, she was happy to be leaving. Shirleen hadn't been at home when they'd stopped by the apartment earlier. Her absence worried Passion.

It took only moments for Dre to herd her out of the restaurant and into the Lexus. "Take me by the apartment. I need to check on Shirleen," she said.

Tracks, gloved hands on the steering wheel, looked into the rearview mirror to see his boss's reaction.

Dre threw his head back dramatically. "You still worried about that old witch?" Without waiting for her answer he waved

102

Tracks on. "Fine. Fine." He pulled a flask from his breast pocket and took a long drink.

Passion's stomach reeled as the strong smell of liquor filled the space between them. Her overall sick feeling increased with the thought of breaking the news to Shirleen. Her friend wouldn't be happy about her decision to move in with Dre.

* * * * * * * * * * * * *

Dre came alert when the mobile phone purred to life on the dashboard. No one called unless trouble started. Tracks reached back to hand it to Dre. "What now?" he wondered.

"Dr. Dre," he said into the receiver.

"Doctor, is it?"

Dre winced at the too-familiar voice. "What the hell do you want now, Reed?" His jaw still had a bruise from where he'd been hit.

"I have to admit, Woods. You got me good the last time we met."

"Yeah, so what's up?" Dre's ringed fingers tightened around the hard plastic.

"Just wanted to let you know I'm holding a press conference tonight at nine o'clock."

"So?"

"I have a thing or two to say that you won't want to miss." He laughed heartily, with an obvious try at intimidation.

Dre didn't like the sound of this at all. "I ain't interested."

Reed stopped his laughing. "You'll be interested. You're not going to like it, though."

The phone clicked. Dre slammed it down. He really hated that man.

"Chill, Dre," he said to himself. He took all ten fingers and drew them over his wavy locks. No way would Reed mess up this night. It was only a matter of time before he got Passion into bed and tasted the sweet honey of her love.

"Who was it?" she asked.

"No one important."

* * * * * * * * * * * *

Passion glanced guardedly across the Lexus at the man she'd agreed to live with. She then listed all the reasons she had for doing it to help ease her mind. It didn't help much. They'd be at Shirleen's apartment soon; she'd have to get her stuff together. Of course, the most important reason, getting a nice first-floor apartment for Shirleen, could never be mentioned.

Passion knew her friend would sooner die than allow such sacrifice on her behalf.

"What's the matter?"

"Just thinking." Passion fidgeted, trying to come up with the words that would keep Shirleen from blowing her stack, once she heard the plan.

Dre, seeming to read her mind, put a possessive arm around her shoulders. "If that witch gives you any trouble, she'll have to reckon with me."

"No." Passion sat up straight. "I don't want any trouble between the two of you. Could you try not to say anything, please?"

"Absolutely."

She didn't like the slight hesitance in his voice. What else could she do but hope he'd keep his word?

The old building loomed ghastly gray against the night sky. Her heart hammered with anxiety as Tracks pulled the car to a stop. "Actually, Dre, you may just want to wait in the car while I talk to Shirleen."

"Fine."

She couldn't allow Shirleen's stubbornness to dissuade her. This move was for her own good.

And mine. She'd get an education and take charge of her life after this.

* * * * * * * * * * * *

Having arrived at Miss Jackson's apartment, Jourdan had

expected Passion to be on the premises. Not so. Nor had she shown up as he and Shirleen ate dinner. Strange, but the old woman didn't seem bothered by Passion's absence.

Jourdan, edgy over the upcoming newscast and anxious about Passion's whereabouts, struggled to remain calm. He made himself settle into the old kitchen chair and pat his stomach appreciatively.

"Shirleen, the Lord has truly blessed you with a gift for making sweet-potato pie."

"Thank you, Reverend." She sliced through the brown-orange dessert once again. "Have another."

"No, thank you." He waved the slice away with a chuckle. "I think I've made quite the glutton of myself already." He rose from his seat and began collecting dirty dishes.

"Now sit yourself down." Shirleen shooed him and took the dishes away. "I'll take care of these."

"Why don't you sit down? Cooking this good deserves a reward." He brooked no argument. After all, he'd watched her grow weaker by the moment. Every movement seemed to be a chore. Every breath a fight.

Jourdan prayed silently for the woman's health and proceeded to wash the dishes. "Are you expecting Passion soon?" he asked, growing more anxious.

Shirleen frowned. "I 'spect so." She didn't seem too sure.

The whole situation got more confusing moment by moment. "How did you meet Passion? It isn't often two people of such diverse ages become best friends."

Shirleen fanned herself with her hand and settled into her chair. "She and her mama moved into the projects next door to me and my husband, William, when she was jus' a little thang."

Jourdan smiled and tried to imagine what a young Passion had looked like.

"Oh, she was cute. Kinda sweet and shy."

"Now that I find hard to believe." Passion had never had any problem telling Jourdan exactly what was on her mind.

"It's true. Shore is." Shirleen got a faraway look in her eyes. "Jus' the circumstances of her life has made her so forward now."

"I see." Jourdan didn't see. How could anyone take up with a man like Dre Woods? How could Passion allow herself to get pregnant with that man's baby? Why did waves of jealousy wash over him every time he thought of them together?

"Forgiveness."

"What's that?" Jourdan had only been half-listening.

"Dat's all she needs. And a chance to start over. She so hard on herself for doing things dat was outta her control."

Jourdan remembered Passion's plea for forgiveness when he'd driven her home. Forgiveness for sleeping with men she was not married to. Forgiveness for . . . "Shirleen?"

"Yes?"

"Does Passion really hate her mother?" Jourdan, thinking of his own parents, rinsed the suds from the clean dishes and placed them in the rack beside the sink. Although he'd never longed to raise pigs, Jourdan had all the respect in the world for his father and mother. He couldn't imagine it any other way.

Shirleen sighed. "Passion thinks she hate her mama, but it ain't so."

Jourdan dried his hands on a small towel and joined her at the table. "Really?"

"It's not so much hate as it is fear." The color came back to the old woman's face. Her breathing seemed normal.

"Was the woman abusive?"

"She slapped her around once and again, but that ain't the reason. Sherrie jus' weren't no good, Reverend. She didn't much care about her daughter. Or anyone else. Seemed t' me like all she wanted was to get men's attention, like if dey slept with her, she was worth somethin'." Weary brown eyes settled on him. "Passion's scairt she gonna turn out like her."

He swallowed the thick lump in his throat, only to have it surface again. "Has she?"

"What? Turned out like her mama?"

One look at the woman's angry face, and Jourdan wished he hadn't asked the question. He wanted to know, though. What was Passion after? And why?

Shirleen leaned in closer to him. "I kin tell you what I thinks, but I'm afraid you gonna haveta make your own mind up about dat, Reverend."

Jourdan wished he *could* make up his mind about Passion. From the moment she'd walked into his church, his emotions had been in turmoil.

He was afraid of her beauty—afraid of how he reacted to her presence. Her eyes spoke of love, free-flowing, waiting to be given each time he looked inside their golden brown depths. But beyond them, he suspected a temptress lay waiting—luring her prey into a dangerous game of seduction.

Yet her voice . . . Sweet songs like prayers and bold songs of praise played in his head and soothed his soul every night before he slept. The only thing Jourdan knew for sure was he wanted Passion without question. Desired her without reason.

A clock with vegetables for numbers caught his attention and steered his thoughts to the time. Reed would be giving his song and dance about now. "Would you mind if I watch television while we wait for Passion to get home?"

"Course not, Reverend. Make yourself at home." Shirleen wrapped the remaining pie in foil and rose to put it in the refrigerator.

Jourdan crossed the room to the television. He turned the channel to seven and adjusted the antenna on the old set. It had been a long time since he'd watched TV without a remote control in hand. He got comfortable on the worn couch and admonished himself for even wanting to watch the district attorney's press conference. It was sure to be a farce.

Still, if there really were leads in Cece's murder, he needed to know. The least he could do was make sure his wife's murderer did ample time behind bars.

The conference began when the channel seven news anchor entered from the wings and explained to the members of the press how the question-and-answer session would work. He then introduced Edmond Reed.

Reed, wearing a navy blue suit and red power tie, addressed the camera rather than the press. Typical politician. All smiles and hot air.

After a long-winded recant of his accomplishments, he finally got to the point. "A suspect is in custody over the Cece Watters murder."

Jourdan's instant relief faded when Reed continued.

"I am pleased to announce we will be pushing for a trial date soon in the murder."

He paused, waiting for the rippling voices to subside.

"Ladies and gentlemen, I now have eyewitness testimony and hospital records that show the Reverend Jourdan Watters, of Zion Baptist Church, was having an affair before his wife's death."

Jourdan couldn't believe his ears.

"Evidence shows that Reverend Watters ordered his wife, Cece, killed," the DA continued, "because his mistress, Passion Adams, became pregnant with his child."

The press went wild. Hands shot up in the air and voices rose in competition with each other to get their questions answered first.

Reed's quarry sat, stunned and disgusted at the bald lies. Where had the DA received such ridiculous "evidence?" Passion? He'd find out what she knew. Tonight.

Chapter VIII

The heel of Italian leather went smashing into the tiny television set that sat between the front seats of the Lexus. Tracks jumped.

"Aahhhhh," Dre wailed like a wounded animal. In the rearview mirror, Tracks watched the man bury his head in his arms.

The Adams chick had gone up to her apartment a few minutes ago. Dre's sudden freak out couldn't be about that. Tracks peered over the back of his seat. "Yo, Dre. Chill, brother."

Dre didn't respond. He'd doubled over, rocking himself as if in acute pain.

"Come on, now. The sister can't be *all that*." Tracks tried again to console his anguished boss. He hadn't seen anyone act like this since his buddy Vince went crazy on PCP. It was like he was possessed or something.

Suddenly, Dre lifted his head and looked past Tracks toward the apartment building. "She played me, Tracks, and now the whole city knows about it. Give me my gun."

"Hell, naw." Tracks put a hand over the glove compartment. "You ain't right, man."

"Give me the damn piece, Tracks!"

Tracks looked at the slit eyes and drool sliding from his lips. "Naw, man. There's too many witnesses in that building. This ain't the time to lose your cool."

Dre crawled over the passenger seat with amazing speed and pushed Tracks against the driver's door. Before Tracks could sit upright, and in one quick movement, Dre opened the glove compartment and grasped the dark weapon.

Tracks threw open the car door in time to see Dre run inside.

"Damn." He rubbed the back of his sore, bald head, not sure whether to leave or stay. They didn't have a getaway planned out this time. And he was sure someone would get hurt. Bad.

* * * * * * * * * * * * *

The TV on, Passion stood silently in the open door watching Jourdan pace Shirleen's living room floor. Her heart twisted painfully at his expression. He knew. This wasn't how she'd wanted him to find out. "I'm so sorry," she managed to say.

Jourdan looked up into Passion's eyes. Rife with anger and confusion, his gaze was glacial—freezing her out.

He spoke to Shirleen. "I can't believe Reed's so desperate to keep his job that he'd make up such an insane story."

"Oooh, Lordy." Shirleen keened quietly from the kitchen doorway. She ducked inside her bedroom.

Passion took a step inside the room. "I don't know how he found out the baby was yours—"

"Mine! Have you flipped out, too?" He took a step in her direction. "I think I'd remember having an affair with you."

Passion closed the door behind her, searching for the words to explain what had happened.

His expression changed to suspicion as he watched her take a seat on the couch. "Did you tell the DA that I got you pregnant?"

No," she said simply, reading a thousand horrors in his eyes. Her heart sank. "But it's your child I'm carrying."

Jourdan looked as if she'd just taken him on a trip to the Twilight Zone. "How can you say that?"

"Sit down. Please." She'd feel better if he weren't standing over her with closed fists.

Jourdan wavered before easing down on the far side of the sofa. "From the moment we met—I've known you'd suck me into scandal." He squinted upward. "Lord, how did I allow this to happen again?"

Again?

She didn't have a moment to ponder his accusation, disgust, or the meaning for his rage. Jourdan demanded to know everything. Now.

Passion swallowed, nervously fiddling with the belt circling her waist. "Four months ago—"

* * * * * * * * * * * * *

Wavy hair on end, as if electrified, Dre slammed through the unlocked door and into Shirleen's apartment; both Passion and Jourdan jumped to their feet. The worst night of her life had just gotten worse.

Dre's small red-rimmed eyes drilled Passion first, then Jourdan. "I won't put up with this."

Passion's eyes had already riveted to the black gun Dre held in his right hand. Jourdan took a cautious step, as if to shield her.

Dre lunged further into the room. "Damn you, Passion!"

Jourdan spoke calmly, with reason, "Give me the gun, Woods."

Dre jerked his head up and pointed the weapon at Jourdan's heart. "Don't take another step," he warned through clenched teeth. "Why're you here, preacher man?" He kept the gun trained on Jourdan and looked over at Passion. "You come to collect your woman?"

"No, Dre. I'm going with you, remember?" Passion's heart pounded against her ribs in fear of Dre, and in shame from the look Jourdan turned in her direction.

The gun drifted unsteadily toward Passion.

"Don't do it, Woods."

"Shut up, preacher man." Dre shuffled around Jourdan, who had blocked his line of fire.

"You played me, didn't you?" said Dre, his eyes wide with fury. "Well, I got news for you. No woman makes me look like a fool in front of the entire city and lives to tell about it."

"Calm down, Dre." She willed her voice to remain steady while looking down the cannon-sized barrel of Dre's gun.

Jourdan stood tense, like a caged lion.

Dre closed some distance between himself and Passion. The gun wobbled in his grip. "Y'all are caught dead to rights now, aren't ya?"

"Enough, Woods."

Passion could barely breathe. "What do you mean?"

"I suppose preacher man is gonna marry you, now that the whole city knows you're carryin' his kid."

"The baby's not mine," Jourdan shouted. "I'm not marrying Passion."

His determined statement sliced her heart in two. Suddenly, dying at Dre's hand didn't seem nearly as bad as a lifetime of Jourdan's hatred.

"I told you I was pregnant, Dre."

The gun wobbled again. Dre's mask of torture transformed to grief. "You told me you'd stay with me—but only if I paid you."

Jourdan gave her a sharp look of distaste.

"That's right, preacher man." Dre pointed the black barrel at Passion once again. "She played both of us."

Dre moved forward, his fingers tightened around the gun. "All I wanted was for you to love me."

A tear rolled down Passion's face. Fear, sadness, and despair went with it. "I know, Dre. I'm sorry." It seemed to be her night for apologies.

Jourdan again stepped between the gun and Passion. He grabbed Dre's wrist and pushed him against the wall. They spun around the room in a desperate struggle, Jourdan trying to knock the gun away, Dre trying to point the weapon at the larger man.

Passion raced across the room to the telephone.

"What's goin' on?" Shirleen rushed from her bedroom to see the weapon shaking to a point just below Jourdan's temple. She ran to help.

"Shirleen, no!" Passion shouted, ignoring the 911 operator's questions.

"Damn!" Dre cried—Shirleen had a finger looped inside his earring, dragging him across the room. "You crazy, woman?"

Shirleen yanked again. "I had enuf-a you, Dre Woods." Shirleen whapped his jaw. "Get your sorry behind outta my house and don't ever come back."

"Why don't you let us take care of him, Miss?" An amused policeman entered and had the gunman on the floor and in handcuffs in a blink of Passion's eye. Summarily, the lawman hauled Dre out of the apartment. Curses ripped through the hallway.

Shirleen slumped to the floor, her hand grasping her breast. "Shirleen!" Passion screamed.

A paramedic rushed in behind the policeman and checked her breathing and pulse. "Cardiac arrest."

A flash of white fear slashed through Passion's brain. The forgotten phone slipped through her fingers. A uniformed woman began pushing on Shirleen's chest.

"Please, God. Let her be all right," Passion prayed.

"Are you able to answer a few questions?" a kind voice asked.

The blue uniform blurred before Passion's tears. She wanted to follow Shirleen to the hospital—her friend's body looked so limp as they loaded her onto the stretcher.

"Can it wait?" she asked.

"Afraid not." The policeman put a warm hand on her shoulder. "We'll need to go to the station."

"Can't we give our statements here?" Jourdan asked.

"No, sir."

Passion watched in confusion as the officer pulled out a pair of handcuffs. "You are Reverend Jourdan Watters, aren't you?"

"Yes, but—"

"You're under arrest." He pushed Jourdan against the wall, then yanked his arms behind him.

Passion began to protest, but the female officer did the same to her. The rough texture of the wall chafed her cheek as steel handcuffs circled her wrists.

"Why are you doing this?" Jourdan demanded. "The entire world has gone crazy tonight."

"You're under arrest for the murder of Cece Watters. You have the right to remain silent . . ."

Passion nodded when the officer finished reading her rights. She did indeed remain silent while being steered toward the flashing lights of the police car. The police woman instructed her to watch her head, then prodded her inside, next to Jourdan.

He too, was quiet, the chill of his cold shoulder more bitter than the night wind. Passion's world spun out of control— Shirleen—Dre—Jourdan. She had none of them now. Even the child she carried wasn't her own. For the second time in her life, she had only herself.

Passion pressed her head against the cold window. Her breath and tears turned to cracked ice on the glass—how appropriate.

The scream of the ambulance siren pierced the air in front of them. *Don't let her die, Lord. Not Shirleen.* If He heard no other prayer, let Him hear this one.

* * * * * * * * * * * * *

Later, Passion squeezed her eyes closed, still seeing the dots from the camera flash. She felt like she'd been dropped in the middle of "NYPD Blue." First mug shots, then fingerprints. She popped an eye open to examine her hands. The small tissue they'd given her was a poor substitute for soap and water.

She was in a tiny room now, furnished only with a table and a couple of foldout chairs. No one could tell her about Shirleen. "Can I go home now?"

The police officer looked so young, with his short dark hair and wide innocent blue eyes. "I'm afraid not, Miss Adams."

114

"Why not?" she asked.

"We need a statement from you. The district attorney will be here as soon as he gets through with Reverend Watters." The policeman headed for the door.

"Where are you going?" Passion didn't want to be left alone. Even a young officer she didn't know had to be better than being left to think about the bad things that were happening.

"I have to man the telephones, ma'am. Is there something I could bring you?"

"I'd like a soda—any kind." Her throat was dry and tight.

"I'll be right back."

He closed the door softly behind him, locking it. Passion surveyed the bare room. The wall sustained a huge mirror, the only accent besides table and chairs. So . . . they really did use those one-way windows to spy on suspects.

Suspect.

That's what they called me. How did the DA ever come up with his murder theory? Jourdan was right, Edmond Reed was desperate.

What about Jourdan? Was he still here? Did he still hate her? She'd tell the truth and they'd both be free soon. There was nothing to worry about.

The officer came bustling into the room with a cola. "Here you go, Miss Adams."

"Thanks . . ." She squinted to see his name tag. "Brad."

His face lit up like a trick-or-treater. "Sure."

Taking advantage of his helpful nature, Passion asked if he could check on Shirleen Jackson.

"What hospital did they take her to?" Brad asked.

"I'm not sure." Her optimism waned.

"I'll see what I can do." He headed for the door again, in time to be pushed back by a very large man. "Excuse me, sir." Brad flattened himself to the door and slid into the hallway.

"Miss Adams, I'm District Attorney Edmond Reed. I'd like you to answer a few questions."

Passion nodded her agreement. Anything so she could get out of here.

The gray-eyed man sat on the opposite side of the table from her. The only other chair in the room was quickly occupied by a pretty black court reporter, a transcriber in front of her. "Are you aware you could have counsel present before you say anything?"

"I don't need a lawyer."

"Make a note for the record that Miss Adams is waiving her right to an attorney," Reed said to the court reporter with a smug grin.

"Just a moment!" A dark brown man with a shock of white fuzz on his head came storming in the door, briefcase in hand.

"Mr. Townsend, I told you—your client will not be released tonight." Reed rose to his full height, which was significantly taller than the lawyer before him.

"I still take exception to your treatment of Reverend Watters, Mr. Reed. Furthermore, I've just been put on retainer to represent Miss Adams as well."

"By whom?" Reed's face went vermillion.

"Jourdan Watters." The attorney lifted thick gray eyebrows toward Passion. "May I introduce myself, Miss Adams? I'm Sherman Townsend."

Jourdan had hired an attorney for her? Passion was shocked and touched. It was the nicest thing anyone besides Shirleen had ever done for her.

Reed exhaled impatiently. "Would you like Mr. Townsend to represent you, Miss Adams?"

"I would." It couldn't hurt.

"Very well." The little lawyer stepped further inside the room and closed the door. "Proceed, Mr. Reed."

"Are you familiar with the accusations being brought before you, Miss Adams?"

Passion didn't appreciate his rude tone. "Yes."

"Would you like to make a full confession at this time?"

"Confess to what, Mr. Reed?"

"Save us some time, honey. Spill your guts."

Passion had the urge to slap him. "My name's not honey."

"She just told you she's not guilty, Mr. Reed." Sherman Townsend's voice boomed grander than his height. "Don't badger my client."

Passion smiled at her new attorney. She liked the little old guy.

"All right." Reed's nostrils flared like an angry bull's. "We'll start from the beginning. Miss Adams, what is your relationship to Reverend Watters?"

"He's my pastor."

Reed smiled in amusement. "Your pastor?"

"Yes."

His pale eyes danced. "Is it true, Miss Adams, that you're carrying Reverend Watters' child?"

"Yes."

"Does your *pastor* make a habit of impregnating women in his congregation?" the DA inquired, a corner of his lip turning upward.

"You don't have to say another word," Mr. Townsend cautioned her.

"Yes, I do." Only the truth could set Passion and Jourdan free. "The fact is, Cece Watters hired me to surrogate for her and Reverend Watters. A few days after we found out the procedure worked, she was killed. She had yet to find a way to tell her husband about the baby."

"You would like us to believe that, wouldn't you?" Reed paced slowly across the small room. "Just exactly *how* did the reverend's wife come to meet you?"

"I was having lunch in one of the restaurants in Crown Center. She just walked up to me with one of those little religious booklets and asked me if I knew Jesus Christ. I was grateful for the company and asked her to have a seat."

The kindly attorney grinned. "That's typical of Cece. She hated to see anyone by themselves." He smiled at Passion.

At Reed's scowl, Passion continued. "We sort of became friends after that. She told me about her wish for a child. Eventually, I agreed to be her surrogate."

Reed scratched his jaw. "We searched for records on this supposed in-vitro deal and came up with nothing. How do you explain that?"

"It depends on where you were looking."

Reed cut her a dangerous look. "We've searched every hospital and specialized clinic in the state of Kansas."

"Last year, Reverend Watters had sperm frozen in a clinic in Maryland," Passion explained.

"Cece insisted they go out of state for the procedure to keep it quiet. They tried twice, but it didn't work." She dropped her head, remembering sadly her friend's severe disappointment at not being able to carry the fertilized eggs.

"Continue," Reed snapped.

Passion sniffed and blinked to clear her eyes. "Since it was so expensive and upsetting to Cece, Reverend Watters refused to let her try again."

Her attorney nodded knowingly.

Reed gave her a wry look. "How touching."

"Anyway, Cece told her husband some story to get out of town for a few days, to go to Maryland with me. The doctor had fertilized Cece's eggs with Jourdan's sperm. Luckily, my womb proved to be a lot more baby friendly than Cece's."

"This is like a damned soap opera," Reed snapped. "And where is this supposed clinic you went to?"

"The Fertility Institute."

The DA's jaw clenched visibly as he jotted down the name. "I'll have someone verify this." He glared at her from across the table.

Passion returned his unblinking stare. "Fine."

"What was your association with Dre Woods, Miss Adams?"

A blaze of shame shot up her face. "What's he got to do with this?"

"Answer the question." The big man's nostrils flared unattractively.

"I was an exotic dancer at his club."

The smile returned to Reed's face. "For how long?"

"Only a few months—eight years ago."

"Miss Adams, did you know Mr. Woods to order executions?"

"No."

"You suspected it?"

"I really don't know enough about it to say." Passion suspected a lot of things about Dre. An innocent babe, he was not.

"You knew he could get rid of anyone he wanted with a quick phone call, didn't you?"

"I—"

"You asked him to take out Cece Watters, didn't you?"

"No." Passion wanted to wipe the predatory look off his pale face.

"You wanted Jourdan Watters *and* his baby," Reed insisted, "so you asked your friend Dre to take care of his wife. Isn't that right, Miss Adams?"

"Absolutely not." He was starting to piss her off. "I liked Cece. She was sweet and kind, wouldn't hurt a fly. All she wanted was a baby to call her own. I wanted to help her."

"Then why doesn't Reverend Watters know anything about this surrogate business?"

"She chose not to tell him until she knew the procedure was successful. Unfortunately, she put it off too long."

"Why didn't you tell him?" As Reed pounded a fist on the table, the liquid in her cola can spilled from the top.

"I tried."

"You expect me to believe you were willing to carry someone else's child for nothing?"

"I did it for $15,000." Passion shoved to her feet.

Reed was silenced by her admission.

Telling him about the money cheapened the real reason.

She'd done it for Cece. But somehow she didn't think the big oaf would understand simple human compassion.

Her attorney stepped forward and placed a hand on Passion's arm, his voice quietly commanding as he said, "You have your statement, Mr. Reed. Not guilty is the plea."

Grateful for the man's understanding, Passion relaxed her defenses.

"I expect you to arrange a release for Miss Adams and Reverend Watters as soon as possible."

Reed gritted his teeth. Passion thought he would hit her new lawyer. His face bloomed an even brighter red as he turned and yanked the door open instead. Without another word, he tore angrily down the hallway.

She looked up at the attorney. "Thank you, Mr. Townsend. When will I be able to leave?"

The old man rubbed his eyes. "Probably not until morning."

Morning? "But my friend is in the hospital. I need to see her."

"I understand, Miss Adams. But a judge has to determine if there's enough evidence to hold you. No one's available until morning."

"Great." Passion wilted and closed her tired eyes. "Mr. Townsend?"

"Yes."

"Tell Jourdan I'm sorry for all this." She kept her eyes closed. Her head was getting too heavy to hold up, so she laid it on her arms.

"I will."

* * * * * * * * * * * *

"Passion?"

Locked in sleep, she tried to open her eyes, but found herself caught in the zone where movement wasn't possible.

"Passion."

This time Jourdan's voice boomed forcefully enough to rouse her. She slowly opened one tired eye, then the other, to see him standing over her in the hospital waiting room. A pang of guilt stabbed at her as she vaguely remembered waking up this morning, long enough to be released from the police precinct. She'd shamelessly requested a ride to the hospital. She hadn't expected Jourdan to stick around.

"I'm awake," she said in a drugged voice, pushing herself to an upright position on the couch. The waiting room turned cool when the blanket slid to her lap. Jourdan must have covered her while she slept. A small kindness. "Must've dozed off."

"It's been a long night." His voice had a raspy quality to it. Dark circles beneath his eyes told of a sleepless night.

She put words to her thoughts. "I'm surprised you're still here."

Jourdan rubbed his face. "I thought we might get a chance to talk. We're free from prosecution, but not the truth."

They were linked now, like a reluctant bride and groom in an arranged marriage. The quality of their lives for the next five months depended on how willingly he accepted impending fatherhood.

"Miss Adams," a voice interrupted.

Glad for the temporary diversion, Passion sought the man behind the voice.

Jourdan moved aside, allowing her to see past him to the door.

A tall, light-complexioned black doctor with a full mustache and deep worry lines between his brows stood beneath the doorframe. His serious look brought back in full measure her reason for being there.

"How is she?" Passion removed the blanket, suddenly impervious to the chill. "How's Shirleen?"

He folded his arms over his stethoscope and rested a shoulder against the door jamb. "She's suffered a severe heart attack."

Stunned, Passion asked, "How bad?"

"It was a pretty serious one, but the paramedics got to her in record time and the bypass surgery went well."

"Can I see her?" Passion stood in an effort to clear the confused messages going through her brain.

"By all means. But keep in mind—she's still heavily sedated and won't be able to respond to you. I'll be back to check on her this afternoon." He left the room.

"Would you like me to go in with you?" Jourdan's dark eyes were now soft with compassion.

"If you wouldn't mind. I'm not sure how I'll react when I see her." Having Jourdan with her somehow made her feel more secure.

She rounded the corner of the intensive care unit and caught sight of Shirleen in one of the sterile rooms. Fresh tears sprang to her eyes when she saw Shirleen on a narrow bed with tubes running in and out of her arms, nose, and mouth. She looked half-machine, half-human as the intermittent beeps, clicks, and whirls sustained her life.

Passion felt the strength leave her legs.

Jourdan caught her, guiding her to a chair near the bed. "Are you all right?"

Passion nodded sadly and forced herself to be strong enough not to run from the room. This was her first opportunity to repay Shirleen's unwavering support. She deserved more than a faint-hearted attempt.

Passion's resolve returned slowly; she rose shakily. Jourdan, never more than a breath away, walked with her to the bed. Her pulse began to slow and her lightheadedness disappeared as she looked upon the serene sleeping face of her dear friend.

She steadied her hand enough to stroke the gray wisps of hair from Shirleen's face. Still, she couldn't stop the tears from dropping onto the white pillowcase and soaking a spot next to that sweet pale cheek.

Jourdan circled the bed to stand on the opposite side. The warm strength of his hand took her own across Shirleen's prone form; the action forced Passion to look up. It occurred to her . . .

"Jourdan?"

"Yes?"

"Could you," she stammered uncomfortably. "God would probably listen to you a lot quicker than to . . . someone like me." She hung her head. "Could you pray for Shirleen?"

Jourdan's grip on her hand became stronger and she dared to look into his handsome face. There was nothing but gentleness in the rich depths of his gaze.

"Of course." His chin dropped in supplication; he laid a hand on Shirleen's shoulder and began his prayer.

Passion bowed her head and closed her eyes, praying with all her strength.

Jourdan beseeched the Father to heal His faithful servant. His commanding voice reverberated against the walls of the small room.

Passion felt a tingling sensation reach her fingertips, as the power of his voice filled her very being. Her own voice, becoming more confident in response, blended with his in a perfect orchestration of prayer.

A warm, cleansing light entered her mind and surged through her veins. She released her grief to embrace the hope that surrounded her, as Jourdan's hand had moments before.

Shirleen would be all right. She knew it without question.

"Amen." Jourdan fell silent.

Passion smiled serenely and opened her eyes.

This time his gaze wasn't gentle, but fiercely magnetic—energizing the air around them. Every cell in her body pulsed. Every breath drawn in sync with his.

Standing there in silent communion, Passion felt a small bud of hope for her own future. Jourdan wanted her. She could feel his need trying to breech the gap between them. Before it happened, he gave her a look of jumbled yearning and confusion.

Jourdan cleared his throat. "Would you care to go home and change, perhaps get some breakfast?"

"I'd like that." Passion smoothed her hair self-consciously. "I must look like ten miles of bad road."

He gave a half-hearted laugh. "I assure you, that's quite impossible."

"Thanks." Passion accepted the awkward compliment. She took one last study of her sleeping friend, then left the room.

The car ride home held silence. Thankfully, Jourdan didn't ask any questions. She needed some time to sort out her feelings. Despite all her rationale that the good reverend would sooner kick her than kiss her, she wanted him now more than ever.

How strange, the turns of human emotions.

Her mind immediately leapt to another problem. Where would Shirleen recuperate after her hospital release? Obviously, all bets were off with Dre—he was locked up.

* * * * * * * * * * * * *

The sun broke through the clouds of the dreary day just as Jourdan parked the car in front of the apartment building. Once inside, she made a beeline for the bathroom to bathe and change quickly, ever aware of Jourdan's presence in the kitchen. Passion dreaded the conversation to come, but was anxious to be done with it.

Chapter IX

Slipping quietly into a vinyl chair, Passion sat at the table. Jourdan flipped an omelette expertly and prepared another by chopping bacon, cheese, and vegetables.

"Who taught you how to cook?" she asked, desperate to break the discomforting silence.

He turned, startled. "My mother." A tiny smile brightened his face. Facing the stove again, he continued, "I was something of a mama's boy when I was young."

"You? That's the last thing I would've suspected."

Dark bronze muscles rippled in his forearms in contrast to the white material of his rolled-up sleeves. She noted with appreciation how his shirt stretched across his wide back, alleviating the rumpled appearance on the top portion of his shirt. The shirttail billowed in loose tucks at the waist of black slacks. Despite wrinkles, the pants emphasized the round firmness of Jourdan's behind. Heavens, Passion thought, the man was fine from every angle.

"You know . . ." She took a swallow of the orange juice he'd poured and placed on the table. "You're the guest around here. I should be cooking for you."

"Miss Shirleen said you aren't a very good cook. In the interest of self-preservation . . ." He cocked his head and grinned, amazingly.

"Ha. Ha. Ha." Passion could feel the tension ease somewhat.

Within moments he placed an omelette before her with an overly generous helping of hash browns and toast.

"I may be pregnant, Jourdan, but I can't eat all this." She gestured at the food before her.

His smile faded, his tone losing all playfulness. "Do the best you can." He filled his own plate but left it untouched. "About this pregnancy . . ."

Passion chewed a forkful of omelette slowly, but why stall? It was past time for the truth. She said softly, "It's yours. Yours and Cece's."

He stared at her for the longest time. "Mine and Cece's."

Passion nodded. "We went to Maryland. I think she told you she was going to some women's retreat."

He studied the floor, rested his backside against the counter. His forehead creased into a frown. "I remember." Jourdan raised his hands to his face. "Were you so desperate, sweetheart?" His words, spoken to the Great Beyond, drifted like sad notes of a song in the stillness of the room.

Passion averted her eyes, touched and pained by his grief.

"Why didn't you tell me?" His eyes remained shut.

Passion wasn't sure if he addressed the living or the dead.

His eyes opened then, still moist with unshed tears. "I asked you a question."

"I meant to—a couple of times. Started to . . . in the hallway . . . that night we kissed." This past evening, Dre had cut her short. "I was afraid."

"Of what?"

"Of you. Of how you'd react."

"You were afraid I wouldn't want my own child?"

"Yes. It's a horrible thing being raised without love," she

126

said, knowing full well the hurt of a loveless childhood. "After you said you wanted children, I was even more afraid to tell you."

Jourdan shook his head once. "I don't understand."

"The only thing I've ever done right was carry this child, Jourdan." She looked up pleadingly into his eyes. "I want more than anything to be a part of its life. I don't want you to take it away from me."

Jourdan moved closer, his voice a deep whisper. "Why would you want to raise a child by yourself?"

"I don't want to raise it by myself. This baby deserves more from life than I've ever had. It deserves a good home—and two parents." She spoke with more optimism than she could afford. Once again, her heart dangled by a thread. *Dear God, let him be gentle this time.*

"Is that why you propositioned me in my church? Because you wanted this child to have two parents?"

Passion's dim light of hope faded. "No." She held his gaze bravely, ignoring the shards of pain created by her shattered heart. "I just wanted to see the baby's father."

"Not to collect the $10,000 Cece had yet to pay you?"

Dropping her head, she studied the chipped edge of the table. "Mr. Townsend told you?"

"Yes."

She felt as cheap as a two-dollar whore at a millionaire's ball. "Cece had already given me $5,000. After she died, I decided I'd lost out on the rest. We didn't have a contract or anything." Passion swallowed. "She said she trusted me to do the right thing when the baby was born."

"How could she do this?" Jourdan turned toward the counter. "What was she thinking?"

"I've never seen anyone so desperate to have a baby." Passion wiped her nose with a paper napkin.

Jourdan whirled around again. "And what were you think-ing, going along with this?"

127

"I told you. I was only trying to help." Why couldn't anyone grasp the concept?

"And this Dr. Dre, where does he fit in?"

"I used to work for him."

"I heard."

He'd heard? How? From whom? It didn't matter. He deserved total candor. Still, it hurt like the devil.

"Was Woods your lover?" he asked in disgust.

She leveled her gaze with his. "When I was sixteen, my mother tried to kill me. I ran." She painted the picture precisely so Jourdan couldn't misread anything. "Dre took me in. He gave friendship when I needed it, that's all."

"I see."

"You see what?" Passion sensed distrust in his tone.

"You were young and scared and Dre took advantage of you."

"That's right. He did." Passion studied him cautiously. "When he told me I had to work in his club to earn my keep, I didn't see any options."

Jourdan braced both hands on the table. "So what kind of *work* kept you there for eight years?"

Passion moved her plate aside. "I only danced for Dre for a few months. Then, I met a man who was nice to me. I left."

"One of the men you slept with to keep a roof over your head, right?"

"I told you about that."

"And, how many of these *nice* friends did you have?"

"A couple." She rose from the table and clutched her arms around herself. "How dare you throw this back in my face when I asked you how you felt about me."

"I didn't know then you were carrying my child."

Passion shoved her chair under the table. "What happened to my clean slate, Jourdan? What happened to 'Jesus forgives you' and all that stuff you babbled about not so long ago?"

"Your loyalties are with the Philistines. You've been manipulating me this whole time." Jourdan curled his fingers at his side.

Of course, she had. Only now did she realize it.

Jourdan circled the table. "Volunteering at Zion was a ploy to get in my good graces. I was going to be another notch on your rhinestone studded belt, wasn't I?"

"I had no such intentions." Passion self-consciously covered the fake jewels around her waist.

"Come on now, Passion. Your other boyfriends bought you food and rent, wasn't I supposed to buy you respectability?"

His words landed too close to the truth, making her all the more irate. "Yes, I volunteered at your church to be near you. Yes, it was a ploy to get in your good graces." She advanced and stood only inches away from him. "I did it because I fell in love with you, Jourdan." Tears of anger and sadness mingled to send warm streams down her cheeks. "God help me, I'm in love with you."

In turmoil, Jourdan's heart pounded at Passion's newest confession. He raged silently. This was wrong. All wrong.

"It's not right for you to love me, Passion," he said.

"Since when does love know right and wrong?" Her face, her voice, her bearing all showed torture.

He'd witnessed, been a part of such pain in the past. When Cece miscarried for the second time. Afraid he could bear no more sadness without breaking, Jourdan had shied from his wife's pain, using excuses about the television deal or scripture study to shield himself from her grief. Perhaps he hadn't been such a great husband, after all.

Jourdan placed a hand on Passion's shoulder in an attempt to comfort her and to ease his guilt. "Right or wrong, I can't disrespect Cece's memory."

Passion shoved his hand away with a quick swipe. "I don't recall asking you to." She held her head high. "Cece was a kind and generous woman. I'd sooner die than damage her reputation. I know I've sullied her good name anyway. For that, I apologize, Jourdan. I'm very, very sorry."

He knew such an admission hadn't come easy to this proud woman. He drank in the fine golden-brown planes of her face.

Tear-streaked, without an ounce of makeup, and eyes puffy from crying, she stood before him as the most stunning woman he'd ever seen. Bold and fearless, she'd captured his heart when they'd first met and held it now even as she rebuked him. And herself.

From the beginning she'd ignited such blazing desire within him that he feared spontaneous combustion, or worse, spontaneous displays of affection.

What he'd attempted in her apartment hallway—well, that display had been only a portion of what he wanted to do now.

Fear kept him rooted at this moment. If he took a step toward accepting her love, he'd surely lose everything else.

It had taken only a hint of wrongdoing to ruin his last ministry.

With but a bat of her gorgeous eyes—a simple shifting movement—Passion had always unleashed a barrage of sinful thoughts in his head. He wouldn't stand a chance of preserving his reputation with her by his side.

As if to prove the point, Passion moved into the living room with her long-legged stride, unwittingly leaving him miserable with longing.

Have mercy.

But God didn't seem in the mood to be merciful.

Jourdan followed her, taking a moment to catch his breath before sinking onto the couch next to her. "Where do we go from here? I'm not certain how to proceed."

"Neither am I."

"Passion . . . after the child is born . . . will you honor your word to Cece and hand it to me?"

She looked away. "Of course. I want it to have a good life."

"Do you need anything?" he asked, at a loss in his new role. "I could pay you the money Cece promised you."

* * * * * * * * * * * * *

He'd pay her the money. Passion noticed the absence of contempt in Jourdan's tone, but she didn't want to accept his offer.

She started to decline and confess how much she wanted to raise the baby, then thought better of it. He'd made clear what he thought of her. Marriage was out of the question.

With the money that she and Cece had agreed on, she'd be back to plan A. She'd have enough to take care of Shirleen for a while and to take some courses at school. Then she'd wash her hands of men forever.

But—oh! How she'd miss the baby.

"I accept." She didn't dare look at Jourdan. Her aching heart couldn't bear any more of his rejection.

An uncomfortable silence fell between them.

"I'd like to know something, Passion. Do you have *any* reason to believe Dre Woods is involved in Cece's murder? The one they arrested—Teardrop—is known around town as his employee."

"What! Jourdan, I can't imagine—as far as I know, Cece and Dre didn't even know each other," she replied earnestly.

"Are you going to testify against Woods?"

Sighing in irritation, she turned to face him. "Why do our conversations always come back to Dre?"

"I have a right to know."

"Why?"

"You're carrying my child. I have a right to ensure that you aren't endangered by that man again."

"He's in jail, Jourdan, for attempted murder. The state is pressing charges and, no doubt, I'll have to testify. Keep in mind you don't own me just because I'm carrying this baby."

"Fine." He put his hands up in a frustrated, surrendering gesture. "Fine."

Another long hush stretched before he spoke again. "Do you have any objections to my checking on your progress from time to time?"

"No." She calmed down. And reasoned it was only natural for him to care about her developing pregnancy. "I'll be at church every Sunday."

"Let me know when you go to the doctor next. I'd like to tag along."

She hadn't expected that. "Okay."

"I'll pay all medical expenses from here on out."

Again, she agreed, relieved she could continue seeing Cece's doctor instead of those on call at the free clinic.

Jourdan, abandoning the couch, retrieved his coat from the rack and returned to stand before her. "Will you need anything for Miss Jackson when she's released from the hospital?"

Passion sighed. "Just a first floor apartment. I'll only be able to keep her in bed awhile before she'll insist on visiting her friends or volunteering. The stairs aren't good for her."

Shoving his hands in his pockets, Jourdan gave her an unreadable expression. "I have a big house."

"That's nice, Jourdan." She didn't know what else he expected her to say.

"There's a good-size bedroom on the first floor and three upstairs. Shirleen could stay with me."

At his generous offer, which made up for many of his hurtful remarks, Passion sprang to her feet. "Really? She just needs a place for a few weeks, until the apartment I leased opens up."

"Let's plan on it." It was the first smile he'd given her all day; it was a dazzler.

It was a heckuva thing to do to a woman who didn't stand a chance of having him. Passion walked him to the door and exchanged good-byes.

She listened for a moment as his footsteps echoed down the hall. When he'd disappeared altogether, she returned to the old couch. The slight scent of his aftershave still lingered; she sank back to enjoy it. Already she missed him.

Why didn't things ever work out for her?

Why ask such a ludicrous question? With every man, she'd gone about it all wrong, not thinking through the consequences. Married men don't leave their wives. Preachers don't marry women with pasts. Jourdan stood as out of her reach as heaven's pearly gates.

* * * * * * * * * * * * *

Somewhere between leaving Passion and turning onto his own street, Jourdan experienced an epiphany. Sudden elation burst inside him. He slapped the steering wheel with joy. "Thank you, Jesus." He filled the interior of his car with his jubilant shout. He was going to be a father.

Finally he'd get the child he and Cece had prayed for. *Why Passion, Lord? Why not Cece?*

It took only a moment for Jourdan to realize the answer. If Cece had gotten pregnant, both she and the child would have died at the hands of an assassin, his loss doubling.

Passion appeared chosen to carry their child. Chosen by Cece. Chosen in essence by his own fickle heart. *Accept it, Watters. What now? Marry her? No.*

She'd never hold up under the scrutiny of his congregation. Her soiled past would muddy a path through Zion and destroy everything he'd worked to build.

Hypocrite. Once, words of forgiveness had fallen from his tongue. He'd given such comfort hundreds of times before. He'd even told Passion he held no judgment against her, yet with each subsequent encounter, he'd proven otherwise.

In his mind he wished she'd made different choices, not prostituted herself as a mistress to married men. In his heart he knew, her choices made her the Passion of today. A woman desperate enough to give birth to another woman's child for a few thousand dollars. A woman wonderful enough to accept responsibility for the child when the deal went bad.

On the whole, a decent woman.

Sunshine spilled through the windshield, making the last drifting snowflakes sparkle like magnificent diamonds before the dark paint of his garage. Absently, he pressed the garage door opener and watched with weary eyes the lumbering ascent of the wooden barrier.

His elation had drained. He was tired. More tired than he'd ever been.

Pulling the keys from the ignition and himself from the warm comfort of the car, Jourdan trudged the short distance to the kitchen door. Once inside, he dropped his keys on the table and headed straight for his small sitting room on the opposite side of the house.

His big house.

A smile tugged at the corner of his lips. Had he really said that?

Inevitably, he thought of Passion. At sixteen she'd been a dancer for Dre Woods. Though she'd insisted they'd never slept together, Jourdan had his doubts. Dre had the bite of an asp. He sucked innocence from the young—not someone who would take "no" for an answer. Images of the man's thin, slimy fingers caressing Passion repulsed him anew.

Another thought made Jourdan shake away the grim images. Last night Dre had appeared tortured, betrayed. The look of a man who'd waited eight years to capture his prize, only to have her publicly rebuke him.

The thought made Jourdan smile.

Passion surely hadn't allowed Dre to touch her. Despite all she'd been through, her courage had carried her through.

He popped a tape in the player; music filled the room. He collapsed on the sofa. Drowsiness dulled his senses. Visions of Passion in his arms permeated his dreams. The fresh scrubbed smell of her was as intoxicating as wine. The feel of her skin was like refined silk.

Aroused, he held her in his arms, her kiss as potent as a drug. It took every ounce of his will to keep his hands from exploring her dangerously soft curves for a second time.

Her honey-flecked eyes put him under some kind of spell.

A distant drumming became louder and sharper as he

surfaced from slumber. Jourdan sat up and looked around the dark room. Shedding his coat, he realized someone was knocking at his door.

"Jourdan, where have you been?" Evelyn scolded, once she and Amos whisked indoors with the cold breeze.

"We've been looking for you since last night, Son." Amos removed his scarf and coat, offering them to his son-in-law.

Evelyn piled her coat on Jourdan's arm as well. "Did you know about District Attorney Reed's press conference?"

"I know. I watched it. Why don't you two come into the kitchen for coffee?" He led them there.

"Why didn't you call us the moment Reed opened his mouth?" Amos asked.

Jourdan rubbed tired eyes. "I was on my way to jail very soon afterward."

"Jail? I need to sit down." Evelyn pulled a white-washed oak chair from beneath the table but remained standing.

"Sherman got me released this morning," Jourdan said, filling the coffeemaker with water. He glanced over his shoulder at Cece's parents.

Amos crinkled his forehead, causing his silvered eyebrows to meet just over his nose. "Why didn't you call us?"

"One phone call," he said simply. Jourdan left the pot to brew and joined his in-laws at the table.

"Did they also arrest that Adams woman?" Evelyn asked, taking her seat.

"Yes. But they released her, too." Jourdan cupped his mother-in-law's hand to calm her.

"What about these accusations?" Amos paced furiously across the linoleum. "Where did Reed come up with such a theory?"

"You know how desperate Cece and I were to have a child?" Jourdan asked.

"Of course," Evelyn replied sadly. "It was all she spoke of for a long time."

135

"After our last in-vitro attempt failed, she went out and found a surrogate."

"What?" Cece's parents spoke in unison.

"Cece went behind my back and had the procedure done on Passion Adams. It worked. And now . . . she's carrying our child." Jourdan waited a moment for the information to sink in. "Your grandchild."

"Our grandchild?" Evelyn whispered. "Before I get too excited, are you absolutely sure of this, Jourdan?" She sent him a wary look.

Jourdan nodded. "Sherman confirmed it last night." He smiled, thoughts of the baby exciting him all over again.

"The Lord sure works in mysterious ways, doesn't He?" Amos shook his head in wonder. "We still have a bit of our Cece."

"Our poor little girl. She must've felt so hopeless." Evelyn's eyes misted. "To let such a wanton woman carry her child . . ."

Her disapproval hit Jourdan like a slap in the face.

Evelyn pulled a tissue from her purse and dabbed at her eyes. "I suppose she told everything to the DA?" She made no attempt to hide her disgust.

"No. Reed discovered it on his own." Jourdan held tight to his rising anger. "Passion was thinking about keeping the baby."

"That's certainly out of the question." Evelyn snorted. "What could she offer a child?"

"A mother's love."

Passion had attempted to protect the baby from its own father's indifference—to make sure he wanted the child before she told him about it. Funny how easily he now saw her honorable motives. "I think she'll make a fine mother."

He rose to pour himself some coffee.

"Come now, Jourdan," Evelyn chided. "Edmond Reed said in the press conference she was an exotic dancer. Obviously, the woman lacks morals."

Jourdan leveled a warning gaze at his mother-in-law. "It was more than generous for Passion to carry a child for me and Cece. I won't have you demeaning her."

"There's no reason for you to get riled." Evelyn gave him a searching look. "Unless you have some affection for her."

Jourdan recognized her remark for the bait that it was, but decided to bite. "As a matter of fact, I do."

She reeled back like a fisherman who'd just hooked a prize bass, only to find a piranha on the line. "I hope you recognize how foolish that is, Jourdan."

"How so?" he challenged, proud that he'd finally taken a stand for Passion.

Evelyn inquired, in a smooth, slippery tone, "Are you so anxious to invite another scandal?"

"The damage has been done," Jourdan argued. "After Reed's press conference last night, everyone believes I've had an affair with Passion. My name won't be cleared until the five-o'clock news."

"Why aggravate the situation?" Amos moved to his wife's side. "After you're cleared, it would be best if you weren't seen in public with Miss Adams."

Irritation chafed at Jourdan. "How is that possible? She's carrying my baby."

"What will your congregation think?" Amos asked, horrified.

The pulse pounded in Jourdan's temple. Why were they making this so difficult? "My congregation will think as I do—that Passion is a wonderful, generous woman."

"You're delusional." Evelyn's eyes nearly popped from her skull. "He's delusional, Amos. Talk some sense into him." She huffed out of the kitchen.

Amos placed a hand on Jourdan's shoulder. "I have to agree with Evelyn, Son."

"You too, Dad?" Jourdan needed him to be rational and objective.

"I understand how grateful you must feel. I really do. But

137

listen to me for a minute." He guided Jourdan to a chair. "You and I both know the faith of a congregation can be swayed by the whisper of scandal, true or not."

"This is different than the last time," Jourdan insisted. "Passion isn't out to damage my reputation."

Amos sighed and paced the floor again. "Neither was that young girl."

Her.

Slumping, Jourdan recalled his fall from grace. Newly a minister, he hadn't been prepared for the accusations of the pregnant fifteen-year-old. Too scared to tell her parents the truth for fear they'd kill her boyfriend, she'd told them Jourdan had taken advantage of her, during a youth retreat.

Within weeks, anger and hostility had run through the church like flood waters over a dam. Although he'd been proven innocent in the end, many in the congregation had refused to let the issue die. The church officers then offered him a severance package, encouraging him to find another ministry.

Cece had defended him—stood by him like a rock—through the whole ordeal.

"You should know by now that we're not judged as other men," Amos continued.

Jourdan hung his head. Old anger rose, yet he realized the old man was right. He'd struggled too long and hard for his dreams to be destroyed once more.

"Don't let your life's work be for nothing, son."

Jourdan looked deeply into the wise eyes of Amos Johnson. Genuine concern and caring shone from them.

"What do you suggest I do?"

"Keep the woman out of sight until the baby's born and there's nothing more to talk about."

"I can't abandon her, Dad. I refuse to let Passion go through the rest of her pregnancy alone."

"Then be discreet. It wouldn't hurt if she wasn't in Zion every Sunday to fuel wagging tongues."

Jourdan grimaced. Could he ask her? Should he? "I'll ask her to stay out of church, but there's a problem."

"What's that?" Amos looked at him curiously.

"Passion has a friend who's just been through bypass surgery. I've asked her to stay with me until she's fully recovered. Passion will want to visit."

"Her friend can stay with Mom and me," Amos offered.

"She can't climb stairs. You don't have a bedroom on your main level."

"I see." Amos pursed his lips in thought. "Make sure her visits happen when you're not home, then."

Jourdan couldn't argue with the man's sound reasoning. He hoped Passion would understand.

Chapter X

Passion spat coffee, once she saw the newspaper's front page. The headline read: *"DA Claims Preacher Commits Crime of* Passion."

Her picture, aligned with Jourdan's, dominated the morning edition. The surprise on her face as the photographer had caught her leaving the hospital yesterday morning looked amazingly like guilt below the bold type.

She rose to leave the hospital cafeteria, feeling watchful eyes follow her every move. Edmond Reed's desperate attempt to get a conviction and the resultant dismissal of charges made up the meat of the story, but once accused . . .

Chin up, she kept walking. It didn't matter what anyone thought.

Exiting the elevator on the third floor, Passion headed for the ICU. Thank goodness for Jourdan's powerful prayer. Shirleen was doing better, although she was not yet well enough to be moved to a lower-risk floor.

Passion rounded the corner to enter Shirleen's room. Thanks to Passion's faith in prayer, she no longer found it scary, seeing tubes snake in and out of her dearest friend. "Any changes?" Passion asked with a hopeful smile.

The nurse looked up from the chart. "She's breathing on her own and she woke for a few minutes and asked where she was. Those are good signs. She'll be just fine." The pleasant woman finished her notes and started to leave. "Oh, Miss Adams. Some people in the waiting room want to speak with you."

"Thanks." She wondered who'd look for her here. Hopefully, no more reporters. If so, they could wait awhile longer.

Passion approached the bed and squeezed Shirleen's plump hand. There was a slight movement of fingers in response. She smoothed wayward gray strands from the peaceful face and kissed her forehead. "I'll be right back," she said softly.

Tired of talking about how she came to be Cece Watters' surrogate, Passion mentally prepared her "no comment" for whomever awaited her. Turning the corner, she stopped cold when she saw him.

"How did you get out of jail?"

Dre sauntered forward, Tracks near the entrance to the waiting room. "I'm out on bail. It's my first offense."

"How is that possible?" she asked, noting Tracks' advance and Dre's widening smile.

"Always a bridesmaid, never a bride." A ringed hand waved. "I have no convictions on my record. Besides, I didn't kill anyone."

Her heart jackhammered. She remembered how close he'd come. "You wanted to. I have nightmares about you pointing that gun at me."

Dre's eyes filled with remorse. "I was just angry, sunshine. You know I wouldn't hurt you." He reached a hand to her face. "Ever."

Passion pulled back instinctively.

"Come on now, Passion," he whined. "You still need a place for the old lady to recuperate, don't you?"

141

"I've made other arrangements." She took another step to the rear. "Leave us alone."

His ringed fingers grabbed her arm forcefully as she turned to go. "Listen lady—" Yellow skin stretched taut over clenched jaws. "You don't just walk out on me and expect to get away with it. You belong to me."

She dug her elbows into his ribs. "I don't belong to you. I don't belong to anybody, Dre. Let me go."

"Tracks and I got your stuff from your apartment. It's time to come home."

"You broke into my apartment?"

Dre didn't answer, just dragged her by the arm toward the elevators. She could hear the bodyguard's heavy footsteps behind them.

She hated to draw attention by screaming and filling the empty halls with curious hospital workers. She dug in her heels and tried yanking her wrist free of Dre's tight grip. It didn't work.

Suddenly, Jourdan stepped out of the open elevator.

Relief mixed with fear rushed through Passion when Jourdan grabbed Dre's arm and pulled her free.

From the corner of her eye, she saw Tracks reach inside his jacket. "Be careful, Jourdan. Tracks . . ."

Jourdan looked at the bald man then at Dre, then back again, pushing Passion behind him. "I believe we've played this game before, Dr. Dre."

Tense, Passion moved just enough to see past her protector. Several smocked hospital workers spilled into the hallway. "Call the police!"

"Shut the—" Dre's hand whipped around Jourdan to back-slap her.

Swiftly, Jourdan grabbed his wrist and twisted it in a direction it wasn't meant to go. "Don't touch her," he threatened through clenched teeth.

The workers stood mute.

Passion stood rooted in fear.

"This ain't no game, preacher man." Dre's face showed pain and just a flicker of intimidation. He glanced at the slowly advancing Tracks. "I just come to get what's mine."

"Don't you think it's about time you stopped preying on innocent young women?"

"I ain't the one who knocked her up and left her for trash."

"It's not like that, Dre," Passion put in.

With his free hand, Jourdan wound a handful of Dre's silk shirt around his fist and drew him to his face. "Listen, you satanic snake—"

Tracks unsheathed a dagger and lunged at Jourdan.

"Stop!" Passion put a hand out to protect Jourdan. Several men standing in the hallway ran up behind the bald black man. Tracks turned abruptly and swiped the knife in a semicircle to keep them at bay.

Jourdan released Dre with a shove. "Leave, before someone gets hurt." He stepped to the side of the elevator door. "The two of you will answer to the Almighty for what you've done in this life."

"Stick that in your Bible and blow, preacher man." Dre smoothed down his crinkled shirt, gave a signal to Tracks, and pushed the button for the elevator.

Tracks replaced his weapon beneath his jacket.

At last, the doors pushed shut on their scowling faces.

Jourdan escorted Passion through the curious throng, back to the empty waiting room. He took her elbows, his grasp gentle, not harsh like Dre's had been.

"Are you all right?" he asked, eyes brimming with concern.

"Yeah. I'm glad you came along."

"There's something desperately wrong with our justice system when serpents like Woods are let loose to slither in the streets."

"Agreed." Passion noted the tired look around his eyes and wondered at his presence. "You here for a reason, Reverend? Or did you just come to play my knight in shining armor?" She managed a weak smile.

"Knight in shining armor?" He chuckled. "That's one I've never been called before."

"It's something I've never had before, so call us even."

He smiled at her compliment. "Okay. We're even." He caressed her cheek. "How's Shirleen doing?"

"Much better," Passion replied. "She's being moved into a regular hospital room soon."

"Praise God," he said, then lapsed into silence and walked the floor.

Passion could tell there was something else on his mind.

A few moments went by before Jourdan finally cleared his throat and stepped in front of her. "Passion? I notice you're on the list to sing solo on Sunday."

"Oh. I'd forgotten. Thanks for the reminder."

"Well . . ." He cleared his throat again, then stared down at his hands. "You don't have to worry about it. We've got someone who can take your place."

"You do?"

"Yes, so you can be here for Shirleen." He looked hopeful as he gazed into her eyes.

Passion didn't know what to make of his awkward generosity. "Under the circumstances, another Sunday would be better."

"Well . . . actually, I need to talk to you about that. I think it would probably be better if you found another church to attend."

Her heart sank to her toes.

"For the time being," he added quickly.

How could he say this to her? Yesterday, they'd ended their talk on an amicable note. What had happened to cause this reaction? She searched his sorrowful eyes for some kind of explanation. "Why?"

Jourdan sighed and peered at the ceiling, as if it could

provide the answer. "The publicity is bound to get out of hand—"

"You're ashamed to have me around, aren't you?" Realization sent hundreds of needle sharp pains to attack her battered heart. It was bad enough, his disapproval of her past, but to push her away—back to the shadows of loneliness—hurt worse than anything. "Aren't you?" she repeated.

"Absolutely not. Please, let me explain—"

"You don't want me in your church," she whispered in agony. Though she hadn't been accepted by everyone, she'd found purpose and worth in the work she'd done at Zion. Even that he snatched from her.

Jourdan reached for her hand. "It's for your own good—"

"For my own good or for yours? You call yourself a man of God, yet you'll do anything in your power to denounce anyone who could make you look bad." She snatched her hand from his, then placed both palms on his chest and shoved. "You're no less a snake than Dre Woods."

"Passion." He grabbed both her shoulders and held her to him.

"Let me go."

"Not until you hear me out." He pulled her closer, despite her struggles.

Passion breathed deeply of his fresh, manly scent, trying hard to hold onto her anger as he lowered his hands to her waist. Reluctantly, she met his gaze, knowing she'd lose her heart all over again.

His deep, brown eyes flashed myriad emotions before softening with remorse. "Dear God, what am I doing?" he asked, softly. "I'm sorry, Passion." He brought both her palms to his mouth and gave each one an impassioned kiss.

The feel of his lips on her flesh was staggering. She wanted desperately—foolishly—to forgive him. Passion cursed her weakness. "Why do you do this to me?"

"What do you mean?"

145

"Treat me like a whore, Jourdan, or treat me like a lady." She struggled to keep her voice from shaking. "Not one first, then the other."

Pulling her completely into his embrace, he murmured, "I've been such a fool."

Since the first time, she'd wanted nothing more than to be in his arms once more. But as inviting as they were now, she couldn't help but wonder when he'd again push her away.

"Don't think you can seduce me after you've insulted me." She freed herself from his embrace.

Jourdan didn't stop her when she moved away, although he ached to continue holding her. "I'm not trying to insult you."

She sighed and shook her head. "Then what in heaven's name *are* you trying to do?"

He ran the backs of his fingers along the tan silk of her cheek and sought the wonder of her caramel-brown eyes. "Wondering how to love you."

Passion didn't speak. Jourdan not only surprised her, but himself, with his revelation. Moving toward her, he breathed a kiss onto her forehead and closed his arms around her. "Come stay with me," he whispered in her ear. Shirleen needs you to look after her." He kissed her cheek, her temple, the top of her head. "And I need to keep you safe from that Woods character."

She trembled in his arms. "I thought you didn't want me near."

Jourdan felt lower than dirt to know he'd caused her unhappiness. "Of course I want you." He ran a hand gently down her hair. "I've always wanted you."

She looked up at him. "What about your reputation?" A silent plea lay in the extraordinary depths of her slanted eyes.

Don't blow it, Jourdan. Say the right thing.

"I'll stand before my Maker one day." He drew the words from the depths of his soul. "He alone will be my judge."

"Do you really mean that?" Passion asked, her voice guarded.

Jourdan breathed another tender kiss on her forehead before

letting his gaze sink to the depths of her exotic irises. "By all that I hold sacred."

She closed her eyes, her lashes fanning silken cheeks.

"I'm worried more about you," he said. "How will you be treated, now that everyone knows about your past?"

"I've been treated like a dog in some of the best places in Kansas City." Devoid of mirth, she laughed. "Why should Zion be any different?"

Her profound statement shot through him like a holy conviction. "Because it's my church—my congregation," he said more to himself than to Passion. "Christians should welcome everyone with open arms, not shoo them away."

"I agree." Her eyes turned soft and loving. "Promise me you won't be the one holding the door open next time it happens."

Jourdan had to convince her, not with words, but with actions, of his unwavering love. He lowered his head and sought her lips. He took her mouth with great care, not wanting this kiss to be like the first—all heat and lust.

Passion wrapped her arms around his neck and parted her lips to accept him.

Encouraged, Jourdan held her tighter, kissed her deeper. She tasted of sweet lust and salty desire, her skin the scent of everything wondrous in the world. He stilled his mouth and let his lips part from hers slowly. There was a glow in her golden eyes that warmed him despite the chill of the waiting room.

She'd asked again, with her soft, probing lips if he'd stand by her whatever the future held. Never before had Jourdan shunned Amos' advice. From now until forever, he'd follow his own instincts. It didn't matter what people thought.

"I promise," he vowed, welcoming her into Zion. And into his heart.

* * * * * * * * * * * *

Passion watched Jourdan depart, her heart so full she nearly burst with ecstasy.

She headed for Shirleen. One more check, then she'd go home and pack for them both. Jourdan would be by that evening to get her.

Passion rounded the corner in time to see Shirleen struggling to sit up with a nurse's assistance.

"Shirleen!" Joyfully, she ran in and grabbed the old woman's hand. "It's so good to see you."

"Now, now. What's all dis fuss about?" Shirleen said wearily.

"You're awake."

"It's good to see you too, chile." Shirleen patted her arm gently.

"What can I get you? Anything?" Passion had to make sure of her comfort.

"Matter-a-fact, yes. Why don't you run on home and gets me my Bible?"

"Bible. Okay. Anything else?"

"Yeah. My robe. No respectin' child a God oughta be runnin' around in a get-up like dis." She pulled at the flowered hospital gown.

Passion laughed. "I'll be back just as soon as the limo can get me here," she joked, referring to public transportation.

"Well, now don't rush yo'self," Shirleen scolded. "Sit down and talk wid me awhile."

Obediently, Passion pulled a chair to the bedside.

"What's been happenin' since I been here? Last I 'member, Dre was up in our house actin' like a crazy man."

Passion settled in and told Shirleen about Dre's release from prison and her own brief incarceration.

"Lordy, chile. It's a good thing that nice reverend got you such a good lawyer."

"Yeah. Lucky thing Jourdan just *happened* to be around, huh?" Passion placed her tongue firmly in her cheek, knowing Shirleen had invited Jourdan to their apartment.

"I was jus tryin' to help is all." Shirleen gave a weak chuckle. Only an echo of her former joviality. "He a good man."

"True." Passion placed a hand on Shirleen's. "He says you can stay with him until that apartment I leased is available."

Shirleen was instantly cantankerous. "He ain't got no call to do dat for a perfect stranger."

"Sure he does, he's a preacher." Passion laughed. "Besides it's no less than you would do."

"Don't matter." Shirleen lay back against her pillows. "Men don't know nuthin' bout takin' care a folks. Even my William, God rest his soul, weren't no good at it."

"I'll be there." Passion watched carefully for the old woman's reaction. "I'll take care of you."

"You means to tell me, the reverend is gonna have us both up in his house?"

Passion nodded and smiled, still giddy that he'd asked.

The grayed head rolled back and forth. "Both y'all done lost yo minds."

In a moment Shirleen lost the battle with sleep.

Passion kissed a healthier brown cheek. "It's good to have you back," she whispered, then made a cautious look upward. "And thank you, Lord, for whatever you had to do with this."

* * * * * * * * * * * * *

Passion retrieved her coat from the waiting room and left the hospital. The sun made a bleak effort to warm the air, but freezing winds stung her nose and cheeks as she waited for the bus.

The ride home seemed short because Passion's thoughts drifted to memories of Jourdan's arms and the ecstasy of his kiss. She stepped from the bus and nearly bounced up the steps to her apartment.

She hit the third floor and saw her door standing slightly open—why? Quickly, she pressed her back against the wall, fearing Dre's intrusion, and listened for sounds.

After what seemed a lifetime of waiting, only the raised voices from her downstairs neighbors pierced the frigid air.

Deciding it was safe to go inside, she released the breath from her pressured lungs and pushed the door open further.

At first glance, nothing seemed amiss. However, once she stepped inside the bedroom, Passion saw that Dre had been true to his word. He'd taken all her clothes. She didn't even have a change of underwear.

Passion tried to think of what to do next. What would it take for Dre to leave her alone forever?

She had to confront him. He had to understand she would never be part of his life and, hopefully, he'd let her live.

It was a sobering thought, but she had to take the chance— call his bluff—to be free of him.

Lifting herself from the bed, she collected the things Shirleen had requested, then packed the rest in battered suitcases, the latter to be collected by Jourdan. She'd call on Dre right after her stop at the hospital.

She realized, halfway out the door, she'd better call Jourdan and let him know what was going on. He answered on the third ring; Passion thought briefly of how wonderful it would be to live with a man whose voice had such a sexy timbre. "It's Passion."

"Are you ready?" He mistook the purpose of her phone call.

"Not quite. I have to see Dre."

"Dre?"

She could almost see Jourdan's face twist with disgust. "He took my clothes."

"I'll buy you new ones," Jourdan said quickly.

Passion smiled. "That's sweet, but I've got a thing or two to say to him while I'm getting them back."

"I'll go with you."

"There's no ne—"

"I'll be there in forty-five minutes."

"But, Jourdan—"

"Stay put."

The droning dial tone halted her further objections. He took this knight in shining armour stuff way too seriously.

Damn. Men were starting to piss her off.

* * * * * * * * * * * *

In a lousy mood, Dre draped a leg over the lip of his black lacquer office desk and looked out at the lights. "We're waiting for Cindy?" he asked his bodyguard.

Tracks traced a thick finger down the ledger. "Yeah. And Chante."

"I'll give 'em another hour." Dre pulled a thin cigarette from his gold case.

Tracks gave a half laugh. "Back in the day, you would've beat the hell out of your ladies if they didn't come in on time with your money."

Dre didn't want to hear any more. For weeks now he'd heard how lax operations had gotten. "What of it?"

"Not to start nothin', but word on the street has it you're goin' soft, Dre."

Dre puffed on his cigarette, eyeing the big man. With those sunglasses permanently shielding his eyes, it was hard to read him. "Do you sleep with those damn glasses on?"

The scars on Tracks's cheeks lifted into a sneering grin. "Don't go tryin' to change the subject."

"Well, I don't want to talk about it."

"Fine. But pretty soon folks'll lose respect, man."

Dre knew, like everyone on the street, once you were known as an easy mark, every small-timer wanted to put you out of business. Truth was, Dre didn't have the same enthusiasm for the game he once had. He might just take his Swiss bank account and leave Tenth and Quindaro for good.

"What would you suggest?" Dre asked, not wanting to know.

"Retaliate."

Dre turned on him once again. "Against whom?"

"Passion." Tracks spread his arms wide, causing muscles to bulge beneath the sleeves of his tight-fitting shirt. "Everybody knows she walked out on you and played you for a—"

"Enough!" Dre didn't want to be reminded how Passion had weaseled out of his grip again. "She'll be back."

"Cool, man." Tracks retreated for a moment. "But you could put a hit on that Reverend Watters character." His meaty fists boxed the air. "I'll put him away for half my normal fee."

"Don't do it, Dre," came a demand from a feminine voice.

He looked up to see Passion standing inside the doorway. Of course, she would remember weekly-payment nights.

"Do what?" Dre took another pull on his cigarette and tried to hide his pleasure at her appearance. "Hurt the reverend?"

Jourdan Watters appeared behind her then. "You don't scare me, Woods."

Dre blew a smoke cloud toward the two of them, forcing himself to remain calm. He'd lost his cool the last time, had acted like a whipped dog. He wouldn't mind seeing that pompous Holy Roller taken down a few pegs, but now wasn't the time. "Tracks was just telling me how bored he's been."

The smack of Tracks' large fist into his palm punctuated Dre's threat.

Passion glared at the big bodyguard, then settled her eyes on Dre. "Can we talk?"

"Sure." Dre pressed the butt of his cigarette into an ashtray and went to stand by another door. "Without him." He pointed at the preacher.

Jourdan took Passion's arm. "Forget it then."

"No. Wait." Passion sent Watters a steady look. "It'll be okay."

"Yeah." Dre smiled. "It'll be just fine."

"I don't think—"

"He won't hurt me." Passion assured him. "Will you, Dre?"

Dre gave a long pause so they would think he might. "Naw." He shrugged. "Won't touch a hair on her head."

The reverend still looked uncertain.

"Good—scared him," Dre thought. Served him right for coming into Midnight Dreams and disrespecting his business.

"I'll be right here." Jourdan moved to Dre's desk.

Tracks watched his progress across the room.

Dre gave his bodyguard a head's-up nod. "Take care of those last two ladies there," he said, as Chante and Cindy walked through the door. "And anyone else if necessary." He glared at Jourdan. Preacher man had to understand who was in control here.

Dre opened the door, motioning Passion inside. It had been a stroke of genius to build his office and a bedroom above Midnight Dreams. Both had come in very handy over the years.

He left Passion standing; he reclined on his white lounger, tucking an arm behind his head. "So talk."

Passion crossed her arms and planted her feet wide.

Instantly aroused, Dre thought about what was between those long legs.

"What will it take for you to leave me, and Shirleen—and Jourdan—alone?"

"Jourdan, is it?" Just as he'd suspected. *Something's truly going on between Passion and the preacher.*

Passion wasn't swayed. "What will it take, Dre?"

Reaching a decision, Dre rose from the lounger and traveled across the room to stand before her. "I won't touch your witchy friend or your Holy Roller . . ." He circled her, letting his eyes feast on all he desired. "If you'll marry me."

The golden blaze of her eyes met his in furious surprise. "You can't be serious."

"Oh, but I am." Dre moved in to nibble on a sweet, soft ear. "Marry me, and I'll give you the world."

Passion pushed him away. "I don't want the world, Dre. I want my clothes. And then I want to be left alone."

Dre took her in his arms roughly. "Agree or I'll kill them both." He squeezed tighter so she'd understand his threat. "I need an answer. Now."

"Then I'll say yes." Passion squirmed her way free of his wiry grasp.

Dre's eyes narrowed. "You mean it?"

"If you're serious about killing Shirleen and Jourdan," she countered.

Dre threw up his arms. "I don't want you like this."

Passion held her position. "What do you want?"

"For you to fall on your knees, grateful for all I've done for you over the years. I want you to come to my house and sleep in my bed and make love to me the way you did your old boyfriends." His smug demeanor was replaced by a desperate pleading.

"Passion, I want you to love me the way I love you."

Passion studied Dre—he'd shed his scales to reveal the vulnerable man beneath.

How ironic to be on this side of the situation for the first time. Passion had him right where she wanted him. Unfortunately, there would be no letting him down easy. She knew this from experience.

Sighing, she pressed on, knowing her words would wound him savagely. "Dre, I know how horrible it feels to love someone who can't love you."

He dropped his arms, obviously taken aback.

"I can't be anything to you, not of my own free will. Not your lover. Not your friend. Let me go."

Staggering, he walked to his lounger and sank down.

The look of pain and sorrow on his face, so heartbreakingly familiar, caused her to say with true sincerity, "I'm sorry."

Someone rapped at the door.

"Passion?" It was Jourdan. "You all right?" He wiggled the knob.

She should have noticed that Dre had locked it. "I'm on my way out."

Her bags sat side-by-side in the corner of the room, she noticed. At least he hadn't taken them to his house.

Dre sat silently, unmoving, as she unlocked the door and let Jourdan in.

"My bags are there." She pointed, growing nervous at Dre's continued silence. "Let's go."

"My pleasure." Jourdan retrieved the bags and gave Dre one last glare before exiting.

* * * * * * * * * * * * *

Passion quickly followed Jourdan. In her rush she nearly ran into Tracks; he stood near Dre's desk, a young woman clinging to his arm.

The girl was a thin waif whose pale yellow skin made her appear sickly. Her bleached blond hair stood out in directions that defied gravity as she struggled to stay balanced on spiked heels. Beneath the remains of makeup—just a child. Fifteen, sixteen at the most. Suddenly, Passion felt ill.

Jourdan paused and gave the young girl a steady look. "If you change your mind—"

"Chante said she isn't interested in your damned church," Tracks interjected. He slid a hand between her thighs. She opened her legs and nearly fell over.

Certain the lewd gesture had been orchestrated to disturb Jourdan, Passion pulled at his arm, urging him to let the situation drop.

The girl's drowsy eyes and uncontrolled giggles were a sure sign of a recent encounter with a mind-altering substance. Passion said, "You can't reason with drugs."

Jourdan closed his eyes briefly. The power of his prayer filled the room with charismatic presence as it did his sanctuary on Sundays.

Passion tingled as the pulsing vibrations moved through her. She'd never tire of these extraordinary rhythms.

"When your mind clears, young lady," Jourdan's voice seemed to echo with new authority, "come to the Lord. He'll be waiting."

Tracks lost his smugness and shifted from side to side. "Don't . . . don't listen to him, Chante."

Chante seemed completely mesmerized under Jourdan's gaze.

How well Passion knew the feeling.

A movement from within Dre's bedroom caught her eye. "Time to go, Jourdan."

"You ain't goin' nowhere." Dre emerged and pushed past his bodyguard, nearly toppling Chante in his haste to reach his desk.

Jourdan dropped the bags.

Passion's heart shot into her throat.

Dre pulled open the desk drawer. His hand emerged wrapped around black metal.

Not again!

Jourdan grabbed her hand and pulled her from the room. A bullet hit the wall behind her.

Passion had no trouble keeping up with Jourdan as he hustled her down the stairs.

Fear tightened her chest and turned her legs rubbery, but she kept running—past the pink-clad blur of the exotic dancer—past the enraptured faces of salivating men.

Swerving and swaying past chairs and topless waitresses, Jourdan escorted Passion into the neon-lit parking lot. "Head for the car," he instructed. He let go of her hand to pull the keys from his pocket.

"Stop."

Dre's shout made her freeze within kissing distance of the back bumper. Wondering whether to raise her hands in submission, Passion pivoted in the cold night to face certain death.

Dre stood not five feet away. Lights from the club's garish sign beat down on him. His chest rose and fell heavily; he pointed the gun at Passion. Maybe it was the light playing tricks on her, but his eyes looked as red as the devil.

Tracks stood behind his employer, surveying the lot.

Jourdan put his arm around Passion's shoulders.

"You said you wouldn't hurt me, Dre." Passion swallowed down a throatful of fear and wintry air.

"You think you ain't good enough for me . . ." He put both hands on the butt of the gun.

Panicked, she uttered, "I never said that."

"If that's the case . . ." He lifted the gun to his open eye.

Passion shrunk back.

"Sunshine, you're much too good for a preacher man." While Tracks gained ground, Dre took another step forward—then turned his aim to Passion.

Her blood chilled—icy as the wind. She shook. Her thoughts centered on the unborn child. Sending a silent prayer to heaven, she asked that the child find itself in the cradle of Cece's arms when it left her dead womb.

Crunching glass and rocks from under Jourdan's foot broke the eerie silence, diverting both Dre's and Tracks' attention momentarily.

Dre's trigger arm moved. The barrel pointed at Jourdan. "Take another step and you're dead, preacher man."

"You're messing with servants of God," Jourdan boomed.

A tremendous gust of wind slammed Dre against the door of his club. Tracks hit the pavement like a big, black anvil.

"Threaten Passion again—" Jourdan's voice dropped to a deep baritone "—and you'll have hell to pay."

As if to fulfill the promise, the gusts became even more fierce. Dre stumbled drunkenly. Tracks' sunglasses flew off his face. Both men curled into tight balls as swirling debris, like a demonic twister, shredded their clothes and slashed the skin beneath.

The wind touched neither Passion nor Jourdan.

Passion stared, dumbfounded, at Jourdan, the holy wizard. It seemed he conjured the furious winds, although she knew it wasn't possible.

He emerged from his strange trance. "Get in the car."

Another whirlwind started—this one inside her. Passion slid inside the Town Car, grateful to Jourdan and his holy powers. Grateful to be alive. Even the discomfort of her numb fingers and toes proved a welcome blessing.

Jourdan joined her a moment later, dropping the knife and gun on the floorboard to the left of Passion's feet.

"How did you—?" She hadn't seen him go near the men. How had he retrieved their weapons? She twisted around. Dre and Tracks floundered, fittingly, amidst a pile of trash, their efforts to pick themselves off the ground comical.

She settled back in her seat and gave thanks for the miracle.

Jourdan put the car in gear and nosed the vehicle away from the club.

"You were magnificent, Jourdan," Passion finally said.

He looked at her and smiled, his face showing no trace of his glorious feat.

"Was that coincidence or . . . ?" She pointed upward.

"It was," he said simply.

"Not to make what you did any less terrific," she said, finding her sense of humor and breaking the surreal atmosphere, "but I think you've watched 'The Ten Commandments' once too often."

He gave her one of his earth-shattering smiles. "That good, huh?"

"So good, you could be Moses in the remake."

He chuckled. "I'll be sure to thank you personally when I accept the Oscar."

She settled back against the seat and closed her eyes. Never in her life had she felt so safe. "Jourdan?"

"Hmm?"

"Thanks."

His hand enclosed hers. "My pleasure, I assure you."

Passion smiled and listened to the slush under the tires as they headed for Jourdan's house.

Chapter XI

It seemed their comfort with each other fled the moment Passion and Jourdan entered his house. All Passion could think about was that Cece had lived there.

Jourdan took her coat and hung it in the closet. "Would you . . . can I get you anything?"

"No. Thanks."

"Let me show you to your room." He started up the stairs.

Passion let her fingers slide along the smooth, dark wood and studied the functional, yet cozy decor. The house suited Cece's personality to a tee.

Jourdan escorted Passion to a bedroom at the end of the upstairs hallway. "This is the guest bedroom." He opened the door to a lovely blue and white room. "You'll have your own bathroom."

Passion followed his gaze. The bathroom was also blue and white and the tiles gleamed as if freshly cleaned. It reminded her of some of the finer hotels she'd seen, with the added benefit of homey touches.

"I'll let you settle in." Jourdan paused before leaving the

room. "I . . . Cece's clothes are still here . . . in boxes." His smile wavered. "You could—"

"I'd feel funny," Passion said, her words rushing out.

Jourdan nodded. "I understand." His smile turned one-sided. "So would I."

Passion fingered the edge of her sweater. She didn't know what else to say. It was strange being here—strange walking in the wake of Cece Watters and wanting her husband more than life itself.

"Make yourself comfortable." Jourdan closed the door softly.

Still cold, Passion blew tension from her lungs and sank to the edge of the bed. A bath. *That's what I need.* Tomorrow, she'd think about how she could get some clothes to wear.

* * * * * * * * * * * * *

Jourdan worried his bedroom carpet with his pacing. He rubbed his stubbled jaw, wondering if he should check on Passion. She'd refused dinner and hadn't made a sound in more than an hour—not that he'd been listening. Maybe she was hungry or thirsty and hesitated to bother him.

Throwing on his robe, he crossed the hall and tapped gently at her door.

"Yes?"

Turning the doorknob, he looked in.

The light was out; she'd burrowed beneath the comforter. "Is there anything you need before I hit the sack?"

"No, thank you."

The moon lit the room just enough for him to see her shiver beneath the covers. "Are you cold? I'll turn up the heat."

"No. That's all right," she assured him. "I don't think the temperature matters. That wind went right through me."

Concerned, he crossed the room and sat on the edge of the bed. "Perhaps some warm tea would help."

"I'd really rather not drink anything. I'm up all night as it is."

160

He chuckled, realizing what she meant. He inclined his head toward the plush room where she'd bathed. "Lucky you have your own bathroom then."

"Yeah." She shivered again.

He reached for her hand. It was like holding an ice cube. "You're freezing. How do you feel?" Instinctively he put a palm to her forehead. It didn't seem unduly warm.

"I'm not sick," she answered. "Just can't shake this chill."

What effect would this have on the baby? "We better take care of that." He climbed over her and slid beneath the covers.

"What are you doing?"

"Body heat," he said simply. "It's the best way to get warm if a hot bath doesn't work."

"Don't you have any electric blankets?"

"No." Jourdan smiled guiltily. "I'm afraid of them shorting out. Don't trust them."

Passion chuckled. A smile curved her perfect lips. "A man who commands the elements and tackles drug-dealing pimps is afraid of electric blankets?"

"'Fraid so," he admitted, sliding over. Jourdan made contact with her bare flesh. A jolt went through him.

"I figured you realized I don't have pajamas," she whispered.

"Of course." He'd completely forgotten. His pulse raced as his hand caressed the tender skin just below her breasts.

Passion chuckled. "You forgot, didn't you?"

Her laugh rang through the room, filling all the dark, empty corners and bringing something alive in the room and in him.

Her eyes glowed in the pale moonlight as her hair fell wild and exotic around her face. Once again he faced the danger of her seduction.

With predatory purpose, Passion rolled on top of him. Willing prey, Jourdan welcomed her kiss—welcomed the slow burn in his loins. He slid a hand down her silky skin to the gentle slope of her bottom. The downward pressure of her hips encouraged the kindling flames of his lust.

She quivered.

"Still cold?"

"No." Her gaze blazed with desire. "Not at all."

Her breath smelled like mint, her body like soap and sex. Jourdan's fate tightened around him. He wanted to do wrong, more than he wanted to do right.

Passion shifted her weight, slid from his chest and out of his arms. One of her breasts still pressed against his arm.

Jourdan despaired of the sudden emptiness he felt.

"Careful, Jourdan." Her voice flowed satiny soft. "We don't want your rock-like control to crumble to dust."

He swallowed hard. What control he had left? It crumbled under waves of needs and wants. Passion presented no ordinary temptation, but enticement of biblical proportions. He wanted to drown in her kiss—to have life everlasting in her arms.

"Do you want me to leave?" He held his breath, hoping for the blessing of her consent.

"Never."

For the first time in his Christian walk, Jourdan sinned—willfully. Allowing the call of her soft, yielding flesh to drown out the screaming implications of his actions, he turned to her and ran his palms over her soft slopes and gentle curves.

Her skin, a velvet confection, made his palm warm and tingly. Awestruck by his first glimpse of her pregnancy, the slight mound of her stomach gave him pause. There was life within her. His life. Cece's.

Without Passion, there would be no child.

A surge of love and gratitude filled his chest, compelling him to kiss the miracle of his unborn child. Tears escaped as he realized the full impact of Passion's generous heart.

* * * * * * * * * * * * *

A lifetime of dreams culminated at this moment. Passion reveled in joy . . . in Jourdan. She gasped, arching under his

162

skilled explorations. His kisses became more needy, more demanding, yet each held caring behind them.

She marveled at his tender, worshipful kisses. He whispered her name in his deep, sensuous voice. Everything within her hummed as he played her body like a song of worship.

He moved inside her and she matched his cadence, her body in fluid harmony to his reverent hymn. It had never been so right. All her life, she'd longed to be loved like this.

Jourdan drove his need deeper within her. Tasting the flowery petals of her neck, suckling the points of her breasts. Filling her so fully . . .

He paused.

"What's wrong?" Passion asked.

"Nothing." Jourdan's body strained. He sought her eyes—kissed her soft lips. "I just want this to last forever."

She whispered, "I don't think I could take anything so good for so long."

Jourdan gave in to sweet inevitability. "Thank you, Lord."

Passion gladly followed.

On a crest of shared ecstasy, they completed their passionate interlude.

* * * * * * * * * * * *

The morning arrived swiftly. Jourdan opened his eyes and awaited the searing pain of regret. He'd strayed from the path of righteousness. Yet . . . he felt only renewed love for the woman who lay staring at him—tears sparkling in her eyes.

"What's the matter?" He panicked at the thought of injuring her or the baby. "Did I hurt you?"

Passion's lips trembled as she shook her head. Her hair spilled in all directions on her pillow. "You stayed," she whispered through tears.

He curled her into his arms, touched that his presence meant so much to her. "Of course I stayed." He kissed her tears and

163

lips, igniting the flames in his blood once again. The second time they made love lasted most of the morning.

* * * * * * * * * * * * *

At noon, Jourdan remembered his appointment with Sherman Townsend. Reality rained down as he showered. Stark reality. Dressing quickly, he set out for the kitchen to check on Passion.

She sat at the table, sipping coffee with his robe wrapped around her. The thought of her skin touching something so intimate kick-started his hormones yet again.

"It looks good on you," he said, wondering if he could live without her touch.

She looked up from the paper to smile. "I'm just borrowing it until my clothes dry."

Jourdan tried to suppress his welling emotions—to face the consequences of his actions. Their actions. "I want you to know, I don't regret a moment of our time together. But."

Passion straightened. "Neither do I."

How did he say this without pushing her away again? "You realize what we did was a sin?"

"The thought crossed my mind." Passion raised a hand to his cheek. "It didn't stick around too long."

Jourdan kissed her palm, wanting her desperately, knowing he mustn't. "We have to repent. We can't do this again."

Her eyes filled with questions. "But, it's so perfect between us."

That was the irony of it. "Because it feels right, doesn't make it right." He shuddered, recalling how he'd thanked God at the moment of ultimate sin. "The consequence of fornication is death. Our souls will burn in the eternal flames of hell."

"I'd gladly burn for you, Jourdan." Her golden gaze welded to his eyes.

"I can't allow it, Passion."

Disappointment clouded her beautiful face.

164

Be strong, Jourdan. "I can't preach the truth to my congregation and live a lie. Please, say you understand."

She didn't answer, just stared at him.

"This is not about my reputation." He tightened his fingers on her hands. "It's about doing the right thing—living the right way."

"You know . . ." Passion curved her body to give him a long, lingering kiss. "It's your damned decency I've liked from the beginning."

Relief flowed like a soothing stream, relieving the tension.

"I need to know, Jourdan." Emotion traced her words and gestures. "Is there a chance for us?"

"Yes." Jourdan knew there was no other answer. She was all he had wanted from the time she swayed down the aisle of Zion. "But we have to wait."

Passion smiled and drew away to sip her coffee. "Then that's what we'll do."

She'd never looked lovelier. Never been more precious to him. Jourdan swallowed a lump of desire and adoration, then leapt to his feet.

"Got to run, or I'll be late for my appointment."

"Tell Mr. Townsend I said 'hi.'"

"I will." He gazed at her for one last, lingering moment before heading for the garage.

"Help me, Lord, or I'm never going to make it," he prayed before backing the car out of the garage.

* * * * * * * * * * * * *

"Passion Adams, the devil's drivin' a fire-red limousine to your door to *personally* escort you to hell." Vanessa shook her braids in amusement.

"Thanks, girlfriend," Passion came back sarcastically. After Jourdan had departed for Townsend's office, she'd hopped the first bus to the north end and had spilled her guts in a flurry, hoping to gain a little sympathy from her friend. Now that she'd

165

been with Jourdan . . . "Hellfire or not, I don't know if I can keep my hands off him."

"He was that good, huh?"

Passion sighed, remembering. "There aren't words."

"Shoot." Vanessa grinned devilishly. "I knew I shoulda hooked that man sooner."

Their conversation was interrupted when Vanessa's attention was drawn by the television: "*After this fiasco, it looks like the end of a very short career for Edmond Reed. Back to you Ron.*"

Relieved and somewhat gleeful, Passion watched the news conference. At least the DA would pay for his false accusations. With any luck, Jourdan's reputation would remain intact.

Vanessa pointed the remote and clicked off the set. "Damn," she swore softly.

"I know Reed's your boss." Assessing her friend's face, Passion could tell the relationship went deeper. "Does this mean you're out of a job?"

Vanessa pointed a hot pink fingernail at her chest. "I work for the state. Whoever gets the position . . . gets me."

Passion followed her into the kitchen. It was decorated in black, white, and teal. Or salt, pepper, and a touch of spice—if she went by Vanessa's description. "Why the long face if you're not worried about your job?" she hinted, hoping for honesty.

"I feel sorry for old Eddie." Vanessa collected two pints of ice cream from the freezer and slid one across the counter toward Passion.

"Why? He got what he deserved for accusing innocent people of adultery and murder." She couldn't help but say it. Her night in the police station still gave her nightmares. She ripped the lid off the creamy vanilla treat and walked to the drawer that held the silverware. "But if Reed means something to you, you have my sympathy."

"I'd rather not discuss Eddie just now." Vanessa accepted the spoon Passion held out and dug into strawberry swirl. "I'm not at liberty to discuss what goes on in the DA's office, but I want you to know that I tried calling to warn you and Reverend Watters about the press conference."

"I understand, girl. Nothing would've come out differently." They ate their ice cream in companionable silence for a few minutes before Vanessa came up for air. "So. What you gonna do when your friend gets out of the hospital? I'd love for the both of you to stay here with me, but . . ." She looked around her small apartment. "We'd be awfully cramped."

"Yeah, I can just see me and Shirleen fighting for position on your pull-out sofa bed." Passion's smile turned up on one side. "Don't worry. We've found a place to stay."

Suspiciously, Vanessa peered over her ice cream. "Where?"

"Jourdan invited both of us to stay with him."

Her mouth and spoon dropped at the same time. "You messin' with me?"

Passion chuckled, trying to swallow her ice cream without choking. "Afraid not."

"Wasn't it bad enough, y'all knockin' boots last night and this morning? How you gonna keep your hands off each other?"

"Have to." Passion shrugged. "Besides, I wouldn't do anything with Shirleen in the house."

Vanessa set down her spoon and reached across the counter. "You know the people at church are gonna talk."

"What else is new?"

Vanessa shook her head, her braids swaying back and forth. "Can't you find somewhere else to stay?"

"I have enough money to rent a nice apartment, but we'd be on the streets in six months."

"I could give you more lessons on computers and I wouldn't mind putting in a good word for you at the courthouse. We have openings now and then."

"That would be great. I need to learn an honest trade. But I doubt anyone'll hire me in this condition."

Vanessa frowned. "That could be a problem." She screwed her tinted lips. "What about this Dre character? Do you think he'll be back?"

"Like a bad penny." Passion knew Dre was too hard-headed to drop his pursuit. If anything, he'd be more pissed at Jourdan for besting him the previous night.

"You need to get a restraining order on that man."

"Jourdan's talking to his lawyer right now."

Vanessa shook her head and muttered something unintelligible before looking at her watch. "We gotta go, if we're gonna get to church on time."

Church. She'd forgotten about choir practice. Thank goodness Jourdan had a change of heart about kicking her out of Zion. "I'll put these clothes in the car. Thanks for helping me. At least I'll have something to wear now that you've given me a donation from your closet."

"That reminds me—gotta change." Braids flying, Vanessa raced for her bedroom.

Passion knew her friend wouldn't be caught dead in public wearing sweats.

Vanessa changed in record time and, twenty minutes later, they were entering Zion.

A mob of people moved in and out of the choir room, many of them volunteers for the upcoming holiday dinner. Passion was delighted that her flyers requesting volunteers had been successful.

"Ladies and gentlemen," John Singletary called out, his bald head beading with sweat. "Let's congregate in the main sanctuary if you please."

The crowd moved into the larger room.

Passion noticed she and Vanessa walked alone. "Is it my imagination, or are people making a point of staying away from us?" she whispered. "Surely they know the DA's accusations were false."

Vanessa glanced around, unconcerned. "One way to find out." She sidled up to Sister Martha Biddle.

Passion could feel the frost from where she stood.

"Sister Biddle, how are you today?"

"Vanessa." Pure ice. Sister Biddle did not halt her step, but continued, nose in air, toward the sanctuary.

"Have I offended you or something?" Vanessa called after the woman.

Sister Biddle stopped and looked down her nose in disapproval. "Now that you mention it. You could wear something less revealing."

"I hate baggy clothes. They make me feel unrestrained," Vanessa said wickedly, running an eye over the biddy's high-collared dress.

Passion stayed a few steps behind, biting her lower lip in an effort not to laugh.

Sister Biddle harumphed and straightened her lace collar. "You might take this next piece of advice very seriously." She cut her eyes at Passion and lowered her voice even more. "You might want to stay away from that Passion woman, if you know what's good for you."

Naturally, Passion was meant to hear the scathing advice.

Vanessa's spine stiffened. "Why's that?"

"Don't you listen to the news?" Mrs. Biddle's voice dripped with disgust. "She extorted tens of thousands of dollars out of dear Cece Watters, rest her soul, to carry a baby for her."

Details in the news said only that Passion had agreed to carry the child for a price. Extortion? How many others believed this version of the truth. She looked around at the crowd entering the sanctuary. One or two looked over their shoulders accusingly, but didn't maintain eye contact with her. "You're joking," Vanessa said to the crone.

"I kid you not," Mrs. Biddle answered. "And now I hear she's trying to lead the good reverend astray."

Vanessa unsheathed bright claws from the crook of her arm and gestured dangerously close to the woman's face. "Listen. I don't know where you've been getting your information, but I know the truth."

"Which is?" The look on the older woman's face said there was no truth but hers.

"Passion volunteered to have Cece and Reverend Watters child out of the kindness of her heart. She was prepared to raise the child herself when Mrs. Watters died."

"That's why she came here looking for the reverend, right?" Passion walked up beside her friend. Apparently, her only one within church walls—except for Jourdan. "I'm here to get closer to God and to serve the church. Why are you here?"

"The only thing you want to help is Reverend Watters into your bed." She spun on pointed heels and marched to the choir bleachers.

Passion decided scratching the woman's eyes out would make a huge improvement to the crone's appearance. She wouldn't do it, of course. Not in Jourdan's church. Vengeance belonged to the Lord, after all.

"Good thing she left," Vanessa fumed. "I was fixin' to knock the starch outta her tight behind."

"Don't worry about it." Passion took a deep breath. "I'm used to it."

Vanessa hugged her friend tightly. "It ain't right, Passion. It ain't."

"It's all right." They released each other after a while and Passion steadied herself for battle. "They don't have to like me, stand next to me, or talk to me." She had her chin up, like Shirleen had taught her. "But they can't keep me from singing and helping feed unfortunate people."

"You go, girl."

Chapter XII

Jourdan sank in the chair opposite Sherman Townsend and sighed heavily. He'd come to his lawyer's office to find out how things were progressing with the television ministry contract. Clutching at the aching heaviness in his chest, he repeated the question, hoping he'd heard the man wrong. "Channel seven canceled my contract?"

Sherman removed his glasses and rubbed old eyes. "'Fraid so."

"There's nothing we can do about it?" Jourdan couldn't believe this turn of bad luck.

"Nope." Sherman shifted in his chair and ran a distracted hand over his mahogany desk. "Say they want no part of any scandal—we can't force the issue without creating another."

"But Passion and I were cleared." Jourdan pushed himself out of the chair and strode to the huge window. He couldn't help but think this was his punishment for last night's delicious decadence. Problem was, he hadn't properly repented. He must pray harder.

"Unfortunately, people are still talking about it." Sherman

171

went around his desk to lift a hand to Jourdan's shoulder. "Amos tells me you're looking to take in the young lady." He raised his eyebrows. "Doing so won't help matters."

True. Jourdan had been thinking more with his groin than with his head when he'd offered shelter. But he wouldn't compromise. He'd promised Passion. "It's for her safety, Sherman, since Dre Woods is on the streets."

Sherman's tone dropped along with his hand. "So you told me last night. This Dre character threatened your lives again?"

Jourdan gave him a quick synopsis of the scene in Woods' seedy establishment. "I want him thrown in jail. It has to be a violation of his bail agreement to attempt murder a second time."

"I contacted the police today. They can't find him. They're staking out his house and club."

"He's got a penthouse." Jourdan offered, concerned for Passion. "Did they check there?"

Sherman nodded. "He's lying low. I suggest you do the same."

"I can't go anywhere. I've got a church—responsibilities." Still stunned by the canceled TV contract and even more concerned for Passion's welfare, Jourdan picked up the phone and dialed his home number. No answer. Where was she?

"It's not safe for either of you," Sherman insisted. "Maybe your parents—"

"I've gotta go." Jourdan shrugged into his overcoat. Fear clutched his chest. He couldn't breathe.

"Take care, Son."

* * * * * * * * * * * *

Take care? Passion's whereabouts were a mystery, his ministry dreams shattered—how could Jourdan take care?

Determined not to dwell on his failure, Jourdan raced around the city for more than an hour. He tried the hospital—Shirleen hadn't seen Passion. He didn't have a clue where Vanessa lived, but her mother tried calling her apartment—no answer.

When his watch alarm went off, he remembered the date and the hour. He should be teaching Bible study and Passion should be at choir practice. He hoped and prayed she'd made her way to the church.

Jourdan pulled into his parking space at Zion. Just the presence of the old, stone church, lights aglow and bustling with midweek activities, calmed his mounting fear.

Two steps inside he was greeted by the sensuous alto of Passion's voice. Thank the Lord, gossip hadn't kept her away.

Jourdan halted, dropped his head, and took his first deep breath since leaving Sherman's office.

"You okay, Reverend?" Pastor Moon rushed to his side, his genuine concern bolstering Jourdan's faith in his flock.

"Fine, Ray." He stood erect and smiled. "Couldn't be better."

"You're a little late." Moon checked his watch. "I'm afraid they started Bible study without you."

"Not a problem." Jourdan listened to Passion's perfect voice, lifted by the depth of feeling that rang through the hallway.

"We have more volunteers than we expected to help with the holiday dinner," Ray continued.

"Praise God."

Jourdan moved to the doors of the sanctuary. Pastor Moon prattled on. Jourdan couldn't concentrate on what he was saying; he'd found Passion.

Clad in leggings and a bright orange oversized blouse, she stood out from the rest of the choir like a spring bud in the dead of winter. He wondered where she'd gotten the change of clothes.

She smiled when she saw him.

Completely enamored, he relaxed a shoulder against the doorjamb and smiled back. His rapture was short-lived, however. Thoughts of her safety pressed at his brain. Where could he take her? Dre could certainly find Jourdan's house. Maybe he should rent an apartment for Passion and Shirleen. Then again, a lease drawn under any of their names would be easy to trace.

Would it be too much to ask Evelyn and Amos? She was carrying their grandchild, after all.

"Reverend?" Pastor Moon touched his arm.

Jourdan fought to focus on his associate pastor. "I'm sorry, Ray. What was that?"

"I was wondering if I could have another moment of your time?" Moon shifted his weight from one foot to the other.

"In the morning, Ray." Jourdan patted the elderly man on his back. He wouldn't be able to focus on business this evening.

"How'd it go at the TV station?"

Jourdan swallowed the bitter taste of failure, admitting, "Not well."

"That pains me, Reverend," said Pastor Moon as he left.

Didn't it, though? Time to forget about reaching beyond Zion's doors. The choir was finishing; he and Passion needed to leave while there were plenty of other people around.

Halfway down the aisle, Martha Biddle came charging Jourdan's way. "Reverend Watters, I'd like to speak to you."

He didn't like the pinched lines around her thin lips. "I'm afraid I don't have time right now, Sister Biddle."

"Hi, Jourdan . . . uh, Reverend Watters." Passion held her coat and purse. Vanessa stood at her side.

Smoke almost visible from Sister Biddle, she glared at Passion. "Is it true? Is this—this woman living with you?"

"For the moment." Jourdan held his ground with defiance and determination. "Someone broke into her apartment yesterday. And an attempt has been made on her life." Certainly the woman could understand this was an emergency.

"Couldn't happen to a more *deserving* person." The sister went bustling past Jourdan.

Jourdan nodded politely as "good evening, Reverends" and questioning looks paraded by.

"How did Sister Biddle know?" Passion stood behind Jourdan, allowing other choir members to pass.

Vanessa did the answering. She unwrapped a piece of gum

and shoved it between shiny red lips, saying, "People talk. The reverend's neighbor, two houses down and across the street, saw y'all go in last night and come out this morning." She sighed. "She's Martha Biddle's cousin."

"Great. Just great." Passion pulled her fingers through her hair. "That's why they whispered and cut their eyes when we came in," Vanessa added.

The dark weight of scandal pressed on Jourdan's shoulders. It was happening again. And this time, Martha Biddle seemed bound and determined to lead the charge against him.

Remember your promises?

He took Passion's arm. "Forget Sister Biddle and her wagging tongue."

"Why? What's the matter?" Passion asked.

"Dre Woods. He's disappeared. After last night, I know he's out for blood."

Passion immediately began scanning the emptying sanctuary.

"I've got to take you somewhere safe."

"Oh, girl," Vanessa worried half the red from her lips. "You sure know how to bring excitement into your life, doncha?"

* * * * * * * * * * * * *

Good thing they didn't do water baptisms on Wednesday nights. Dre pushed aside the heavy draperies of his hiding place. He emerged to watch how fast preacher man pulled Passion out of church.

He slid a manila envelope from his pocket, pained by the effort. It had taken three hours at the emergency care center to get his arm and leg wounds treated and bandaged. He'd paid in cash and answered no questions.

The lights dimmed; he crossed to the pulpit and stood there surveying the shadowed sanctuary. He should have been a preacher. It was the biggest scam of all.

Dre took the stairs carefully, grimacing with pain with every step. The hammer and nails in his other pocket slammed against a particularly tender scrape that traveled the length of his outer thigh.

If it hadn't been for that freakish wind last night, he would've killed Passion and the Holy Roller. Better that he hadn't done it. Death was too good for them.

He poked his head from the sanctuary and scanned the wide hall. No lights, no sounds. No witnesses to watch him create his work of art.

* * * * * * * * * * * * *

"A work of art," Jourdan complimented.

"Would you like more roast beef?" Evelyn, plump with pride, held out the serving dish to see if there were any takers.

Passion had eaten only to be polite. She couldn't put another bite inside the tight confines of her stomach. Apparently, neither could the rest of the small dinner party because they shook their heads and pushed back from the table.

Passion's lack of appetite had little to do with food consumption. His request had everything to do with it. Jourdan had asked her "for safety's sake" to stay with the Johnsons.

After choir practice, Jourdan had driven her to his in-law's home. They had arrived as Evelyn finished preparing dinner. Despite their shock at the bizarre request, Amos had agreed.

Jourdan, Amos, and Sherman moved into the living room. They occupied themselves with idle chitchat that failed to mask the room's tension.

"Let me help you with the dishes," Passion offered as the petite woman began to clear the last plates from the table.

"Thank you." Evelyn smiled graciously.

Passion got the feeling her politeness went only smile deep. Wasn't that to be expected? She had been Cece's mother. She was being asked to shelter a woman who had been implicated in her daughter's murder.

Passion took what remained of the food into the kitchen and placed it on a long counter.

"Do you have storage bowls?"

"Yes, right in that cabinet." Evelyn indicated a location over Passion's head.

Passion filled the Tupperware with the candied yams, fresh green beans, and leftover roast beef. She tried to think of the best way to break the ice.

"Mrs. Johnson—"

"Evelyn, please."

"Evelyn," she corrected. Passion took the empty platters and bowls to the edge of the sink, where Evelyn rinsed the dishes before placing them in the dishwasher. "Did you have any idea Cece hired a surrogate mother to carry her child?"

"No." She looked directly at Passion. "I had no idea whatsoever."

"Must've been quite a shock when Jourdan told you."

"Yes, it was. But tell me something, Miss Adams—"

"Passion."

"Passion." Evelyn nodded. "Why did you decide to do it? Carry our grandchild, that is."

Taking a wet cloth, Passion wiped down the already sparkling counters. "For two reasons." She rubbed at an imaginary spot, trying to phrase her answer in the best possible way.

"The money?" Evelyn looked at her, one eyebrow arched high on her forehead.

Passion nodded. "For one."

"And the other?" Evelyn stopped working to face her.

Passion looked her directly in the eye. "Because I didn't think it was fair for anyone to want something so much and not be able to have it."

Evelyn's brown eyes clouded with emotion just before she turned away. She brushed at her cheek before rinsing more dishes. "I don't know who wanted this baby more. Her or me."

Passion certainly knew the feeling. It was hard not to want something for Cece.

"So tell me, Passion. What do you want?" Evelyn closed the

dishwasher, wiped her hands on her apron, and turned for an answer.

"I want to be accepted for who I am, not judged by what I've done." She matched the woman's level gaze. "I want this baby." She yearned to say, "And I want Jourdan."

"Even if you ruin the child's life?"

Defensive, Passion squared her shoulders. "Why would it ruin a child's life to have me for a mother?"

"There's more to motherhood than dressing a baby up like a doll."

Passion's cheeks stung like she'd been slapped. "I've done nothing to make you think I'd fail this child."

"I'm not trying to offend you, Passion. But a child who has the benefit of a loving family and a safe home has a much better chance of becoming successful in the world. I'm sure if you'd come from a better home, you wouldn't have had to make such tough choices in your life."

Silence hung thick in the room while her words sank in. Passion ached to argue, but knew from experience that Evelyn was right.

"You know, dear, there are other ways of making a living—"

"You don't know what it's like having to take to the streets— more afraid of home than the unknown. It's tough to find a safe place to sleep. One without rapists." Emotion caught in Passion's throat, making her voice shaky. "You don't know what it's like to want love and find only men who treat you like a tramp." She paused to recall Evelyn's exact charge. "Men who think they'll make you happy, dressing you up like a doll."

Passion eyed Evelyn, waiting for a reaction.

The kitchen door swung open as Jourdan pushed his way into the room. "What are the chances of a body getting some dessert around here?" he asked, a little too merrily.

Passion ducked her head and composed herself.

"What's the matter?"

"Nothing." Evelyn dismissed his concern with a flick of her

hand. "Girl talk." She uncovered two beautiful cherry pies. "Passion, be a dear and bring over those dessert plates."

Passion did as instructed, glad to avoid Jourdan's curious eyes. "Why don't you go sit down, Jourdan?" She forced a smile. "We'll bring these along."

"Great." He paused for a moment before leaving the room.

Evelyn placed a healthy slice of pie on each plate. She looked at Passion. "I wasn't trying to hurt your feelings, you know."

"Weren't you?"

"I didn't realize how hard your life has been, but that doesn't change anything."

"What do you mean?" Passion held her breath.

"Once the baby's born and you're paid, I expect you to go far, far away. And leave my son-in-law and grandchild alone. I hope you understand. We intend to see the *last* of you."

The daggered words from this preacher's wife ripped new cuts in Passion's scarred heart. Tightly clenched eyelids and a few deep breaths helped her fight back tears. She wouldn't allow the woman to see how deeply she'd been wounded. Instead, she clung to Jourdan's promise about their being together "someday."

Evelyn butted her way through the swinging door to the dining area.

* * * * * * * * * * * * *

Fifteen minutes later, the entire dinner party, except for Passion, sat patting their pie-stuffed stomachs, watching embers glow orange and red in the fireplace. Passion wished to flee into the cold night, to be anywhere but here.

"That was excellent pie, Evelyn." Sherman fished in his pocket for a pipe. He struck a dignified figure with his handsomely aged features and white hair.

"Thank you." Evelyn accepted the compliment with a smug smile. "What you got there, cherry tobacco?"

"I do. Do you mind?" He lifted a thick eyebrow.

"Not at all." She turned to her husband. "Amos, why don't you buy cherry? That stuff you smoke is just awful."

Reverend Johnson made some comment about a select brand and started to light his pipe as well.

Smoke wafted in Passion's direction, upsetting her still-sensitive digestive system. "Excuse me, everyone." She rose quickly. "I need some air."

"Oh, Passion, don't leave on my account." Sherman moved his pipe to an ashtray.

"Don't be silly. I just need to walk around a little."

"I'll go with you," Jourdan volunteered.

Passion could feel Evelyn's frown like a dark cloud over her head. An extended stay at the Johnson residence would be intolerable.

Jourdan met her at the coat closet. "Before we go out, I have something for you. I was hoping to get you alone." He looked around the corner, then reached inside his sweater. He pulled a small box from his shirt pocket and offered it to her. "For you."

Passion reached slowly for it, waves of electricity traveling up her arm as his fingers trailed the bottom of her hand. There wasn't much that could fit in a box that small.

She couldn't keep her hands from shaking as she untied the ribbon. Next, she peeled away the red wrap, revealing a very pretty black velvet box. Running her fingers across the soft material for a moment, she wondered what had prompted Jourdan to give her a gift.

"Go ahead, Passion." His voice carried a soft invitation.

Biting her lip, she lifted the lid. She gasped at the beauty of a deep-green gem and the sparkling white stones that danced around it. Nothing about it implied a marriage proposal.

"I guessed your ring size." Jourdan's eyes were warm and soft as he smiled. "Try it on."

Tamping down the silly expectation that had risen before she realized a marriage proposal wouldn't be forthcoming, she wondered why he'd given her the ring. Then she noticed the flash of white paper stuffed snugly on the top of the box. She looked at Jourdan. He nodded, meaning for her to read it.

Her hands shook unfolding the note. *"Passion,"* it began.

"Enclosed is a Mother's ring for you to keep with you always. Although you have not given this child your blood, you have given it something more precious. Life. Thank you with all my heart. Jourdan."

Passion tried to refold the note. Apparently he hadn't meant his "someday."

Jourdan pulled the box from her hand, lifted the ring from the box, and placed it on her right ring finger. She couldn't tell him that the ring would serve only to remind her of the child she couldn't raise—if Evelyn had anything to do with it.

"Hush, now." He pulled a handkerchief from his back pocket and wiped the tears from her cheeks. "We have to go back through the living room to get outside. I don't want them to think I've been mean to you."

Passion managed to bank her tears. After a moment, she and Jourdan strode through the living room, dining room, and kitchen to exit the sliding glass doors.

On the deck they had a view of an enormous backyard. The moon and the stars twinkled brightly in the black, clear sky, reflecting off pure white snow.

"This is a beautiful evening," Passion spoke, trying to make safe conversation.

Jourdan moved close enough so that their shoulders touched as they leaned against the railing. "Not as beautiful as you."

Again, tears threatened. "I don't feel very beautiful."

Jourdan placed a hand on her stomach. "I've heard that's common for expectant mothers."

Unable to keep up pretenses, Passion shook her head. "I can't stay here, Jourdan. Evelyn doesn't like me."

"Don't worry. She just needs time to adjust."

"She hates me. Hates that I'm carrying her grandchild."

"She'll get over it." Jourdan shifted his position and leaned an elbow on the railing. "Besides, where would you go?"

"I've got an apartment opening up soon. Shirleen and I can stay with Vanessa or something until then."

"Your new apartment's the first place Dre will look for you. Be reasonable."

"Why? Why should I be the only one in this whole stupid city who's reasonable?" Passion's emotions broke through the dam of restraint. "Dre's acting like a lunatic, Martha Biddle thinks she's God's right hand, and Evelyn wants to pay me off and send me packing."

"What?"

She hadn't meant to tell him, but the words gushed as fast as her tears. "I need to get out of here."

Jourdan pulled her close. "Did Evelyn actually say those things?"

Passion nodded against his chest.

His embrace tightened. He held her until she stopped sobbing. "I'm sorry. I know how you feel." His voice was low and intimate. "I was an outcast once."

She moved back to study him, pulling her coat tighter at the increasing chill. "Really?"

"I lost my first ministry some four years before I came to Zion," he reflected.

"What happened?"

"I was naive enough to think the church was a place where sin didn't exist," he said, then looked away, "that lies were never told and everyone always turned the other cheek."

"You were wrong." Passion recalled her recent encounter with Mrs. Biddle and company.

He nodded soberly. "There was a young girl—fifteen. She said she was having trouble at home and needed someone to talk to. When I asked if her family could come in for counseling, she told me she'd be beaten for bringing an outsider into family problems. So I agreed to meet with her in my office."

Passion began to understand the direction his story was taking. "Behind closed doors with no witnesses?"

"Precisely." Jourdan blew a clouded sigh. "We met on several occasions for about two months. It soon became clear the things she accused her parents of couldn't be happening. There would have been hospital records of some sort."

Passion shivered against the wind that kicked up. "Not a scratch on her?"

"Nope." Jourdan shrugged off his coat and threw it over Passion's shoulders. He hugged himself against the cold air.

"So why did she need you?" The delicious smell of him surrounded her as black wool and his particular scent settled around her body.

"Apparently she'd gotten herself pregnant and didn't want to reveal the father, so she accused me of taking advantage of her."

Passion could almost feel the pain of betrayal that still haunted him. "Did you have to go to court?"

"Yes. Of course, blood tests proved me innocent, but the church didn't want me to preach anymore—there was still some doubt as to whether I had slept with the girl."

"And here I come, pregnant and claiming the baby is yours."

He smiled and shivered. "Yeah, talk about déjà vu."

In him, Passion saw the brilliant lights of a thousand compassions. "Will you lose Zion because of me?"

He stopped rubbing his hands and stepped in to wrap her in his arms. "Not if the Lord is merciful."

Passion placed her hands on his chest and lifted her mouth for his kiss. Their cold lips warmed quickly. She'd gladly endure a few weeks of hell on earth for a lifetime of heaven in his arms.

"We'd better go in," Jourdan said. "I can feel you trembling."

"It's not because of the cold air." She smiled at him seductively, forgetting his blunder with the ring.

Jourdan threw back his head. "Please. Don't do that to me."

Passion opened the sliding glass door. "Jourdan?"

"Yes?"

"I'm not staying in this woman's house tonight or any other night."

"You're sure?"

"Afraid so." Passion stared directly into his eyes.

Jourdan shook his head, obviously wondering what to do next.

* * * * * * * * * * * *

Jourdan stood before the fire while Passion reclaimed her seat in the Johnson's living room. Flames in the hearth danced hypnotically. The crackling sap sang backup to his thoughts. What would he do about Passion? How could he keep her safe if his in-laws refused to treat her kindly?

"Jourdan?"

His name, spoken in anger, had been cast across the room. Immediately he sensed something wrong.

"Have you talked to people in your congregation lately?" Evelyn asked hotly as she rose to her feet.

"I always have time for the people of Zion," he replied.

"Amos and I discussed this while you were outside." Veins stood out on her neck. "We can't believe you're going to let this happen again."

Jourdan gave Evelyn a wary look. "And just what am I allowing to happen, Mom?"

"You want me to say it, don't you?" Her mouth drew down into an ugly frown.

"Evelyn—" Amos warned.

She shrugged him off rudely. "It's bad enough that my grandchild is being carried by a whore, but I can't believe you'd embarrass our family again by letting her parade around your church every Sunday."

Passion stiffened in her chair.

Jourdan had to bite down his own fury to force a civil tone. "Wait just a minute . . ."

Evelyn's arms began flailing. "I can't take this nightmarish affair anymore."

"How can you be so cruel, Mom?"

Passion's muscles beneath Jourdan's palms were hard and tight. He wouldn't allow her feelings to be trampled. Not by his mother-in-law, not by anyone.

"It's okay, Jourdan," Passion whispered.

No it wasn't.

"Evelyn. I'm extremely disappointed in you. I expected you, of all people, to have more compassion," he said quietly.

A quick glance at Passion's face told him how tightly reigned her emotions were. A pang of guilt encased his heart. The woman he'd trusted for the past fifteen years had hurt the woman who was kind enough to carry her grandchild—the woman he *loved*.

"Let's go, Passion."

Jourdan looked over his shoulder to see Sherman patting Amos on the back consolingly as Evelyn sobbed in her husband's arms.

Amos's sorrowful eyes harbored pain. "I hope he knows what he's doing," he said to Sherman.

"I'm sure he does," Sherman answered.

"I do," Jourdan replied under his breath and reached for the door.

Chapter XIII

Jourdan had charged to her defense. For that, Passion was grateful. Now what? It seemed the more he gave, the more he lost. After leaving the Johnsons' home, Passion hugged herself tightly, the car heater doing little to warm her. Even though Jourdan's support thrilled her, Evelyn's vicious words and the subsequent showdown still stung like icicles on exposed flesh.

Passion's normal barrier against censure hadn't been enough to withstand the attack. How could kindly Cece have such a glacially mean mother?

"You okay?" Jourdan asked in a warm, caring tone.

Passion welcomed his hand as it covered hers in the Town Car's dark interior. Her hand that wore a Mother's ring, more a symbol of good-bye than a promised future. She took a deep breath before answering, "I'm fine."

His hand tightened comfortingly.

"Take a right at the next intersection," Passion instructed Jourdan.

"Where are we going?"

"Vanessa's." *Even if she doesn't have room.* "Dre doesn't know about her."

"I'm taking you to my house," he stated.

"No. I can't allow it. I won't have you run out of your church because of me. I refuse to create more scandal and embarrassment for you."

His only argument was a sigh of frustration.

Grateful, Passion directed Jourdan to the north end of town and the front curb of Vanessa's building. "That's her apartment." She pointed to the dark windows of the second story.

"Doesn't look like she's home," Jourdan observed.

"She could be asleep. But I don't see her car." Passion moaned. "All I want to do is put this horrible night behind me."

The leather seat scrunched noisily when Jourdan shifted. He pulled Passion close to give her forehead a tender kiss. "I'm sorry. What can I do to make it better?"

"Nothing. It's not your fault." She relaxed her head against his chest and ran a hand over its sweatered expanse.

Jourdan planted soft kisses on her nose, her cheeks, and finally, her mouth. This kiss grew long, slow, deep, and sensuous. Nothing else in the world existed beyond this embrace. Beyond this man.

Passion craved his touch, yearned for his lovemaking. Pursuing him, she guided his hands beneath her sweater to her breasts.

He undid the bra's front clasp and filled his palms.

Moaning under his erotic massage, Passion unzipped his pants and ran her fingers over his hardening flesh.

"Wait." Jourdan clasped her wrist.

"Don't stop," she pleaded, knowing he had an attack of conscience.

He twisted away and let his head fall back against the headrest. "Have some mercy, woman."

She sat back and refastened her bra. "Heaven better be worth the wait."

"I agree." Jourdan laughed and made the appropriate adjustments to his pants.

Passion sighed. Again, he'd asked her to wait. With the ring, now his reticence, she wondered if he truly intended to build a future with her. "What now?"

"I've still got an empty room," he offered.

"We settled that already."

"Things have changed." He started the car. "I'll say a few extra prayers to prevent temptation."

"What if Dre shows up?"

Jourdan shrugged. "My Moses act?"

Passion smiled, but couldn't shake the chills that crawled up her spine.

* * * * * * * * * * * * *

Reed swallowed the last drop of Scotch, enjoying the burn that traveled down his throat into his belly. He sat staring at the empty screen of his television, his feet propped up on the glass cocktail table—the one his wife had won in the divorce settlement but had yet to snatch. He'd make sure it was sufficiently scratched by the time she picked it up, along with the other things that were rightfully his.

"Vanessa, pour me another," he barked from his easy chair.

"I'm right here—you ain't gotta shout." Vanessa rose from the sofa beside him and poured more whisky over the remaining ice in his glass. "You're gonna feel like crap in the mornin', you know?"

"I feel like crap now. What's the damn difference?" He tossed another large dose to the back of his throat.

Ohhh, yeahhh.

He closed his eyes and let the magic liquid soothe the pain of impending defeat. The polls all showed his career in public office would end badly. Asked to tender his resignation over the Watter's fiasco, Reed had spent the last six hours trying to give himself an oral transfusion of alcohol.

"I wish you'd listen to me sometimes. I told you to get more facts before you went on TV."

He raised an eyelid to look at her. She was polishing her clawlike nails for the third time that day. "Who the hell do you think you are? Marcia Clark? My information was accurate."

"Yeah. As far as it went." Vanessa blew on shiny crimson polish. "Even I coulda told you the Reverend Watters wasn't guilty of adultery."

"And what makes you so sure of that?" He hated it when she stood up for that hypocritical preacher.

"Because I tried to entice him once." She raised an eyebrow. "I wore that black spandex dress—the one you say makes me look like a hooker in heat—and invited myself to his house for dinner."

"Am I supposed to be jealous?"

She inclined her torso, resting her abundant breasts on top of the couch's arm. "I don't know. Are you?"

The seductive pout of her lips caused his libido to rise. "Hell no," he said chugging his drink, feeling it, too. Maybe too much.

"Well, if you were, you'd be happy to know he didn't even make a move on me. The man's a pillar of strength."

She sat back and began work on the nails of her right hand.

"He's a pile of something, all right," Reed grumbled, slamming the glass on the end table, the contents sloshing. "Gimme another."

She rose to pour the potent liquid, careful not to damage her wet nails.

No longer able to resist her tempting flesh, he pulled at Vanessa with both hands until she plopped into his lap, then ran a pale hand up and down the smooth curve of her hips, drugged by the painkillers of woman and whisky.

"Tell me somethin', Eddie." Vanessa wrapped her arms around his neck and spread her fingers like cat claws on his shoulder.

189

"What?" He kissed one large breast over the tight lace blouse and watched the center emerge in budding hardness, not unlike the reaction he had beneath his trousers.

"Do you really think anyone murdered Cece Watters? It coulda just been a nut shooting into the restaurant like you said at first, couldn't it?"

"Coulda, but it wasn't." He nuzzled his head between her twin peaks, reveling in her spicy, seductive scent. His head then reeled. His insides reeled, period. *I'm drunk.*

"What makes you so sure?" she asked.

"Becush, he was told to kill only the woman fitting Sheshe's description." He laughed at how funny he sounded.

"Who woulda told him such a thing? You?" Vanessa teased.

"Yep." It was hysterical, how wide her brown eyes got. He gave a long, guffawing laugh and pulled her tighter against him. "If you could see your face, darlin'... ha, ha, ha... bet you never thought I'd tell you shumthing like that."

Vanessa eyed him with an uneasy grin. "You're just messin' with me, huh?"

Reed tried to get his face to cooperate in giving her a wink. "Shhhh." He struggled to boost his wobbling finger to his lips. "It's jush our little secret now."

"Okay," Vanessa agreed, pouring more alcohol into his glass. "Just our secret." She laughed with him and allowed his hand to explore the depths of her brassiere.

A loud rapping at the front door made Vanessa jump and Reed sober, somewhat.

"You expecting company at this hour?" she asked.

A quick glance at his Rolex put the time at one o'clock in the morning. "No."

He pushed her off his lap, finding it funny how she struggled before landing butt first on the carpet. He made his way to the door that seemed to be in three places all at once. Finally, he found the knob and twisted it open.

"I know you won the house in the divorce, Edmond, but I

can't believe you'd change the locks this quickly." His ex-wife, wearing fur and fury, stormed through the door into the house.

He sobered further. Sobered a lot.

"It's nice to see you too, Victoria."

Reed slammed the door, wishing he'd been a few seconds quicker about it.

As usual, his ex-wife's face was saved from being homely by an excellent makeup application and wonderfully smooth, cinnamon-brown skin. Her hair was swept into a tight French roll—a perfect match for her personality.

She walked directly to Vanessa, who had just found her way back to her feet. Victoria put her hands on her slim hips. "So what are you supposed to be? My replacement?"

Vanessa crossed her arms. "What of it?"

Edmond watched in amusement. It would make his night to have two women fight over him. Victoria shattered that bit of whimsy in a millisecond.

"Pssh. You can have him." She waved her diamond-studded hand and adjusted the mink coat that swept her ankles, then swung in Reed's direction. "I just came to tell my ex-husband how sorry I am he's losing his job." She cackled unbecomingly.

The Scotch's last effects wore off, replaced by his mounting anger. "I don't need your damn money, Victoria. I'll do just fine without your snobbish black behind."

"Oh. Looka here, looka here." Victoria bobbed her head. "Just because you got light skin and gray eyes from your daddy don't mean you can forget how black your mama is. And don't think I'll forget that last large withdrawal from our joint account before we settled this divorce."

"Listen, you all. I'm gonna step on outta this." Vanessa went to the closet and grabbed her black wool coat.

"Don't you leave me, too!" He didn't mean to shout, but he couldn't stand another woman walking out on him. He felt worthless enough.

Vanessa deliberated, way too long for his comfort. Relief

came when she placed the coat back on a hanger and closed the closet door.

Edmond regained his composure and regarded his former wife.

"How sweet." Sarcasm dripped from Victoria's red lips like blood from a vampire's fangs. "Such loyalty."

"Did you need something, or are you here to continue making my life a living hell?" he asked, thoroughly embarrassed at having begged Vanessa to stay in front of Victoria.

"The living hell part is very tempting." She sucked in her cheeks and studied her bracelets. "But I'm here to retrieve the keys to the Mercedes." She opened a palm and turned it up.

"How the hell am I supposed to get to work?" He'd have at least a couple weeks of grace time to turn over the reigns.

"Two words." She held up the appropriate number of fingers. "Public transportation." Her palm opened again.

"I'll get you there, Eddie." Vanessa shot daggers at the woman. "Give the skank her keys."

Edmond fumed and retrieved them from the table. Damn it all! He should have insisted the car title be put in his name. Careful not to touch Victoria in any way, he dropped the keys in her outstretched hand.

"Thanks, you're a real peach, sweetie," she said smugly and turned on expensive two-inch heels. "I hope he's paying you well," she tossed over her shoulder at Vanessa before she and her dead rodents went sailing into the night.

Edmond crossed the room in two strides to slam the door again, the rattling windows only a small consolation for the damage he wanted to do to Victoria.

He looked at the fuming Vanessa and pulled her into his arms roughly, covering her mouth, her neck, and the top of her breasts with rude kisses.

"Oh, Eddie," she breathed at his almost brutal assault.

He slid his hands down her thighs and raised her knees to his waist. Her long legs wrapped around him in a vicelike grip, and he anchored her against the closet door. His pent-up anger and frustration was soon replaced by a primal, throbbing need that strained against the material of his suit pants, demanding release.

Nipping at the juggling flesh before him, he slid his fingers beneath her panties to feel her sweet spot. He dipped inside, again and again. There would be no tickling and teasing this time. He needed to use her, to take her.

"Now, Eddie," she gasped. "Now."

He dropped to his knees and laid her down roughly. He ripped her clothes away, saving the tight bit of cloth covering her breasts for last. He watched as they burst into motion.

Burying his face in the soft, dark flesh he kissed the valley between the pair of mounds. Taking one large, sucking mouthful after another, he worked his way up a tip of one sweet breast, then the other.

Vanessa's fingers dug into his shoulders. Her gasping moans fueled his appetite. He sucked hungrily at the peaks.

Straddling her writhing hips between his knees, Edmond pulled at the catch of his trousers. He shoved them and his briefs down in one swift movement.

She sat up to rub him. Her fingers were hot as they closed around him and pulled gently.

"Now, Eddie," she repeated and guided him into the warm, wet tunnel between her legs. She squeezed herself around him and lunged her hips to meet his.

He thrust deeply, quickly, viciously. Shattering her after only a couple of strokes.

Riding on the wave of their shared desire, he dove deeper and deeper. The warm, wet tingle of her encompassed him and took him to the place where there was no pain—no defeat.

"Oh, Vanessa!" He exploded in jerking spasms, spilling himself inside her, releasing the anger, the frustration, and the need. Afterward, a calmness spread through him, more potent than the alcohol. He covered her body with his own.

The gentle stroking of her hands up and down his back made him drowsy.

"You really know how to treat me right, Eddie."

He'd never been good enough for Victoria. All she'd ever done was complain that he didn't have a more important position, or his lovemaking was substandard. The rest of the time, she'd lamented picking Reed over Grant William Wescott the third.

Served Reed right for marrying her money. He shifted his weight on his secretary. "It's too bad he shot the wrong one."

"What did you say, Eddie?" Vanessa asked.

He didn't know what he'd said. The sweet dark comfort of sleep began to overtake him. She might be too sassy, but Vanessa was loyal. He decided there could be an outside chance he'd actually learn to love her.

* * * * * * * * * * * *

The next morning Vanessa plucked a nail file from her desk drawer. Her thoughts were of Eddie. He hadn't seemed to remember much about last night, except for how much he hated Victoria.

True to her word, she'd given him a ride to work. It was the least she could do to repay him for his awesome performance the night before. But what he'd said still clawed at her conscience.

The sounds of his cursing spilled from his office, punctuating the air. Vanessa sighed and rushed to him. There was no telling what he fussed about now.

She surveyed the disheveled room. Eddie tore through the papers on his desk.

"Amazin' how much junk you can get into one office in two years." Vanessa stepped gingerly over a box lying on the floor.

"Quit griping and help me out," Reed said gruffly.

She hoped he'd last in his job without killing somebody. Suddenly, the mere thought of murder made her uneasy. Had he really ordered a hit on Cece? Why? And what had he meant when he'd said the wrong one got shot?

Vanessa shook her head. Her imagination had run away with her. Best not to pay serious attention to someone who'd been three sheets to the wind. "Whatcha lookin' for?" She slid a stick of gum from her cleavage, unwrapped it, and stuck it in her mouth. It was warm and soft.

"For a damn reason to live, what the hell else?" he glared nastily, with more than a hint of disgust.

"Testy, testy."

"The key, Vanessa. I can't find the key to my private desk files." He sank to his knees on the thin carpet and began searching beneath his desk.

"Tell you what." Vanessa stepped behind him and pulled him out by his belt. "I'll look for the key. You go for a sweet roll or somethin'." If she didn't get him out of there for a while, he'd drive her bananas.

"Oh, all right." He stood and adjusted his clothing. "I know I had it here yesterday. Give me your keys. I'll go home and check my suit pockets."

"Fine." Vanessa pointed to the objects. "They're on my desk."

"I'll be back. If you find it—" a thick finger poked her face "—put it on top of my desk. Don't go getting efficient and packing up that stuff. It's for my eyes only."

His pale eyes looked like a wild animal's.

She wanted to whack the wildness right out of him. "Fine," she repeated, pressing her lips together.

Anything further would set him off again.

A sigh of relief passed her lips as he vanished through the outer office door. Fear of losing his job had driven the man stark raving mad, she decided. Vanessa carefully redistributed papers and books he'd thrown carelessly into boxes to make them easier to cover and stack. Half an hour later she moved the last box into place. Beneath it, a shiny metal object glistened.

"What a relief." She plucked the key from the carpet.

She flipped the key between her fingers for a moment, then rose to stand. "No." He'd told her not to touch anything.

Obediently, she placed the key in the middle of his desk and went back to her typing. Unable to concentrate, she made mistake after mistake.

Darned if that thing ain't callin' my name.

"I really shouldn't be doing this," she said under her breath, but left her desk anyhow.

Her pulse quickened as she stuck the key into the appropriate lock and opened the drawer. Files with meaningless names caught her attention. Looking closer, she decided they were a rough code of some sort.

She popped her gum. Eddie probably thought she wouldn't be able to figure them out if she saw them. It became obvious while looking through the file labeled PIMPSIGOT that he'd kept a detailed list of crimes on the city's pimps. He probably held them for some future need.

Running a fingernail down the list, she stopped on the name Dre Woods. While each pimp had his own ledger, Woods had two or three. In wonder, she pored over his list of crimes until an entry jumped off the page at her.

Aug 3rd. Hit Victoria.

Vanessa's blood ran cold as she fumbled to replace the file. August third had been the day Cece Watters was murdered. Had she been the *wrong one* Eddie had spoken about?

Cece had been active in the church; Vanessa had spoken with her on many occasions. Remembering Victoria's plain features, slight build, and dark complexion, Vanessa knew someone could have mistaken her for Victoria, from a distance. But up close, the predatory, catlike stare of Victoria Reed could never be confused with the gentle kindness in Cece Watters' eyes.

Vanessa's fingers shook. It took her three attempts to lock the drawer. She placed the key on the desk where she wished she'd left it.

"So . . . you found it."

Vanessa jumped. "Oh, Eddie. Don't scare me like that." How long had he been there?

He didn't say anything, but his expression said his mood hadn't changed.

"Where was it?" He snatched the key from the desk.

"Under one of those boxes you had all over the room." She tried to sound sassy, hoping he couldn't catch her false tone.

"Don't start with me, Vanessa." Rounding his desk, he plopped in his chair. "Get me some coffee. I've got work to do."

He pulled open the drawer she'd been nosing around in and brought out a file.

Terror caught in her throat, as she saw the streak of her passionate plum fingernail polish standing out like crayon on the folder. Of all the days to forget a topcoat.

He looked over his papers at her. "Coffee. *Now.*"

"Oh, yeah. Be right back." She tried to walk calmly out of the office. If he'd seen her going through his drawer, he would have gone ballistic, she assured herself.

Vanessa checked the clock on her desk. Five minutes after ten. Would this day never end?

"Vanessa!"

She jumped again, this time from her chair, knocking her knee against the edge of her desk.

Child, you're gonna have to chill out.

Rubbing her knee, too nervous even to pop her gum, she limped slightly going into his office. "Yeah, Eddie?"

"Victoria's coming over for the last of her stuff tonight. After she's gone, I'll need you. Come by about ten."

"Okay, Eddie." She turned to leave, but halted midway. "Oh, on second thought, I can't tonight."

He looked ready to kill. "What?"

"I promised a friend I'd—"

197

"Well, unpromise."

"I can't. Honest." She didn't need Eddie making her nervous.

He didn't bother to answer, just lifted his hand and dismissed her with a flick of his wrist. He concentrated on his files, shoving each document, one by one, into the portable shredder he'd placed beside his chair.

Well, so much for that, Vanessa thought. Any evidence linking Eddie to Cece's murder was gone now. Still . . . her conscience gnawed, urging her to tell someone what she knew, even if there was no way to prove it.

Chapter XIV

Even though the night had passed without incident, Jourdan had gotten little sleep. Odd noises from outside had kept him awake. More than once, he'd checked to see if Dre or his ugly bodyguard had attempted to break in.

The urgent, yet vague call from Associate Pastor Moon caught Jourdan with poker in hand and stinging, sleep-deprived eyes. Nonetheless, he rushed to dress in order to meet the man.

Jourdan opened the garage, escorted Passion to the car's passenger side, then went around the front bumper to slide behind the wheel.

"He didn't give you any idea what's wrong?" Passion asked as he started the engine. She appeared as nervous as Jourdan felt.

"Just said it was serious." Ray Moon wasn't the excitable sort. He usually took crises, solved them, then let Jourdan know the results. The man had barely been able to stutter his words this morning.

Silence spoke volumes between Jourdan and Passion on the

trip to Zion. Knots of tension made his shoulders ache. *What now, Lord?*

Before he entered Zion's doors, Jourdan felt the presence of evil. One step inside, and it nearly blew him over.

"Sweet Jesus," he whispered, shocked.

Pictures were pounded into the old concrete walls with huge nails. Lewd, disgusting photographs of Passion in poses Jourdan had never imagined—in costumes from lace to leather that covered less than nothing. Above the rest, he saw a picture of Dre's club, Midnight Dreams.

"Oh, God," Passion choked out.

Jourdan grabbed her by the shoulders, trying to give comfort. He failed.

"I've got to go, Jourdan. Now!" She wrenched away, and when he tried to stop her, she pleaded, "Don't. Please don't. I need time *alone*. You need time. Respect my wishes. Please!"

This time, there was no stopping her.

Pastor Moon approached Jourdan unsteadily, a dozen or so people following in his wake. "Reverend—"

"Take them down," Jourdan commanded, ripping the first one from the wall. "*Now.*"

"I refuse to touch such filth." Martha Biddle twisted her thin lips and marched down the hall.

Jourdan glared at those tempted to follow her. "No one deserves this." He lowered his voice. "Please, take them down."

Ray Moon pulled in earnest and several others did as well.

Trembling with rage, Jourdan ripped at the photos like a man possessed. He pulled nails from the wall with his bare hands.

Someone had provided a trash can; it quickly filled to overflowing.

"Somebody hand me a match." Jourdan stared down at the offensive photos and railed inwardly against Dre Woods's depravity.

Staring long and hard at one photograph, Jourdan noted the

full cheeks and wide, innocent eyes of Passion's youth. She'd been almost a baby when these were taken.

A young man solemnly pressed a matchbook into Jourdan's hand.

In ritualistic silence Jourdan picked up the garbage can, walked outside, and placed it on the bottom step. Igniting the head with his thumbnail, Jourdan dropped the blazing matchstick into the collage of Passion's past.

He found no joy, no consolation from the fire. Only pain. In one photo, Passion's full, painted lips turned down. As if, at any moment, they would tremble with a lifetime of sorrows.

He scanned the parking lot, wondering where she'd gone. Though no tears fell, Jourdan wept inside for the pain she must be feeling. He wouldn't run from her grief like he'd done with Cece—didn't want to make the same cowardly mistake again.

Jourdan searched the parking lot and his car, but couldn't find her. Obviously, she did need time alone. He'd have to respect that.

When the photos turned to gray ash, he reentered the church. Moving toward his office, he ran his fingers over blistered holes the nails had left. The walls could be repaired. But he wondered if Passion's pride or his ministry would ever survive the damage of reckless gossip over Woods' sick, vicious act.

He slumped at his desk; Pastor Moon walked into his office.

The old man's jowls were pulled down like a basset hound's. "The deacons have called a meeting."

"Of course." Jourdan ran a hand over his face. "When?"

"As soon as you can make it." The man made a quiet exit.

Jourdan heard a voice calling him. He followed the sound to the sanctuary, touching each pew on his journey to the altar. Each step grew heavier as he sensed the time for reckoning.

He bowed his head and bent his knees—slowly sinking into the familiar position of prayer. No sooner had his knees touched the carpet than flashing bolts of contrition began to pervade his spirit.

201

He'd failed to love his wife the way she deserved. He'd failed his congregation, allowing them to believe God's house had room for hate and prejudice. He'd led Passion to sin with his craving flesh.

Jourdan bowed all the way over until his forehead touched the carpet of the bottom step. He cried for grace and mercy. He cried for the strength to turn things around. Praying opened his mind and allowed him to settle into the calm of pure white light. The Lord spoke to him, fed his soul, offered forgiveness.

Perhaps he had been too proud, too greedy to keep the biggest, most successful ministry in the city. Had he done it more for himself than the Lord? If so, then he deserved to lose it all. If not, then he deserved so much more than a scandalized dismissal.

Jourdan had no idea how long he prayed, yet his knees ached and his legs tingled when he rose slowly, painfully to his numb feet. He sensed a presence at his back.

He turned to face Ray Moon. "They're anxious to get started?"

"Yes."

Jourdan tucked in his shirt, taking care to button it to the neck. He smoothed what he could of the wrinkles and followed Ray out of the sanctuary.

The conference room was deadly silent. Condemnation hung in the air like fog. He took his seat at the head of the table and surveyed the deacons and associate pastors assembled and seated. Men he had known for so long. Men who'd helped to make Zion Baptist Church the best in the city.

Brother Wilson cleared his throat nervously; Pastor Moon tapped his pencil in double time on the hard wood. No one made eye contact.

Jourdan exhaled. "Gentlemen, it's you who've called this meeting. Tell me what's on your minds."

Pastor Moon spoke first. "Reverend Watters, we've been the governing body of this church since it began."

"That's right," Deacon Jones called out loudly.

"And we've seen good times and bad times in those years."
Jourdan waited patiently for him to get to the point.

"But never have we had a low point as we do now." He dropped his eyes, avoiding Jourdan's level gaze.

"Shall we get to the point, gentlemen?"

Pastor Moon finally met his gaze. "I . . . that is we . . . feel that your living with Miss Adams—"

"Is an abomination and a sin!" Deacon Jones pounded the table.

"Jourdan," Ray Moon pleaded, "you saw what she was."

"Are you alluding to those pictures?" Outraged, Jourdan tried to explain, "She was only a naive child—"

"A scandalous, wicked whore!" Deacon Jones boomed. "What kind of example is she for the young people?"

"The best kind." Jourdan clenched his teeth. "We have sinners every day who come to Christ and lead new lives. This is the hope for our youth. The hope for us all."

"A preacher has to be respected, Jourdan. You know that." Pastor Moon's rheumy eyes watered.

"I understand, gentlemen, that as the leader of this flock, my moral character must be above reproach." Jourdan rose from his chair. "But I refuse to have all the good I've done be reduced to nothing because someone doesn't like Miss Adams staying in my guest bedroom."

"We have the right to take your position away from you if we feel it's in the best interest of the church." Deacon Jones rose as well.

Hot blood pulsed dangerously in Jourdan's neck. "What right do you have to take what is mine?"

"Every right as the governing body of Zion." Spittle flew from Deacon Jones' mouth.

"It does take a unanimous vote, gentlemen." Michael Mills, the youth pastor, spoke up. "And I, for one, think supporting Reverend Watters during this difficult time is in the best interest of the church."

Every man began to talk at once.

Pastor Moon paced behind his chair and rubbed his sparsely covered brown head in disbelief. "You can't be serious, Michael. There's not a single member of our congregation who wants to be part of a scandalized church."

"This church can be shamed only if we allow it to be," Michael argued. "Don't you see, our getting rid of Jourdan only gives credence to the prejudice and ostracizing that some members of our congregation practice on a regular basis."

"That's right." Jourdan, relieved to have an ally, nodded. "We must act as Jesus did and not allow stones to be cast at someone whose sin is judged by other sinners."

Ray hung his head in silence for a minute. "But, Reverend, you're living in sin with the woman."

He couldn't deny his wrongdoing. But God's grace was his. "Vengeance is our Lord's. He passes judgment, not mortals."

"We'd be no better than Philistines, if everyone did as they pleased, waiting for Judgment Day."

Ray's voice cut through the room. "What do you plan to do about that woman?"

"I'll marry her."

"Let's not make things worse." Deacon Jones circled the conference table. "Miss Adams could no more be a preacher's wife than a pig could stop squealing."

"I say who will be my wife, Deacon. No one else!"

Jourdan regained his composure and flattened his palms on the table. Leaning forward, he made his final plea. "Gentlemen. Let us not get so caught up in the politics of religion that we can't see what is right."

No one spoke. No one moved. Nothing stirred.

"As leaders of Zion Baptist Church we must make the effort to reach out to those who need us most and not turn them away. Forgive Passion Adams the sins of her youth. All she's ever wanted is a kind word and loving friends." He scanned the room. "Jesus has forgiven her already. As followers of his teachings, can I expect less of you?"

Silence.

Jourdan took his seat. "Someone is trying very hard to discredit Miss Adams, myself—and this church. It will depend upon our actions to guide Zion through this satanic attack. Agreed?"

"Agreed," Michael Mills said quickly.

Eventually, the whole governing body was in agreement as to what needed to be done.

Ray Moon rubbed his flabby cheeks. "Who will convince the congregation?"

"Leave that to the Lord." Jourdan felt energized as the pendulum swung back to his side. "It's only right that I marry the woman I love."

There were no arguments.

Now he needed to find Passion and propose.

* * * * * * * * * * * * *

Passion closed the door to the musty motel room. Covering her mouth, she raced to the bathroom to vomit. Her stomach muscles tightened like a fist, but nothing came up.

She hadn't eaten that morning, which made things worse.

Sinking to the cold tile, Passion covered her face and cried. Cried for her own humiliation, but mostly for Jourdan's.

Never again could she return to Zion. Her dreams of a lifetime with Jourdan were gone. She had to spare his further disgrace by staying away from him.

For a moment she wondered if it would be better to die.

"No, it wouldn't," she answered herself. Who would take care of Shirleen? Who would give Jourdan his child?

Passion wasn't quite sure how to solve the last problem.

* * * * * * * * * * * * *

"Chile, you look a sight. Dem bags under yore eyes is big as skillets."

Passion placed her hands on the wheelchair, forcing a smile. "I'm all right."

Shirleen doubted that.

"Are you ready to leave this hospital?"

"I is." Shirleen shuffled her way to the wheelchair while the tall, handsome doctor explained Shirleen's prescriptions to Passion.

"Lordy, seem like I be taking pills till Judgment Day."

"Now, Miss Shirleen." The doctor bent to her eye level. "Make sure you take your medicine when you're supposed to. I don't want to see back in the ICU."

"Don't you worry none. I ain't comin' back," she assured him. "Even for those purty brown eyes a yours."

He grinned. "That's the spirit."

"C'mon, Passion. I needs to get home so I kin get some rest." Shirleen was careful not to bend her elbow. "My arm's still tender from them pokin' and proddin' on me all hours uh da day 'n' night."

Obediently, Passion pushed her toward the elevators.

"Where's da reverend?" Shirleen had assumed he'd be with her.

"He's not coming."

"Oh." Shirleen got a funny feeling from the hollow sound in Passion's voice. "Y'all have a fight?"

"No. I don't want to talk about it."

Lordy, she was snappish today. "I guess we ain't stayin' at da reverend's house now?"

"That's right." Passion punched the elevator button and stayed quiet down to the first floor.

The child was in a mood all right. Shirleen decided it would be best not to ask too many more questions.

Passion fussed over Shirleen the whole time they waited on the bus, adjusting her coat and scarf to make sure she didn't catch a chill. Though she grew a little irritated at all the attention, Shirleen knew the girl needed to do something to take her mind off her worries.

The motel wasn't much to look at, but neither was their old apartment. "You say dis is justa temporary place?"

"Yeah." Passion released Shirleen's arm.

Shirleen sank onto the hard bed.

"I've canceled the lease for our apartment. I'm afraid Dre could find us. We're just staying here at the motel until I can figure things out."

"What about our furniture?"

"I put it in storage."

Shirleen watched her unpack her bag and transfer a dirty nightgown to a laundry bag. Ordinarily she would've waited patiently for Passion to explain things, but she couldn't take the suspense. "You gonna tell me what's goin' on b'tween you and Reverend Watters?"

Passion shook her head. "It's not something that I'll ever want to talk about, Shirleen. So please stop asking."

The grief on her friend's face hurt Shirleen to her toes. She could see powerful pain affecting her. "Well, you let me knows if there anythin' I kin do."

"I will." Passion hugged her. "Thanks."

* * * * * * * * * * * * *

Tracks came down the apartment stairs slowly and Dre knew every step hurt like hell. He'd been cut up in the weird storm, even worse than Dre. Healing was taking too long for both of them.

"She ain't here."

"Damn." Dre pulled off one black leather glove, careful of the bandage on his wrist, and fished inside his jacket for a pack of cigarettes. He glanced up the staircase leading to Passion's abandoned apartment. "I thought for sure she'd run back home."

But she hadn't—not during the long week since Dre had nailed art to the walls of the Holy Roller's church.

"All the old lady's stuff is gone too," Tracks added.

Dre's shoulders slackened. If anything could convince Passion she had nowhere to go but to him, those pictures should have done the trick. She had to know she didn't belong in that plastic world with all those plastic people.

Dre puffed on his cigarette. He'd been ready to take her back with open arms. Why hadn't she called?

A police cruiser turned down the street.

"Heads up." Tracks pulled his coat collar around his ears and his cap lower.

Dre ducked toward the building. The police were all over his territory, staking out his house and club.

He'd been able to find a safehouse, though, when he'd learned the district attorney had left office.

With Reed off his back, Dre had felt safe enough to visit Passion's old residence. 'Til now.

"Let's go."

"Where to?" Tracks asked.

"The bank. I need to transact a little business." He had hired a realtor to sell his house and cancel his lease on the penthouse. Where he was going, he wouldn't need them anymore. The only thing left to do was retrieve his cash and have it wired to the islands.

"Did I tell you two more of your ladies skipped out last night?"

All his business had been going to crap lately. "Who?" Dre asked, not surprised.

"Trixie and Chante."

"I never figured Chante had it together enough to put one foot in front of the other." She'd grown quite fond of crack—one of his best customers, Chante.

Tracks, arms folded, scanned the street behind his dark sunglasses. He didn't seem to be in any hurry about leaving.

"Where did they go?"

"Don't matter." Tracks shrugged. "The deed is done."

It was only a matter of time before the rookie pimps and drug dealers started infringing on his territory. Dre blew a long trail of smoke. So what? Let them have it. "Well, let's move. Unless you've got more good news."

Tracks whipped off his sunglasses for the first time since Dre had known him. "Just thought I'd let you know, I'll be working for Rocko."

"What the—?" Dre dropped his cigarette to the concrete.

The big man smiled. "He's offering me more money, and he ain't got voodoo-practicing preachers after him."

Since the night Watters had taken Passion, Dre noticed Tracks unusual aversion to drive past churches. Without Tracks, his foothold in the Hood would be gone. Well, he had other plans.

"I don't want to go down with you. No offense."

"Then step." Dre opened the driver's door. "I don't need you anyhow."

"Cool." Tracks donned his sunglasses and flagged down a taxi. He looked back before hopping in. "Oh, by the way, the girls you're missin' . . ." He smiled. "They comin' with me."

He jumped into the taxi and slammed the door before Dre could get an answer past his lips. Dre slid behind the steering wheel of the Lexus for the first time.

Good thing he was retiring. He had enough money put away to live very large in the Bahamas. The rest of these two-bit hoods could kiss his black behind.

If only Passion had come to her senses he would be taking her with him. No matter how much he wanted to hate her, the woman burned in his veins.

He turned the key and ignited the engine. *Bump her.* He refused to keep giving her chances. There were plenty of beautiful women where he was going and, with all his money, they would worship him like a god. One Bahama Mama was all it would take to cool his desire for the woman who had refused him one too many times.

So long, Passion. I hope you enjoy being tossed out on your behind by those hypocritical church folk.

* * * * * * * * * * * * *

Jourdan rubbed his aching temples, then checked the time. One o'clock. He had half an hour to get downtown to meet with the station owner at channel eleven, the first to show an interest in televising Jourdan's ministry since channel seven's cancellation.

His dream seemed lifeless without Passion. Where was she? Weeks had passed since she disappeared. The holiday feast had come and gone, Sister Biddle taking Passion's place. Christmas was just around the corner. There would be nothing to celebrate without Passion, not for Jourdan.

He couldn't even find relief in Edmond Reed's departure from office. Furthermore, the new DA had promised to give the murder investigation his full attention since Reed's bungling. Nothing had come of it yet.

"Jourdan?"

"Ray." Jourdan stood as his associate pastor walked into the room.

"I just wanted to wish you well. I've been praying this meeting comes out all right. I know how much it means to you—to all of us."

Jourdan smiled, but not broadly, at his old friend. "Thanks, Ray. I appreciate your support."

The men shook hands. Jourdan took some comfort in having his old friend on his side again.

A tapping at the door interrupted their handshake. Vanessa. Lately, she hadn't attended services. Jourdan invited her in. Did she have news of Passion?

She passed Pastor Moon, who excused himself. "I have a problem." She took a seat in front of Jourdan's desk. "I hope you can help me."

"I'll certainly try." He rocked back in his chair, waiting for her to continue.

Vanessa smoothed her short skirt. "A while back, I ran across some information that seems to implicate a friend of mine in a crime."

Jourdan nodded, disappointed she didn't mention Passion. "Go on."

"I don't know if my hunch is true. That's why I've been keeping it to myself. If I'm right, my friend would go to jail for sure."

"Continue."

"If I choose not to say anything, then everything would be okay, because the person who actually committed the crime is already in jail. My friend didn't pull the trigger."

"If your friend is involved, doesn't that make your friend just as guilty?"

"Under the law, I suppose it does." Vanessa dropped her head. "Would it be wrong to say nothing?"

"The truth is always the right answer." It would be wrong to tell her differently. "Search your soul, say a prayer. You'll find the strength to do what's right."

She sighed heavily, looking as tired as Jourdan felt.

"I'll give it a try." She lay a soft, dark hand on his. "You should try getting some rest. You've got circles the size of circus rings beneath your eyes, Reverend."

He patted her hand. "I do feel like a few elephants are dancing all over me." Sadness clogged his throat. "I miss Passion." He looked pleadingly into her eyes. "If you see her, will you tell her that?"

Fuschia lips trembled slightly. "Yeah, I sure will." She picked up her tiny purse and crossed the room to leave.

Alone, Jourdan buried his face in his hands and tried to rub some life back into it. If he didn't get moving, he'd miss his appointment.

* * * * * * * * * * * *

Sherman Townsend was waiting when Jourdan tore up the steps to channel eleven. "Slow down, Jourdan. You're not late yet." His dentures sparkled brightly as he opened the door to the lobby.

"I know, Sherman. It's just this station is our last chance now that nine and four have turned us down." The thought still

211

angered him. You would've thought he *had* been convicted of murder, the way they'd treated him.

"Keep the faith." Amos picked up the briefcase at his side as two men pushed their way through the security doors.

A large man with squinty blue eyes and a crew cut stuck his hand out first. "I'm Otto Graves, the station owner." He spoke around a large cigar extending from his mouth. "This here is Hugh Matthews, my program director." He nearly shoved the short black man in front of Jourdan and Sherman.

Introductions complete, they were buzzed through another security door and led through a maze of hallways.

"Make sure you all don't make too much noise when we go past the red lights," Otto cautioned in a slight southern drawl.

The lights he spoke about signaled television shows being taped behind the closed doors.

Finally, they came to a door marked Conference Room and entered. Jourdan took a seat on the side of the large desk where he could have a view of the river. He wondered if his child would like riding the riverboats as much as he had. Would he ever see his son or daughter? Or Passion?

"Jourdan?"

He brought his attention back to the assemblage. "I'm sorry, I must've drifted off. Shall we begin?"

Sherman Townsend sifted through a short stack of papers. "The station agrees to give you airtime, as long as you provide them with at least a reasonable share of the audience on Sundays at ten o'clock."

"But my services don't start until ten-thirty, gentlemen," Jourdan pointed out. It would be difficult to gather his members in at an earlier hour.

Amos waved his palm back and forth. "No, Son. They're going to tape your sermon and play it over the air at ten o'clock at night."

Another bubble burst. He'd thought he would get time in the morning when the other services were on, like Billy Graham's or Kenneth Copeland's.

Otto Graves' small blue eyes met Jourdan's accusingly. "This is only if the thing with the DA's office doesn't flare up again, you understand?"

"Of course," he replied and tightened his jaw.

Otto relaxed against the back of his chair, his ample stomach quivering with the movement. "I wouldn't want my station to be the center of scandal."

"We understand completely, Mr. Graves," Sherman assured him. "Since the DA has retracted his statement, these accusations have been laid to rest."

"Very good," the large man replied.

Hugh Matthews spoke for the first time in the meeting. "We're planning to place you as early as next Sunday. Will you be prepared?"

"I'll be ready." Jourdan said a silent prayer of thanks to the Almighty. His dream lived. If only he had Passion to share this triumph with.

"Jourdan, we need your signature here." Sherman pointed to a small X on the document.

Overwhelmed with gratitude, Jourdan took delight in formalizing the agreement.

The men exchanged handshakes.

"Thank you for the opportunity, Mr. Graves. I hope you'll be pleased with my ministry."

Once Jourdan and his attorney reached the parking lot, he smiled. "Do you believe it, Sherman? We're finally going to be televised. I could turn a somersault."

"Congratulations." Sherman reached up to pat him on the back. "Better tell that Kenneth Copeland fellow he's got competition."

"If only Passion was here, everything would be perfect," Jourdan admitted.

Sherman frowned. "I'm sure she'll be watching when it happens."

"Maybe so." Jourdan had to stop thinking, stop grieving,

and get himself together. "I've got work to do. I need to practice preaching to the camera, don't I?"

Sherman laughed. "You'll do just fine."

"Thanks for everything, Sherman." Jourdan offered his hand. He owed a lot to this steadfast man. "By the way, how are Evelyn and Amos doing? You seen them lately?"

"Evelyn's still pissin' vinegar about this whole thing. Wants me to put a warrant out for your friend Passion's arrest."

"For what?" Jourdan asked, incredulous.

"Kidnapping." Sherman laughed. "I told her the woman couldn't kidnap what wasn't born yet."

"Evelyn's amazing."

"Don't you worry, Son." Sherman gave his shoulder a pat. "I've seen the way she looks at you. She'll be back. Forgiving and forgetting."

Jourdan prayed he was right.

* * * * * * * * * * * *

Passion cautiously opened the motel door. She thought she'd heard a woman scream. She closed the door. Again, she heard a high-pitched scream. This time it was followed by "Oooh, Timmy!"

Great. She was about to drop and their new next-door neighbors were getting it on. Passion dragged her feet to the bed and dropped onto the musty, faded spread.

Shirleen sat in the corner, crocheting a decoration for the tree they didn't have. "Gonna be tough to sleep through dat."

"Can't last long." Passion yawned. She kicked off both shoes and covered herself with her coat.

The baby tried to get comfortable, too. Passion wondered if it would resemble Jourdan.

Fatigue weighed down her eyelids and every muscle in her body; she tucked her hands between her cheek and the bed.

"I know dis ain't none of my business . . ."

Passion lifted one lid, sensing a confrontation. Actually,

214

she was surprised her friend had waited this long. "What, Shirleen?"

"When you plannin' on lettin' that nice Reverend Watters know where you is?"

"Not yet."

"Why not? You ain't 'specially happy without him."

Passion punched her flat pillow. "I'm not especially happy about not being able to find a job."

"What about dat baby you carryin'?" Shirleen persisted.

"Here we go again. Same song, second verse."

"Stop dat sassin' and listen up." Shirleen stood and placed a hand on her hip. "Dat man got every right to know what's goin' on with you and his chile."

Passion smiled at Shirleen. "You must be feeling a lot better."

"Don't go changin' the subject."

"You're right." Passion sat up. "I know I should tell him. But after what happened—" She stopped, not sure if she could stand repeating the story.

"Go 'head. Tell ole Shirleen all about it." She sat on the bed beside her and opened her arms.

Comforted by her familiar embrace, Passion told Shirleen about her humiliation at Zion. "You can see why I can't go back." She let a tear roll onto Shirleen's flower-print housecoat.

"Mmm hmm. I can see why you doesn't want to." Shirleen hugged her tighter. "But hidin' don't seem like da same Passion I knows."

Startled, Passion pulled away. "What's that supposed to mean?"

"Since when does you let other folks tell you what you worth?"

"But, Shirleen." Passion was on her feet. "Dre had me displayed on those church walls like some kind of profane art show. I was stripped bare for everybody to see."

"So dey saw a bit more of ya than you liked. So what? Ain't like you got nothin' to be shamed of. God made you same as dem." Shirleen lifted her chins.

She made it sound logical, not scandalous. Passion asked, "And I suppose you expect me to tell them that?"

"Suit yo'self." Fingers again worked crochet needles. "But da Passion I know always fights for what she want. Mmm hmm."

Female cries of passionate worship came through the thin walls again. Passion looked at the dark, horrid motel room. It was a prison of her own making because she was too scared of people's opinions to do anything but hide and cry.

"You're right, Shirleen." Living like this was ridiculous, especially when she'd come so close to having everything she'd ever wanted. She missed Jourdan. Oh, how she missed him.

"I guess I'd better take my tail from between my legs and go get what's mine, hmmm?"

Shirleen winked. "Dat's my girl."

* * * * * * * * * * * * *

Passion heard the crunch of tires outside their motel room door. "She's here." She turned to the scratched mirror of the vanity and adjusted the bright yellow dress. If she was going to Zion, she'd go in style.

"No need for all dat primpin'," Shirleen rose and ran a hand over her own dress. "You looks beautiful."

Passion answered the door before Vanessa could knock. "It's so good to see you."

"Girl, it seems more like years than weeks." She threw her arm around Passion's neck.

"I know. It does." Passion hugged her tight. "I've missed you."

"Don't disappear on me again. Hear?" She gave her a glare beneath layers of mascara.

"I won't. Promise." Passion couldn't wait another moment— "Did Jourdan . . . has he lost his ministry?"

"No. The church council is behind him now. I don't know what he told them in their meeting, but Martha Biddle is mad as a wet hen he's still pastoring," Vanessa explained.

What relief!

Vanessa said, "I know you don't want to be late to hear his sermon. Are you ready to go?"

"Can't wait." Passion went to help Shirleen to the car, although she was getting around better every day.

"That smock looks good. Even motherhood becomes you. I hate that," Vanessa teased, once the threesome settled in the Escort. "It's good to see you gettin' around, Miss Shirleen."

"I happy to be around, chile." Shirleen chuckled and sank back in the seat.

It was so good to have her friends back that Passion felt inspired by their good humor and the brightness of the day.

"Just let Martha Biddle try to bring me down. She'll regret it."

"I hate to ruin our reunion but I have some bad news," Vanessa announced.

"What?" Passion sat up straighter. She hoped it wasn't anything too horrible, especially if it concerned Jourdan.

"Eddie, you know, my boss?"

"Yeah?"

Vanessa's fingers grasped the steering wheel—hard. "He's in jail."

Passion, confused, asked, "Why?"

"I ratted on him."

"Praise da Lord," Shirleen interjected. "Dat man had no bizness puttin' my Passion through hard times."

"This is incredible. I thought you liked him," Passion said to the confessing Vanessa.

"I do." Vanessa chewed crimson from her lips. "But he did something horribly wrong."

Passion, not particularly upset about the district attorney going to prison, knew it wasn't easy for Vanessa.

"He had Cece Watters killed."

"Vanessa! You knew about it?" Passion couldn't believe she'd held back information from the police.

Both Passion and Shirleen spoke at once, firing more

217

questions at her. Vanessa pleaded for quiet, then gave full explanation of how Reed had contacted Dre to kill his wife.

"You have to understand—I love Eddie. I wasn't sure my information was correct." Vanessa sniffed. "I went through his private drawer and saw a file on Dre Woods with an order that said "August third, hit Victoria?"

"Who's Victoria?"

"Reed's wife."

"He was trying to kill his wife?"

Vanessa nodded. "And got the wrong woman. Cece and Victoria could be twins."

"Lordy, Lordy." Shirleen tsked from the backseat. "Ain't this sumthin'?"

Something? No! Extraordinary news. Jourdan had to be thankful to know Cece's real murderers would finally be brought to justice.

"There's a warrant for Dre Woods' arrest, too," Vanessa concluded.

Cold comfort.

Passion could tell the whole thing upset Vanessa. "You must feel awful to be the one to tell . . . "

"It's killing me." Shirleen handed Vanessa a tissue from her purse.

"Stop that, girlfriend, you'll ruin your makeup." Passion smiled tentatively at her tortured friend's profile. "If it makes you feel any better, you did the right thing."

"It makes me feel like crap." Vanessa blew her nose. "Poor Eddie."

"Here, stop. Get out." Passion ordered. "I'll drive to church so you can have a good cry."

Vanessa nodded and did as she was told.

Once they arrived, Passion and Vanessa each took an arm and escorted Shirleen up the steps of Zion. Inside, Passion looked at the walls, where they'd been desecrated. No evidence of Dre's handiwork remained.

Rochelle and Laticia ground to a halt when they saw her. Their hatred reached across to Passion. Their angry glares were no threat, not after all that had happened over the past months. Passion shrugged off their contempt, lifted her head, and moved forward.

The disapproving sisters disappeared inside the sanctuary before Passion, Shirleen, and Vanessa reached the double doors.

Shirleen tiring, Passion thought it best to sit in the back.

The choir was singing. Passion longed to be with them, praising the Lord. For now, it was enough just to be here. To be in the same place with Jourdan. Eagerly, she waited for him to appear at his pulpit.

Chapter XV

A pretty woman eyed him, smiling. Dre Woods stepped forward in the charter flight terminal to accept paperwork from her. "Good-bye Kansas City," he said to himself.

"Your charter flight to the Bahamas is ready to board, sir," the attendant announced. "Have a nice trip."

Trip? He'd stay in the islands. Forever. Passing a crowd that milled through the terminal, Dre pointed his fancy shoes toward the flight line.

"Mr. Woodson?" a deep voice from his rear inquired.

Who would know he was here? "What?"

Dre turned to see a badge flash in his eyes.

"Detective Thurman, KCPD."

This couldn't be happening. Dre tried to sound irritated, tried to cover his dismay. He asked, "What's going on?"

"Dre Woods, you're under arrest for conspiracy in the murder of Mrs. Cece Watters. Come with us."

Dre noticed a smaller man in sunglasses standing next to the detective. Another cop, no doubt.

"I'm not going down like this. Hell, no—I'm not!" Dre

dropped back, shoved past the detectives, and ran as fast as he could toward the front exit.

"Stop, or I'll shoot!" one of the detectives shouted.

They wouldn't shoot. Too many innocent bystanders. Dre kept running. Just as his lungs felt like bursting, he reached the double glass doors. Perfect. He could get lost in the parking lot.

He pushed through the doors, hearing footsteps race to his rear. He searched frantically for the perfect spot to hide and caught sight of a cluster of vans and trucks. Dre headed for them at breakneck speed.

"Stop, or I'll shoot," one detective repeated.

No way. Dre kept running.

A warning shot rang in the freezing December air. Dre slipped, slid on the icy concrete, but righted himself. *Just a few more steps.*

He heard another shot, felt a burning sensation in his back. His face met the pavement with a hard slap. His last picture of Passion had fallen from his pocket. He grasped it. Her beautiful pout . . . It was the last thing he saw. Before everything went black.

* * * * * * * * * * * *

"Dear Lord, make me worthy to carry your message. Give me the words, strengthen my delivery, and let those who need Your message most—let them open their hearts and hear the truth. In Jesus' name, Amen."

The unflagging power of God surged through Jourdan's veins. Robed, he lowered his Bible from his bowed forehead and stepped into the over-brightened sanctuary. The choir had sung its final song before services. TV cameras were in place.

The audience grew unusually quiet as Jourdan reached the podium, as if they sensed the gravity of his impending sermon. His word would reach beyond Zion today, yet he'd speak to his flock alone. For the Lord, he had to win back the stragglers who had yet to forgive Passion.

He waited to speak.

Soon they began to squirm in the pews. A cough here, a baby's cry there. It was time.

"And thou shalt love the Lord thy God with all thy heart, and with all thy soul, and with all thy mind, and with all thy strength: this is the First Commandment."

The sanctuary went silent.

Jourdan slid his Bible into the other hand, turning to the New Testament, and stepped away from the pulpit. "And the second is this. Thou shalt love thy neighbor as thyself."

He slapped the book closed and descended the steps until he stood level with the congregation. Their opening eyes were windows to their souls. Jourdan said, "Study 12 Mark, verses thirty and thirty-one."

Many dutiful members thumbed their Bibles to scripture. Jourdan noted that several near the front seemed to wonder what was to come, Sister Biddle among them.

"How many of you know that, as Christians, we must follow those two commandments and hold them above all others?"

A majority of hands met the air, some half-heartedly.

"And how many of you know that, often as Christians, we are guilty of doing just the opposite?"

Very few responded.

Jourdan strode slowly to the right. "It's true. For instance, has anyone said to you, 'Did you see that dress Sister so-and-so had on?'" He raised his voice an octave. "'Ooooh, child—scandalous!'"

For emphasis he hitched a hip and placed a fist on it.

Laughter erupted.

He strode to the left. "Or how about 'I wouldn't sit by *those* people if they were the last seats in here.' Come on. Tell me you know what I'm talking about!"

"Amen."

"Preach."

The energy had loosened, as he'd wanted.

"Have we, church, become so enraptured by the scent of our own perfume that we don't realize we emit the foul stench of prejudice?"

Shouts of approval floated toward him. Understanding caught fire. Pacing the altar, Jourdan took heart.

"'But, Reverend,' you may argue." He stopped. "'We can't associate with *sinners!*'" He'd exaggerated that last word. "'If we do, we might become like them.'"

"Come on and preach," a man shouted.

"I say that the more sinners we let in this house of the Lord, the more sinners we sit next to, the more sinners we bring to Christ—" he threw arms wide "—the less sinners we have to deal with in the outside world."

Praise and applause ruptured throughout the sanctuary.

"Tell 'em, preacher!"

"Go 'head!"

"Don't tell me it's my job to let you persecute others, just because you feel they've committed worse sins than you."

"Preach!"

Before speaking again, Jourdan leveled a direct gaze at Martha Biddle. "All sins are washed clean when you come to Jesus!"

Sister Martha looked downward. Apparently her glasses needed a cleaning. But the congregation was on their feet, clapping and shouting.

Jourdan knew his message had gotten through. If only Passion were here to experience it.

* * * * * * * * * * * * *

Tears streamed down Passion's face. "Tell 'em, Jourdan."

"I sees why you like him, sugah."

"She likes *and* loves him," Vanessa pointed out.

How very true. Passion watched Jourdan wipe the sweat

from his brow, in the aftermath of defending her. Never had she loved him more.

Vanessa dabbed at her eyes. "You better let that man know you're here. He's been worried sick."

Jourdan asked for an altar call. Passion moved to the aisle. Ahead of her, Sister Biddle slid out of her pew and ducked up the aisle.

Passion stepped into her path. It would be easy to hate her, but Jourdan had preached too well. She couldn't hate the sister. Instead, she sang a particular hymn at the top of her voice. "Precious Lord . . ."

Martha Biddle broke down in tears.

* * * * * * * * * * * * *

Passion's perfect voice caused Jourdan's heart to thunder with joy. His line of sight traveled up the aisle to find her. She walked forward, arm in arm with a sobbing, obviously repentant Sister Biddle.

Thank you, Jesus.

Jourdan smiled and gazed at his beloved. Stunning, his Passion, a bright yellow beam of perfection. Even her swollen stomach became her. She created havoc in his thoughts, his emotions, his desires. *Have mercy. Let it not be too late for us.*

He stepped down to meet her. Rays as intense as the sun burst from her golden-brown irises.

Jourdan opened his arms. "Have you come to accept Jesus Christ as your savior?"

"I already have, Reverend." Passion smiled. "What I want now is . . . *you.*"

She stepped into his outstretched arms. Folding his robes around her and the growing babe, Jourdan thanked the Lord for this blessing. He kissed the warm, sweet nectar of Passion's lips, not knowing how many people were left in the sanctuary or if cameras still rolled. Not caring. All that mattered? Passion's return.

He laid a cheek against her perfumed hair. "You left before I could ask you something very important. Will you marry me?"

Arms roping around Jourdan's neck, Passion grinned. "I thought you'd never ask. But, yes! I accept."

The Lord's will had been done.

Epilogue

Passion closed her jacket against the chill of the April day and watched Jourdan make his way between the headstones. He carefully carried the blanketed bundle, as if the baby would break with any sudden movement.

The bright day reflected off Passion's wedding ring like a bouquet of iridescent lights. She'd been Mrs. Jourdan Watters since their wedding the past Christmas Eve, with Sherman and Shirleen standing up for them. They still celebrated every day like an anniversary. Passion couldn't remember being happier.

A small gurgle escaped from the bundle, carried to Passion's ears by the wind. She smiled. Adam Cecil Watters was the spitting image of his father. He'd been a happy baby since birth. Of course, the world was still new to him and he didn't have much to complain about, but Passion believed he'd inherited his mother's disposition.

As for Evelyn and Amos, they'd lost their hard feelings at the first sight of their grandson. The scars between Evelyn and Passion had healed. Praise Jesus.

Finding the large, marble headstone, Jourdan stopped and knelt on the damp grass.

Passion felt a pang of sadness as he balanced the baby in one arm and drew a long caress along the top of the stone with the other. For long moments he stayed there, introducing Cece to the child she had wanted so desperately.

Passion would never regret having done this for Cece, and she was grateful for being given the chance.

"Thank you, Cece," she whispered to the wind, knowing her voice would carry to heaven. "Walk with the angels."

Coming Soon...

FALL/WINTER 1997–1998 RELEASES

October 1997

Glory of Love
Sinclair LeBeau
1-885478-19-4 $10.95

Dr. Nina Sterling overcomes the emotional scars of foster care and becomes a successful OB-GYN. But years of serious academic study rob Nina of pleasurable indulgences until she becomes reacquainted with the infamous Dr. Wagner. And together, finally . . . Nina enjoys the glory of love!

November 1997

Secret Obsession
Charlene Berry
1-885478-20-8 $10.95

Allysse Dobson is intrigued by the romantic interest of Wes and Gabriel, and comfortably shares her love for both. But Wes and Gabriel have secrets that, if revealed, will shatter their triangular love affair!

Also by Charlene Berry, *Love's Deceptions*.

January 1998

Again, My Love
Kayla Perrin
1-885478-23-2 $10.95

Gavin's ultimatum makes Marcia's choice a painful one—her career or him.

Forced to make a decision, Marcia follows her career, leaving Gavin behind but taking with her the pain of parting ways.

Marcia does find love again, and enjoys a great career and then . . . Gavin! After a long absence he decides to claim his first and only love, Marcia!

February 1998

Gentle Yearning
Rochelle Alers
1-885478-24-0 $10.95

Daniel Clinton's affair with his best friend's beautiful widow, Rebecca, yields more than love. Nearly torn apart by guilt and deceit, both yield to their overwhelming desires and love for each other, forever.

Also by Rochelle Alers, *Careless Whispers* and *Reckless Surrender*.

March 1998

Midnight Peril
Vicki Andrews
1-885478-27-5 $10.95

Leslie, a bright and attractive corporate attorney, is divorced and a single mother of a teenage daughter. Somehow she finds the time to fall in love, but falls for two very different men, before intriguing events and circumstances narrow her love interest to the one man she really needs.

March 1998

Quiet Storm
Donna Hill
1-885478-29-1 $10.95

Deanna is beautiful and immensely talented. As a concert pianist and accomplished equestrian, she is constantly in the public eye touring the world. Many admire, yet envy, her beauty, talent, and relationship with actor Cord Herrera. But in one moment, tragedy casts a dark shadow over Deanna's bright future . . . producing a quiet storm, calmed only by an unexpected liaison.

ORDER FORM

Mail to:
Genesis Press, Inc.
406A 3rd Avenue North
Columbus, MS 39701

> **Visit our Web page for latest**
> **releases and other information**
> **http://www.colom.com/genesis**

Name _____

Address _____

City/State _____ Zip _____

Telephone _____

Ship to (if different from above)

Name _____

Address _____

City/State _____ Zip _____

Telephone _____

Qty.	Author	Title	Price	Total
	Robin Hampton	Breeze	$10.95	
	Monica White	Shades of Desire	8.95	
	LaFlorya Gauthier	Whispers in the Sand	10.95	
	Rochelle Alers	Careless Whispers	8.95	
	Charlene A. Berry	Love's Deceptions	10.95	
	Chinelu Moore	Dark Storm Rising	10.95	
	Gay G. Gunn	Everlastin' Love	10.95	
	Gloria Greene	Love Unveiled	10.95	
	Rochelle Alers	Reckless Surrender	6.95	
	Beverly Clark	Yesterday Is Gone	10.95	
	Gay G. Gunn	Nowhere to Run	10.95	
	Mildred E. Riley	Love Always	10.95	
	Robin Hampton Allen	Hidden Memories	10.95	
	T. T. Henderson	Passion	10.95	

Use this order form
or call
1.888.INDIGO-1

Total for books _____

Shipping and handling:
 $3 first book, $1 each _____
 additional book

Shpg. & handling subtotal _____

Total amount enclosed _____

  MS residents add 7% sales tax

Indigo love stories at quality book stores everywhere